LAST CHANCE AT Love

APR 1 4

LAST CHANCE AT Love

ESSENCE BESTSELLING AUTHOR

GWYNNE FORSTER

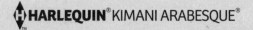
HARLEQUIN® KIMANI ARABESQUE®

Recycling programs
for this product may
not exist in your area.

LAST CHANCE AT LOVE

ISBN-13: 978-0-373-09151-5

Copyright © 2004 by Gwendolyn Johnson-Acsadi

First published by BET Publications, LLC in 2004

⊕ HARLEQUIN®
™ www.Harlequin.com

Printed in U.S.A.

Acknowledgments

To the memory of my beloved husband, Professor George Forster Acsadi, and to my stepson, Peter, who, in spite of the tremendous demands of his own profession, supported and relieved me during the difficult time of my husband's illness.

Chapter 1

"I want you to bring me a day in the life of Jacob Covington. He's hot copy and I want your story to sizzle." It was an order, and Allison Wakefield knew that Bill Jenkins, editor of *The Journal* and her boss, meant what he said. *The Journal* was known for its titillating accounts of the lives of celebrities.

"You said you wanted a story on a typical day in his life. Are you telling me to dig into the man's privacy, to snoop? I'm a reporter, Bill, not a private eye, and I'm not interested in digging up anybody's skeletons." She'd heard that careers were destroyed hourly in Washington, D.C., and after her own experience, she didn't doubt it. She brushed her long brown fingers back and forth beneath her chin and straightened her shoulders.

"I can't stoop to that, Bill. I won't."

He lifted his shoulders in what appeared to be a careless shrug. "You said you didn't want any more assignments on the wives of visiting dignitaries; you wanted hard news. Well, this is your chance. You're after a story, and whatever you find had better go in it." He paused, allowing a grin to slide over his face. "But if you're chicken…" He let the thought dangle, but she understood what he didn't say.

"Refusing to muckrake is not the same as being cowardly." She knew she should hold her tongue, because she didn't want to leave *The Journal* until she had another job.

Oblivious to the implied insult, his gaze swept over her. "A reporter has to be tough, Allison. So get used to it. If you don't, the job's not for you. Bring me the story."

Allison turned away from her editor without thanking him for the chance of a lifetime. She collected her briefcase and pocketbook from her office several doors away and walked out of the building. Pausing in front of the eight-story structure at Fourteenth and H Streets, N.W., Washington, D.C., she breathed deeply of the warm, late June air. She hadn't regained her status as a top reporter, but she still had her soul. Maybe she should have shown some gratitude, but why thank him for the double-edged gift when she knew it could be her undoing?

Jacob Covington had an impeccable reputation, or at least that was the opinion of other reporters who had interviewed him since he'd become a bestselling author. Cut him to pieces? She knew her uneasiness was well founded; Bill Jenkins kept *The Journal* afloat with scandal, searing his subjects, and if she let him, he'd treat this story no differently; he wanted the dirt. Muckraking was what he expected, and she'd need all of her wits to circumvent him. Top-of-the-line editors didn't hire reporters who built their reputations on sleazy copy, and she wanted another chance at working for one of the best newspapers. But she couldn't do that until she erased that blot from her record. She meant to show her detractors that she could reestablish herself as a journalist, and she wouldn't trash Jacob Covington's reputation to do it.

Warren Jacob "Jake" Covington paused in front of his town house near the Ellington School of the Arts in Georgetown and took a deep breath of warm, dry, early morning air, appreciating the unusually low humidity for the nation's capital. Returning from the steaming tropics, the type of climate he least liked, he walked into his house and dropped his luggage at the closet door in his bedroom. After hanging up his jacket and kicking off his shoes, he stretched out on his bed and gloried in the feel of his own hard mattress under his back.

He had just completed his first trip for the department in four years, and the experience increased his appreciation for his current job as the department's chief policy analyst. He wondered how he ever thought of his former job as an undercover agent as exciting and fascinating. He wanted no more of it.

An hour later, at the beginning of the working day, he reached for the phone on his night table and dialed his chief. "I got home an hour ago," he said. As a policy, he didn't identify himself over the phone. "We can't expect success with the present strategy. I'll have to come up with a better plan. I've got some ideas."

"All right. Glad you're back," the chief said. "Get some rest and check in with me tomorrow morning."

Jake stretched out again and grasped at sleep, only to have it elude him. As always, hours passed while he tried to climb down from the emotional high that consumed him when he was on a department mission. Long before he changed assignments, he had begun to tire of the ever-present danger and to want a home and family, something that he couldn't contemplate as long as he held that post.

"We don't have anyone else who can do this as well as you can and get back here safely," his chief had said, trying as usual to inveigle him back into his former job. Well, if he got caught or died, they'd find someone else; he wasn't indispensable. He had paid his dues, and he was out, a fact of which he intended to remind the chief as soon as he saw him.

Allison had never feared an assignment; indeed, the prospect of digging into a topic or an individual and finding something new and interesting always excited her. But she hadn't worked for a newspaper that touted the sensational or for a boss who reveled in it.

Roaming around her small town house in Alexandria, she considered giving her boss an ultimatum: take her off that assignment or accept her resignation. But until Bill Jenkins hired her a month earlier, she hadn't worked in eighteen months, had lived off her now-depleted savings.

I'll write the story, but I won't scandalize the man, and I won't cover up for him, either. That's a lesson I don't have to learn again.

The muffled sound of the telephone interrupted her musings. "Hello? Auntie! How *are* you?"

"Lazy. I just caught a huge striped bass, and that set

me to thinking about you. Fishing's real good right now. You ought to come up here for a few days. It ought to be nice this weekend."

Allison thought for a second. "You know…that's not a bad idea. I'll be starting a new assignment in a few days, and it wouldn't hurt to rest up. I'll fly to Reed City, pick up a rental car, and get to Idlewild around eight Friday evening."

At exactly seven-thirty in the evening, Allison's rented Toyota stopped in front of her aunt's house, a yellow frame structure built in the 1920s, but renovated and well preserved. Frances Upshaw, tall and regal at eighty, rushed off the front porch to greet her niece who, along with Allison's brother, Sydney, constituted the total of the family members that she cared about. She made it a point to tell her friends that the other members of her family were "too supercilious" for her taste.

"We've got another hour before dark," she told Allison. "You're just in time for us to get our supper. Mr. Hawks passed here a few minutes ago with a good dozen catfish and pike. They must be jumping."

"Okay," Allison said, hugging her aunt. "Let me put on some sneakers. I have to wear leather soles when I drive."

She followed her aunt to the northern end of Little Idlewild Lake, baited her hook, and cast as far as she could.

"I'm getting rusty at this, Auntie."

"No such thing. Child, I've been rusty for years, but not when I'm fishing." Her laugh emphasized the insinuation. "When are you and Sydney going to settle down?"

Here it comes, she thought. "We're settled, Auntie."

"You know what I mean. Find yourself a— Oops! Will you look at what I got?" She reeled in a pike of about four pounds, the gleam of her white teeth expressing her pleasure as she put the fish in her basket. In less than half an hour, they had three fish each, enough for the weekend.

Around seven the next morning, Allison got her copy of *Flying High,* a folding chair, a big straw hat and dark glasses, and headed for the beach. As she sat facing Idlewild Lake and enjoying the crisp morning breeze, she thrilled at the thought that she could be sitting in the same spot where Ethel Waters, Duke Ellington, Louis Armstrong, Count Basie, or W.E.B. Du Bois once reclined. In its heyday, Idlewild, known as Black Eden, was famous as a black resort area, the first in the Midwest, attracting the most prominent black entertainers and scores of black intellectuals seeking a place to unwind.

Allison had often wondered how such a charming place with its winding roads, virgin forests, and beautiful lakes could have fallen into decline. She'd heard that integration made it redundant. She dug her bare toes into the powdered sand, leaned back, and opened her book. She liked being there alone when the birds chirped in the trees, a few people sailed on the lake, and a kind of peace flowed around her.

At the sound of a bird singing, she twisted around in the hope of getting a glimpse of it and gasped. Who was that giant of a man with a mouthwatering body rising from the lake like an amphibious Adonis, clad in only the tiniest of swimsuits? As he neared her, she lowered her glasses for a better look and could see the droplets of lake water on his flesh. Long, beautiful legs, tapered waist. Openly, she ogled the man, happy to acknowledge that example of God's perfect handiwork. He didn't glance her way, and she had never been happier to be ignored.

She returned her attention to her book, but the hero of *Flying High* took on the image of the handsome stranger, teasing and mocking her on every page. She closed the book and wondered about the identity of that spiritlike Adonis. Too bad, she would probably never see him again. Besides, he was probably married.

"Aunt Frances," she said, "I saw a really tall man, maybe six feet five or six, on the beach. He had a tan complexion and black silky hair. I'd say he's African-American with some Native American ancestors, and a knockout."

"Well, well, hit you where you felt it, did he? Sorry, but he doesn't live here in Idlewild. Must be a tourist. Why don't you stay for the week? You might see him again."

"Believe me, I'm tempted, but if I do that I'll probably lose my job, and you know how long I've been trying to get one. I have to leave here Sunday noon."

Frances rinsed her cup and saucer and rubbed her sides to dry her hands. "I'll keep an eye out for him, and you know I'll walk right up to him and ask him about himself. When you get to be my age, you can get away with anything."

On Monday morning, Allison telephoned Jacob Covington. The deep baritone voice invited her to leave a message but, struck by the beauty of his voice, she merely stared at the receiver. Recovering quickly, she said, "Mr. Covington, this is Allison Wakefield of

The Journal. My editor says you've agreed to give us a story. Please call me at your convenience." She gave her phone number, hung up, and pondered her next move. Later, checking *The Journal*'s calendar of events for a potential story, as she regularly did, she noted Covington's scheduled lecture that night at Howard University's Andrew Rankin Chapel. She'd be there.

Allison took an aisle seat on the first row and nearly sprang out of it when Jacob Covington strode to the rostrum. Her awareness of him as a man surprised and disconcerted her, as her gaze caught the big giant of a man, who looked directly at her with long-lashed hazel eyes. With so little space separating them, he had to see that a glance at him had left her disoriented, so that she responded to him as surely as flowers rise to greet the sun. At the end of his lecture, she hardly recalled the gist of his talk, so intent had she been on concealing her feminine reaction. She stood in line for an opportunity to speak with him and stared in disbelief when he looked beyond those closest to him in the line and let his gaze linger on her. Common sense told her that she should tell Bill Jenkins to give the assignment to another reporter.

"Hello." The deep, sonorous voice curled around her, and the hazel eyes that punctuated the elegance of his rich, brown face seemed to look into her soul. Without thinking, she extended her hand. And he took it. Nobody had to tell her that, at that moment, she dealt with fate.

"Hello, Mr. Covington." She managed to keep her tone cool. "I enjoyed your talk, but I have a business reason for wanting to meet you."

His left eyebrow arched. Then he winked, bewitching her. "What kind of business?"

She handed him her card. "I'm the reporter Mr. Jenkins assigned for *The Journal*'s story on you."

He looked at the card, then at her. "Your name's not familiar."

"I hope you don't have a case of gender insensitivity."

That wink, again. "Hardly. My concern is for competence and experience."

With so much at stake, she couldn't afford to show vexation. "And you can look at a reporter and know whether she's competent?"

"There are still a lot of people behind you. If you'll step aside, we can settle this later." Settle it? How? This was her chance, and if he had thoughts of refusing her interviews, he could forget it. Right then, she had the upper hand, because he didn't need bad press just as he was about to begin a national book tour.

"Suppose we walk out together," he suggested when the last of his audience had left. "I agreed to be interviewed reluctantly, because my publisher thinks a story in *The Journal* will widen my readership, but I have to tell you I have misgivings. What kind of story are you planning?"

She noticed that he shortened his steps to accommodate her and wondered at his height. "A day in the life of Jacob Covington. What do you say?"

He didn't miss a beat. "A *working* day in the life of Jacob Covington is what you'll get. My private life is my business, so if you've got plans to start on the day of my birth, and not miss a second of my existence until the day before the story goes to press, forget about it."

As they reached the door, she stopped walking and

looked up at him. "I can write the story without a word from you, or I can do the decent, professional thing and interview you. I'm giving my boss a story one way or the other."

His hazel eyes took on a glaze, and his stare might well have been a laser, slicing through her. "Has some of Bill Jenkins rubbed off on you? A story at any cost? Damn the individual; the public has a right to know?"

She told herself to remember the stakes. "Let's start over, Mr. Covington. This assignment is important to me, and I'm sure you know that. Give me your ground rules, and I'll try to follow them."

He breathed deeply, as though resigned. "All right, Ms. Wakefield, nine to five, Monday through Friday, and whenever I'm lecturing, signing books, or being interviewed on radio or TV. At all other times I'm a private citizen. Okay?"

"Fair enough. Are you married?" He seemed taken aback at the abruptness of the question, and she could have kicked herself for having asked it in that fashion.

He winked again, and her heartbeat accelerated. "No. Was that question for the interview or personal use?"

She wished he wouldn't look at her so intently, because she couldn't use the pleasant weather to explain the moisture that matted her forehead. Self-consciously, she lowered her eyelids, annoyed at her warm feminine response to him.

He's just a man, Allison, she admonished herself, and recovered her equilibrium. "I know you're thirty-five— the next logical question is marital status."

He inclined his head slightly and quirked his brow, verifying her suspicion that he didn't believe her, but she appreciated that he softened his voice and manner as if to put her at ease. "This isn't a convenient time for your interview. I'm about to leave on the first leg of my national tour."

"Why can't I travel with you?"

"You couldn't be serious, Ms. Wakefield. I don't want the press chronicling my every breath."

In her exasperation, she permitted herself a withering stare, but realizing that she might provoke him, she immediately changed her demeanor. "Mr. Covington, I am not asking to spend every minute with you, only for the chance to carry out my assignment as best I can."

After seeming to weigh the pros and cons, he said, with obvious reluctance, "All right, if you can manage to stay out of the way."

Boldly, she met his eyes straight on and tried to ignore the bouncing of her heart in her chest. "Would you please try to be less patronizing. I can't observe you if I have to stay out of sight. I'm a professional, and I know how to do my job. It wouldn't hurt you to remember that."

He ran his fingers through the thick, silky black hair that belied his African heritage and told of his Seneca ancestors—traits that had once enhanced his value as an undercover agent; one couldn't be certain of his racial identity.

"All right," he said and grimaced, "but if it doesn't work, we'll have to drop it. I'll let you know when I'm ready to leave." At the bottom of the hill, he asked, "Are you driving, or should I help you get a cab? They seldom cruise on this part of Georgia Avenue at night."

"I'm driving."

"Then you can give me a lift?"

She stopped the car in front of his town house in an upscale section of Georgetown and turned toward him.

"This is a lovely neighborhood," she said, reluctant to voice the words that rested uneasily in her thoughts. He nodded and reached for the door handle. "Mind if I ask…" He stiffened, and she decided not to coat it. "You have a habit…I mean… Why do you wink at me?"

"What? Oh! I didn't realize I'd done that. It isn't something I control; it's involuntary. I… It does whatever it pleases. Thanks for the lift. Good night." Puzzled at his sudden diffidence, the man filled her with wonder as she drove across the Williams Bridge and took the Shirley Memorial Highway to Alexandria and her small, two-story frame house near Bren Mar Park.

Jake thought he'd been around so many indescribably beautiful women that one long-legged black woman with big eyes the color of pinecones and the shape of almonds and a come-to-me expression couldn't knock him off balance. But like a freight train charging through the night, Allison Wakefield had done exactly that. For what other reason would he have given her permission to follow him around and record his every gesture? And why else would the damned wink have returned? That alone was positive proof that she'd gotten to him. The wink hadn't bothered him since he overcame a short, feverish attachment to Henrietta Beech. He distrusted reporters and for good reason; the eagerness of one to expose his former State Department activities had nearly cost him his life. Covering up the incident and guaranteeing his protection for some months afterward had cost the government a bundle. And *The Journal!* Did he dare risk it? He secured the front door and leaned against it for a full twenty minutes, musing on the evening's surprises. Suddenly, he strode into his office and lifted the phone receiver. He stopped. Why did he want to telephone Allison Wakefield? Nonplussed, he pressed the fingers of his left hand first to his right cheek, then to his temples, and closed his eyes. What the devil was going on?

Annoyed with himself for letting Allison get to him, Jake paced around in his bedroom, stopped, and swore; he needed a haircut. Nobody and nothing could have persuaded him to get one in that bastion of intrigue he'd just left, with a terrorist lurking in every other house, every store, and around any corner. In that environment, he wouldn't be fool enough to sit in a barber's chair and expose his throat to a razor. The ring of the phone jarred him. Wondering who would call him at half past eleven at night, he answered it.

"Covington."

"Come in early tomorrow. I've got something for you. Can you make it in by eight o'clock?"

Jake held the receiver at arm's length and glared at it. "You couldn't wait until tomorrow morning to tell me? Did you forget I'm on a year's leave of absence, chief, and that I just got back from a mission this morning?"

"No, I didn't forget. I need your savvy. I want you to check these plans because if anything goes wrong on this job, Congress will have my head."

"Eight o'clock," Jake said and hung up. Right then, he hardly cared whose head came off. He hadn't had a decent night's sleep in ten days, and who knew when he'd get another one if he had to worry about keeping Allison Wakefield out of his business?

Three days later, his job for the chief completed, he prepared for his first book-signing tour.

Rested, after a sound night's sleep, Jake pulled himself out of bed, got a cup of black coffee, and tried to think. Considering the way he had responded to Allison Wakefield, all the way to the pit of his gut, he'd probably relax with her, slip up, and reveal more than he should. And she was bound to get suspicious if he periodically interrupted his book tour and disappeared for days at a time, as he would if the chief called on him. Any good journalist would want to know why he disappeared and where he went. He promised himself he'd get out of that commitment.

"I've rethought it," he told Allison when he called her at her office later that morning, "and I'd prefer not to be encumbered on this tour. It'll be tiring enough without having a reporter around to record every breath I take."

He'd disappointed her, and he couldn't help it, but when he'd looked down at the audience and had seen her there with her right hand at her throat and her lips a little apart, he hadn't known what hit him. In his thirty-five years, he didn't remember having had such a powerful reaction to a woman. He'd gotten through that lecture, though he didn't remember how. Then she'd walked up to him and held out her hand, and for a moment he'd thought he'd conjured up a vision.

The extent of her frustration came through when she spoke. "If I can't tour with you," she bargained in a voice that lacked her previous toughness, "could you give me a list of people to interview who you'd trust to tell me the truth?"

"Your generosity astonishes me," he said, clearly baffled. "I don't get it."

"I wouldn't worry about that," she replied, her tone more confident. "I won't have any trouble finding people who'll do you in. If I put an ad in the paper, they'll come running."

"That's blackmail, woman."

"Tut-tut. Don't be so harsh. There's more than one way to ride a horse; you know that. So what do you say? Do I tour with you, or don't I?"

She sounded tough, and she might be, but something about her reached him, and he didn't want to hurt her. She inspired in him exactly the opposite response. But he had to protect himself from damage, too. And he didn't doubt that, if she dug into his private life, she could twist what she found sufficiently to torpedo his dreams of becoming scholar-in-residence at his alma mater.

"Are you equating me with a horse?" he chided. "Your choice of metaphors intrigues me."

"I didn't mean… Well, n-no."

He couldn't resist a dig. "Don't apologize, Allison. When you ride, be considerate enough to make it enjoyable." Oh, if phone lines had mirrors! From her long silence, he knew she'd gone slightly out of joint. Still, he couldn't help needling her. "It isn't always what we hear that causes trouble, but how we interpret it. You get my point, I hope."

"If you're trying to convince me that six weeks of your company will be unpleasant, don't squander your energy," she replied. "And off-color innuendos are wasted on me."

"Off-color innuendos? I didn't insinuate anything; I meant what I said. Plain and simple."

"Like your wink?"

"Like your handshake, lady. Meaningful." She could hold her own, he saw, as he waited for her reply.

"When do we leave?"

If he hadn't spent the last thirty minutes talking with her, his answer probably would have been, "We don't." But he suspected she'd be good company. *And face it,* he told himself, *you want to know whether that clap of thunder you heard and the lightning fire that roared through you when you first saw her signaled the real thing.*

"All right. I'll give it a shot," he told her, "but please do your homework. I don't mind telling you that I've had enough of fledgling reporters and their inept questions."

"This is your first book, but I've worked as a reporter for six years. Which one of us is a fledgling?"

A warm flush spread through him, and he couldn't help laughing; a woman who could hold her own with him was to be prized. And encouraged. "Touché. My publicist will give you my schedule for the next six weeks." He hung up, and his smile faded. He'd have to make certain that she didn't tail him on Friday and Saturday nights.

Jake couldn't decide whether to rent a car, drive out to Rock Creek Park and spend a couple of hours horseback riding, or call a buddy for a game of tennis. He hadn't had any useful exercise in ten days. He needed a good workout. "Dunc was always good for an early morning set or two," he said to himself and telephoned his friend, a freelance journalist who worked at home.

"Jake here. How's it going, buddy?" he asked Duncan Banks when his friend answered the phone.

"How am I? Man, I need a vacation. I just finished a piece on undertaker scams, and damned near wound up the victim of one of 'em myself. Don't tell me you want a game. I just told my wife I needed some exercise."

"I can be ready for a couple of sets in half an hour. How are Justine and Tonya?"

"Still spicing my life. I'll pick you up in forty-five minutes."

"You look as if you've been hanging out on a beach," Duncan told Jake when he opened the door.

"Hardly," Jake said. He didn't discuss his work for the department, and especially not his trips, and Duncan never asked him where he'd been. However, Jake didn't doubt that a news reporter of Duncan Banks's stature had done his research, knew the answers, and kept his thoughts to himself.

"I hope you're paid up with your club dues," Jake told him, "because I forgot to pay mine." He didn't mention that the notice arrived while he was on a department mission.

"I forget sometimes, too," Duncan said, "but they won't throw us out."

They practiced hitting the ball for several minutes, tossed a coin, and Duncan served first.

"Brother, that was one wicked lob you sent over here," Duncan called to Jake after returning it for a point. After winning a set each during nearly two hours of play, they sat on a bench and helped themselves to the lemonade that Justine had made and sent in a cooler.

"You've been married to Justine how long now?"

"Two years. The happiest and the most productive of my life. I hardly remember who I was before I met Justine. Looking back—and I often do—I realize my first marriage was a sham."

Jake stretched out his legs and leaned back against the bench. "Marriage is a risk any way you slice it."

A frown slid over Duncan's face. "Sure. And so is taking a shower. It's simple, Jake; if you don't gamble— I mean, take a chance—you can't win. From the first time I looked at Justine, I was a changed man."

Jake sat forward, remembering his reaction to Allison Wakefield. "You mean as soon as you laid eyes on her?"

"That's just what I mean. Man, I did everything, told myself all kind of lies about how she wasn't for me, even left my own house to stay at the lodge so I wouldn't see her…trying to avoid the inevitable. I didn't stand a chance."

"Damn!" Jake sat back, put his hands in the pockets of his tennis shorts, and shook his head. "Man, I don't like the sound of that."

"Whoa! Wait a minute," Duncan said, coloring his words with barely restrained laughter. "What's her name?"

Jake shook his head again as if perplexed. "There isn't any *her*. I am not even going to repeat her name. It's too ridiculous. I am definitely not going *there!*" He spoke forcibly.

"Go ahead and convince yourself." Jake didn't like the laughter that spilled out of Duncan like water cascading from a mountaintop. "That's just what I said," Duncan told him. "I'd be honored to be your best man."

With that, Jake stood, ready to leave. "You're off your rocker."

Duncan permitted himself a long laugh. "Whatever you say. In the thirteen years we've known each other, you've intimated a serious interest in one woman. One.

And for that particular one, your youth was ample excuse." He stood and looked Jake in the eye. "Getting a jolt at the age of twenty-two is nothing compared to being poleaxed at this age."

A look of fond remembrance claimed Duncan's face. "I'll never forget the day and the minute I gave in to it; oceans roared."

"That was you. This is me. Tell Justine I want some of Mattie's stuffed roast loin of pork and lemon-roast potatoes. That woman can really cook."

"That, she can. When are you leaving on your book tour?"

"Monday, but I'll probably be back home on weekends."

"I thought most book signings were held on weekends."

"Or at lunchtime, like mine. Thanks for the workout, Dunc."

"My pleasure."

"The guy's a lucky man," Jake said to himself later as he stood beside his kitchen sink, eating a ham sandwich. "One long year of trouble, and then his ship came in. I should be so fortunate."

"Covington goes on national tour pretty soon, and he's agreed to let me accompany him," Allison told her boss.

"Atta girl."

Without commenting, she turned to her computer and began to sketch the questions that would guide her interviews with Jacob Covington. She worked on them until two o'clock, packed her briefcase, and headed for her home on Monroe Avenue in the outskirts of Alexandria, Virginia, en route to her other life. Her boss and her peers thought her tough, and she *had* developed a crust of self-protection against their slurs and slights, had hardened herself. But not even for the sake of her ambitions would she step on anyone for personal gain. *Let them think whatever they like.* She had their respect, and that was what she wanted.

Allison changed into casual clothes and prepared to enjoy the happiest two hours of her week. She parked in front of the two-story redbrick structure whose colonial front gave it the appearance of a gracious private home. Mother's Rest was a temporary haven for eleven children under the age of two who were awaiting foster homes. A child rarely remained there more than six months.

Zena Carter, the head nurse, greeted Allison as she entered the house. "I've got a brand-new one for you today," she said. "Cute little tyke, too. She's in a fit of temper, and I sure hope you can calm her down."

Allison followed Zena down the hall. "Is she sick?"

"Doctor said she wasn't. Just hates yet another environment and more strangers, I guess. Your things are in there."

Allison stepped into the little cubicle, washed her face and hands, put on a white gown, and covered her mouth with a small mask. She took the baby, and her little charge stared up at her with big brown eyes that beautified her dark face. *How could anybody...* Quickly, she put a stop to that train of thought. Hadn't the social worker warned her not to judge the mothers or to become attached to any of the children? It was one thing to give that advice; as far as she was concerned, the ability to follow it required superhuman command of one's emotions.

For two hours, she coddled, stroked, and chatted with the seven-month-old baby girl who, like the other babies there, was awaiting a foster home or an adoption. The child's bubbly personality tore at her heart, and when she sang, the baby clapped her hands and tried to join her. The time passed too quickly. To avoid bonding, the volunteer mothers, as they were called, were not allowed to stay for more than two hours, nor could they visit with the same baby twice in one month. Her coworkers wouldn't believe her capable of those gentle, tender moments with the children, and she didn't want them to know. But the hours spent there nourished her for the rest of the week.

She walked out into the warm summer drizzle and raced half a block to her car, shielding her hair as the moisture rid it of its elegance, dampening her and shrinking her rayon shirt. At Matty's Gourmet Shop, she bought her dinner and two boxes of Arlington Fair Blue Ribbon gingersnaps and went home with the intention of preparing for her interview with Jacob Covington. She answered the phone with reluctance.

"Yes?"

"Hi, Allison. Want to go to Blues Alley tonight?"

Of course she did. Connie knew she never got enough of good jazz. "I'm all set to work because I didn't have other plans. But it'll be a while before I can get back there, so why not? Who's there?"

"Buddy Dee, and Mac Connelly is with him tonight."

"No kidding? I'll meet you there at quarter to eight."

"I thought that would get your juices flowing. First one there takes a table. Say, I ran into Carly Thompson this morning. She's here sealing a deal with Woodie's to carry a full line of her Scarlet Woman Cosmetics. Can you beat that? The girl is gone."

"She sure is. Last time we spoke, she said she had some hot irons in the fire, but I thought she was talking about a man."

"She's headed for Martha's Vineyard," Connie said, releasing a sigh of longing. "Wish I could go with her."

"Me too, but I'll settle for my new assignment. See you later."

Jake dressed in the style associated with jazzmen of the thirties and forties, picked up his guitar, and headed for Blues Alley. Half a block from the club, he put on dark glasses to hide his telltale hazel eyes, conceal his wink, and complete his masquerade.

When that curtain rose, he was Mac Connelly. He wasn't ashamed of what he did, but he couldn't afford to have his name associated with the jazz subculture. If his association with the musicians was known, the reputation could deny him his coveted goal of an appointment as scholar-in-residence at his alma mater. Furthermore, his boss at the department had warned him that, on a nightclub bandstand, he was a sitting duck for the enemies he had incurred in his former work, and the bullet wound in his left shoulder was a testimonial to his boss's wisdom. He'd taken that bullet three blocks from the department, proof at that time—if he needed any—that his enemies knew where to find him.

When the lights came up, he was already seated, tuning his guitar and waiting for the six other band members to walk onstage. His blood accelerated its pace through his veins the minute he heard Buddy's downbeat. As usual, the dance of his magic fingers up and down the strings brought cries of "Right on, Mac", "Kill it, man" and "Take it on home, baby" from his devoted fans. And as they did whenever he played, the crowd clamored for his rendition of "Back Home in Indiana," his signature piece.

The third and last set ended too quickly. As always, he remained seated while the band took a bow and the lights dimmed. Still high from total immersion in his music, he picked up the glass of iced tea that he'd placed on the floor beside him to resemble liquor, emptied it, and ducked out back. He'd had a ball, but uneasiness pervaded him because, unlikely as it seemed, he was fairly certain that Allison Wakefield had been in the audience. Allison wore her hair up, and this woman's hair hung around her shoulders, but an African-American woman with big, almond-shaped brown eyes and long sweeping lashes in a flawless, oval-shaped ebony face was not the most common sight. Besides, he not only had the facial similarity for a clue, his reaction to the woman was similar to what he felt when he first saw Allison. He'd thought her the Bach fugue type; it wouldn't have occurred to him that she'd pay to hear jazz.

He took every conceivable precaution to conceal his identity at the club, including never being seen standing, since his six-feet-five-and-a-half-inch height and 215-pound weight might give him away. His music was his life, and he cherished those few hours on Friday and Saturday nights with Buddy Dee's band. He'd have to watch his every move, because a reporter could damage him almost irreparably.

"He got away again," Allison grumbled to Connie, as they waited outside the club.

Connie scrutinized Allison's face. "Are you sweet on Mac?"

Allison glared at her. "Of course not. With those black glasses, I don't even know what he looked like. But pins and needles shoot all through me when that man plays, and he sits there, in his element. He's so mysterious."

Connie's shoulders lifted in a quick shrug. "You reporters are all alike. You have to know everything. It's a wonder you don't walk up to the man and interrogate him."

"Can you see anybody intimidating that big guy?"

"Yeah. You might not try to browbeat him, but you'd dig into his business just to talk to him. He's your type."

"My type?"

"Sure he is. You like a man who's four or five inches taller than your five feet nine, and you could really luxuriate and feel tiny with this guy. He must be near six feet six. Of course, I'm just guessing; he's always sitting down."

"Yeah, he is," Allison replied, bemused. He'd already taken his seat when the lights went up and remained sitting after they went down, while other band members walked in and out in full view of the audience. She could only conclude that he had a disability. Maybe he couldn't walk. She dismissed the matter with a shrug. It was of no import. A jazz musician would be the last man who'd interest her.

She put on her Ella Fitzgerald and Louis Armstrong CDs as soon as she got home and sang along with them while she sorted out her clothes for the tour. With gentle strokes, her fingers brushed the once-yellow leather rose that had long since turned brown from her loving caresses. Half a dozen times, she'd thrown it into the wastebasket, only to retrieve it and return it to her little collection of treasures—the green quilted silk box in which she kept her first bra, the lace handkerchief she'd carried to her freshman high school prom, the empty perfume bottle that had held the first gift she received from a man. The yellow rose had nestled in the elegant bow on the box in which the perfume had been wrapped. Edna Wakefield hadn't approved of a deliveryman for her daughter, and she'd let him go. But unlike opportunistic Roland Farr—her betrayer—that man had loved her, she now knew.

What of Mac Connelly? She couldn't get him out of her mind. Tonight, she'd sensed in him a peculiarly erotic aura that she hadn't detected the many other nights she'd seen him play. As she watched his fingers tease those strings, an unfamiliar heat had pulsated in her. A laugh rumbled in her throat. First Jacob Covington had poleaxed her, and now this. No doubt about it; she was a late bloomer.

Early Sunday afternoon, two days later, as Allison stepped out of her Jacuzzi, she heard Covington's voice on her answering machine, interrupted it, and took the call.

"Don't forget that our flight leaves at eight tomorrow morning, Allison. We might as well use first names. I'm called Jake. As I was saying, please be on time. I have a ten o'clock appointment, and I don't want to miss that plane."

As soon as her heartbeat returned to normal, she summoned her most professional demeanor. "Mr. Covington, I'm assuming that you don't make these statements because you want to rile me, but because you're deficient in the art of conversation. I will be on time, dear, and I will wash behind my ears before I leave home." His uproarious laughter cooled her temper, and she vowed not to react negatively to every one of his incautious remarks.

"Did anybody ever try to blunt that sharp tongue of yours?"

"Now, you…" she began, remembered her counsel of seconds earlier, and stopped. "Jake, do you think we automatically rub each other the wrong way?"

That deep, dark, sexy laugh again. "I think we rub each other, but I'd be the last one to suggest it's the wrong way. Rubbing with you gives me a good feeling."

"Well, it irritates me," she huffed.

"In what way? I'd be happy to soothe whatever I irritate. Just let me know what I've…uh…inflamed, and I'll gladly cool it off." His laugher caressed her. Warmed her. If she didn't watch out, she could find herself enamored of… Was she out of her mind?

"I don't suppose it has occurred to you that you can keep your thoughts to yourself."

"It has, but doing that wouldn't be fun."

She could imagine that a grin covered his face. "You're not going to tease me into letting you trap me with innuendos. I'm onto you. Aren't you ever serious?"

"I'm always serious," he shot back, "but I'm not a rash man. If I told you in plain English what's on my mind, I could damage our relationship. I don't want that."

She wondered if her nerves would riot. After that comment, he might as well dump it out, but she refrained from saying it. "Thanks for being circumspect," she replied instead, and she did appreciate it. "Having to suffer my boss's coarseness is a big enough price for getting ahead in this business."

"I can well imagine that. See you at eight in the morning." As though he'd received an unpleasant reminder, his manner changed when she mentioned Bill Jenkins. Who could blame him? She told him goodbye, dressed quickly, and made her way to Mother's Rest.

Allison took Leda from the nurse, looked into the child's sad face, and told herself that, if she were ever fortunate enough to have one of her own, she'd love it so much that it would bubble with joy all the time.

"Leda," she cooed to the solemn little girl, "smile for me." She sang "Summertime" and was rewarded with the baby's rapt attention. She cuddled Leda to her breast and paced the colorful, well-lighted room, singing as she did so. Leda quickly learned that a smile brought another chorus and, when the two hours had passed, Allison surmised that she had sung the famous song well over a dozen times. The nurses let her stay beyond the allotted two hours because the child fretted when she attempted to leave. Finally she managed to sing her to sleep, but for the first time, pangs of separation after leaving one of the children tore at her, and she vowed to have some of her own. But when?

She got home, saw the house's dark windows, and realized she'd forgotten to set her automatic timer. She searched for the small flashlight that she always carried in her pocketbook, found it, and opened the door.

After sleeping fitfully that night, she arose before daylight, dressed in leisure, and stood leaning against the check-in counter for the Delta Air Lines Washington to New York flight when Jake Covington got there. Captivated, she watched him approach her, his gait loose and his stride lazy. Suggestive. He walked up to her and grinned. Then he winked. Unaccustomed to a promiscuous onslaught of desire for a man, she had to battle the frissons of heat that swirled within her, unsettling her. Six weeks of him could be her undoing.

"What's the matter?" he asked, replacing the smile with a look of genuine concern.

She wasn't so foolish as to tell him what seeing him had done to her. She turned to the ticket agent and handed him her credit card. "New York. One way, please."

They took their seats in business class, and Allison immediately opened a newspaper, but Jake couldn't resist closing the paper and relaxed when her inquiring look bore no censorship.

"I want us to get along well, Allison," he began. "I grew up in a peaceful, loving family, and I've accepted that as the kind of life I need. I do not allow myself to spend a lot of time with contentious people. If you can't stand my company, I'd rather we called this off before the plane leaves the gate."

"I'm a little unsettled. It'll pass over, *I hope.* In any case, Jake, contentiousness is not part of my disposition, so if that's what you detect, you probably precipitated it."

He ignored the remark. "What happened to you back there?" Whatever it was, it had plowed right through him. Oddly, he didn't expect an explanation, because the incident had the appearance of spontaneity, a phenomenon unto itself and of its own power, so her answer held no surprise.

"I wish I knew. Don't worry, though; I'm fine."

He let his hand touch the side of hers; he couldn't help it. Something in her called out to him, sparked a need in him, and it wasn't one-sided. He knew she'd deny it, but there it was. She reacted to him exactly as he responded to her, and though he wasn't anxious for them to get involved, he knew from experience that when nature decided to take a hand in such things, it didn't ask permission. So he told himself he'd better take his mind off the matter, because the more he thought about her, the more she intrigued him. When the odor of fresh, perking coffee wafted into the cabin, he inhaled deeply, savoring its aroma, grateful that it overrode Allison's tantalizing scent.

"I'd like some coffee. Sugar and cream," he told the flight attendant.

Allison asked for plain black coffee and didn't reply when he commented, "Unadorned, huh?"

She also hadn't moved her hand from beside his fingers. What was he supposed to make of that?

Trying for a reaction, he teased, "Scared of gaining weight? From where I sit, you're perfect." He wouldn't have thought that a simple blush could give him so much pleasure, but he relished the sight of her embarrassment as evidence that his compliment pleased her.

He sensed her uneasiness, too, but he didn't think she'd want to be questioned about it, so he opted for impersonal conversation. "My network appearances will be taped at seven-thirty in the mornings and aired at nine-thirty," he said, "and I have to be there an hour early. You want to go with me, or would you rather—"

That did it; immediately she removed her hand. "You're not losing me, Mr. Covington, so please don't try it. If I had wanted to watch you on television, I could have stayed home and done so in the comfort of my bedroom."

His left hand went to his forehead. How did a man deal with such suspicions? He decided to ask her.

"Do you distrust everybody? Or just me? Allison, I cannot and I will not spend the next six weeks tiptoeing around your tender feelings."

He watched her lift her chin in a display of aristocratic disdain. *For heaven's sake, not a stuffed shirt,* he said to himself.

"My feelings are not tender," she corrected him. "I want to make it clear that I won't let anything or anybody prevent my carrying out this assignment, and that includes you." Tired of hassling when he wanted to be gracious, he resorted to silence.

"I didn't mean to snap at you," she said after a time. "I'm not usually so touchy, but you seem to... I don't know... I haven't been my best self this morning."

He rewarded her with an obliging smile, though it wasn't what he felt. She'd glanced up at him for his reaction, and he'd smiled because she needed to be absolved.

Allison hadn't considered that the simple business of registering at their hotel could prove embarrassing. After determining that they really did want separate rooms, the Drake Hotel registration clerk asked if they were traveling together. Jake said no, but she said yes, not realizing that they were being asked if they wanted adjoining rooms with a door that opened between them.

"Which is it?" the clerk asked. Heat singed her face when Jake replied that they didn't want to be together. Flustered, she looked everywhere but at him and cringed before the clerk's knowing gaze. She'd rather neither of them had known that she'd never checked into a hotel in the company of a man, not that it was their business.

"I'll be ready in twenty minutes," he said when she walked out of the elevator. "Can you make that? We're going first to my publisher, then lunch, after which I sign at Barnes and Noble. Okay?"

She nodded. It was one thing to be attracted to him, but if she wasn't careful she'd like him more than was healthy. Her reaction to him in the Washington Airport had distressed her, and when he'd sensed her unease and almost covered her hand with his, he'd told her more about himself than she needed to know right then. She changed into a burnt-orange suit and brown accessories, refreshed her makeup, and met him in the lobby with minutes to spare. His smile of approval had nothing to do with business and everything to do with a man liking the looks of the woman who approached him.

He held the taxi door for her and took his seat beside her. "I may not be in this evening, Allison; bright lights hold a lot of fascination for a country boy."

She turned her body fully to face him. "Did you say you're a country boy?"

"Surprised?"

She nodded. "I am, indeed."

He winked. Voluntarily or not, she couldn't tell. "Yep. I was born in Reed Hollow, Maryland, about a mile from the Chesapeake Bay Bridge. I was wondering when you'd get around to asking. Couldn't be that you intend to stick to my present daytime activities, as you promised?"

She glanced down at her long, perfectly manicured fingers. "As a man of the world, you ought to know the folly of whetting a reporter's appetite. The obvious is far less interesting than that which is obscure or hidden."

She felt the tension in him, as one feels a speeding object just before it hits, and wondered at his anxiety. "Don't get antsy. I promise to write nothing but the truth." She watched in astonishment as he withdrew.

"Another person's truth isn't necessarily yours to tell. A man's privacy is sacred."

She refused to give quarter. "Public figures have to forgo some of their cherished privacy."

He eased into the corner, away from her. "And the public has a right to know, damn the individual and what disclosure does to him. Right?"

Stunned, her breath lodged in her throat, and she stared at him. When she regained her equilibrium, she told him, "I'm not a monster, and I never write lies. Never."

But her words evidently didn't placate him, for he stared straight ahead, his expression grim. "That's more than I've come to expect from reporters. Some of you can twist the truth to the point that…that love of country seems like a crime. I want to see your text as you go along, and if at any point it's out of line, this deal is off."

"In your dreams, mister," she sputtered. "Not even my editor sees my copy until I've finished it."

"We'll see about that" was his dark reply.

Allison figured she'd better check in with her boss, though as always she dreaded talking with him.

"Jenkins."

"Just checking in, Bill. We're at the Drake."

"*We?* Now you're talking. Squeeze everything out of him. I've never yet seen a man that couldn't be had if a woman played her cards right."

She swallowed hard. Didn't he ever elevate his mind? "I called to let you know where I am. My room number is eleven-B, and I believe Mr. Covington is in sixteen-H."

She imagined his look of incredulity when he said, "You're joking. I gave you credit for more than that."

"I hope I didn't misunderstand what you said, Bill."

His snort reached her through the wires. "Sorry to disappoint you, but I'm in the business of scooping other papers. Play it any way you choose. Just bring me a good story, and if you find out that the guy smokes opium or sniffs coke, it had better be in your story."

She didn't know why she laughed, because his words hadn't amused her. When she could control it, she asked him, "Have you ever met Jacob Covington?"

"No, and never wanted to. Why?"

"He's a gentleman. If he'd heard your reaction to our room arrangements, he'd probably cancel this deal; he doesn't trust *The Journal*. If you want this story, you'd better ease up and let me handle it my way."

His long silence told volumes, but she waited. "I've been in this business thirty years," he said at last, "and you're a lamb born yesterday, but you know it better. Do what you please, but you get me that story just like I want it."

A sense of foreboding seeped through her, and she wished she hadn't called him.

While Jake met privately with his editor, Allison reviewed her notes in the publishing company's waiting room. Keeping her mind on her work proved difficult; the friction between Jake and herself worried her because she sensed that they had on their hands an attraction that could erupt into full-blown passion. And she didn't want that, at least not until she'd turned in her story. It was never far from her thoughts that she'd lost her first job because she'd fallen for Roland Farr, on whom she'd been assigned to write a story. She hoped Jacob Covington didn't have any secrets and that, if he did, she didn't find out about them, because whatever she discovered was going in that story. After covering for Farr, a gesture that had almost ruined her life, she had learned a painful lesson.

Chapter 2

Allison watched Jake fold his papers and prepare to leave the store after the first book signing. "You certainly know how to work a crowd," she told him. "I never saw so much easy charm in my life. How could you smile nonstop for three hours?"

She supposed it was human to appreciate compliments, but his broad grin and warm flush suggested that her remark meant more to him than she'd anticipated.

"When people say nice things to me, I'm a sweetheart," he offered in an apparent attempt to cover his embarrassment. Then he winked, not once but twice. "A real pussycat. Try me; you'll like me."

She had to laugh. This man had many sides to his personality, and every element of it fascinated her. "Try to stay humble, Jake," she teased. "It won't be easy, I know, with hundreds of women lining up for a glimpse of you and the chance to own your unreadable signature. But try. Otherwise, you might sail right up into the clouds, and I'll be unable to reach you."

This won't be easy, she cautioned herself, as he continued to smile with hazel eyes that gleamed with pleasure. Worse still, she had to finesse his mesmerizing gaze while the scent of his tangy cologne teased her nostrils. Well, she was a big girl; she'd just make herself ignore it. Fat chance. Could that wink possibly be beyond his control, as he'd said? Built-in sex appeal, she thought, when he winked twice—a half smile playing around his full bottom lip, reinforcing his impact.

"You can reach me anytime you want to," he assured her, responding to her comment. "And if you think you're having problems finding me, just let me know and I'll tell you exactly how to get to me. Come to think of it, you don't need any advice about that."

Her gaze took in his rough masculinity, set off with those mesmerizing eyes, rich tan skin, and thick black wavy hair. She feigned displeasure.

"Don't you ever stick to the subject? No matter what I say, you manage to give it a double meaning."

His left shoulder lifted quickly, as though by reflex. "I got where I am by taking advantage of every opportunity, and I haven't found a reason to break the habit." He stared directly into her face. "Oh, yes. And you'll find that I'm a patient man. I'm willing to wait for what I want, but that doesn't mean I'm not busy ensuring that I get it. If you're ready, we can leave."

He'd just given notice that he controlled his life and a good deal of what happened to him, and he'd apparently had more success at that than she'd had. She looked around, glad for the opportunity to release herself from his gaze.

"Let me get that bag of books I bought," she said. "They're behind the counter over there."

The light pressure of his fingers on her arms sent heat spiraling through her body. God help her if she was going to react that way every time he touched her.

"I'll get them," he said, and left before she could reply.

"How many did you buy, a hundred?" he asked as he walked back to her with the bag. She reached for it, but he added her laptop computer to his burden and started off.

"Wait a minute. I can carry my stuff," she called after him. He was not going to treat her as if she were helpless.

He stopped, turned, and looked at her, an expression of incredulity masking his face. "Allison, if you think I'm going to walk up Madison Avenue with a woman who's struggling under thirty or forty pounds of whatever, while I carry my four-pound briefcase, you're a few bricks short of a full load. Please be reasonable."

"I'm not going to let you treat me as though I'm an incompetent little something or other. Hand me my things, please."

He smiled in that special way of his that seemed to bless everything around him. "You have to realize that my father didn't let my mother lift anything heavy, and he taught me to be protective of her and all other women. I can't ignore my upbringing just because you're out to prove you're the equal of, or better than, any of *The Journal*'s other reporters. I'm carrying this stuff, and if you don't like that, next time don't bring it. What do you say?"

"Okay." She said it grudgingly. "But I like bossy people about as well as you like contentious ones. And you don't have to make such a big thing out of this, either. I wouldn't want you to disobey your parents."

"What?" His deep laughter rolled with merriment. She loved the sound of it, and if she knew how, she'd keep him laughing.

"I'm thirty-five years old," he reminded her, "and at this age, I obey selectively. Does this mean you're going to stop bickering with me and let us be friends?" The gleam in his eyes told her she'd be foolish to react, that he had her number and needled her out of devilment.

She laughed, though she was less assured than her manner suggested. "Bees will stop stinging long before we get chummy, pal." If only she could be sure of it.

His gaze sauntered over her but, apparently not satisfied that his eyes had telegraphed his message, he told her, "Lie to the world if you must, but tell yourself the unvarnished truth. Self-deception can be dangerous."

"I certainly hope you're not speaking from experience," she replied. But he'd come close to her vulnerable spot, and flippancy wasn't what she felt, as the memory of Roland Farr's cunning floated back to her.

In her room, she got a handful of gingersnaps and crawled into bed with Jake's book, *For the Sake of Diplomacy,* hoping to find something of the man in his work. She didn't relish the idea that her interest in him might exceed the professional preoccupation that she normally brought to her work and hoped she hadn't set a trap for herself. Words danced before her in black-and-white confusion, challenging her to concentrate. When

Jacob Covington's face appeared among the tangled alphabets, she closed the book.

He'd been ungracious in not asking if she'd like company, Jake decided, and rang her room. "I forgot to ask whether you have friends here, Allison. I'd hate to think of your not taking advantage of this great town. So if you won't be busy this evening, how about spending a couple of hours with me?"

"Sure. What will we do?"

He welcomed her honest, straightforward answer, because he disliked women who played games with him. She had nothing planned and didn't pretend that she did have.

"After we eat, we can take in a show, go to one of the jazz clubs in the Village, watch the skaters in Rockefeller Plaza, whatever. Depends on how you want to dress."

"I vote for food and skaters," she said, causing him to wonder why she hadn't suggested the music. He'd been certain she'd choose the jazz, and he'd have proof that he had indeed seen her at Blues Alley, but he didn't exclude the possibility that her choice could be a ruse.

He hung up, made dinner reservations at a small West Side restaurant, and remembered to call his mother.

"I'll be down there in a couple of weeks," he told Annie Covington.

She'd be glad to see him, she said and then voiced what he knew was her real concern. "Son, have you found a nice girl? I hate to think of you always by yourself."

"Not yet. You'll be the first to know." He wanted

to get off the subject, because she wouldn't hesitate to complain about the grandchildren he hadn't given her.

"Married men live longer than loners," she warned. "And don't let your success keep you out of church, Jake; it's prayers that got you where you are."

"Plus hard work and my parents' support," he said, gave her his phone number, and added, "Don't forget to keep my itinerary posted on your refrigerator, in the bathroom, and beside your bed."

Her hearty laugh always filled him with joy, reminding him that she no longer struggled in abject poverty because he made certain that she had every modern home convenience, more money that she could use, and that she worked only if she wanted to.

"That falls pretty easily off your tongue," she told him. "But don't you forget that for the first forty-five years of my life—the refrigerator was a zinc tub filled with ice when we could get it, the bathroom was wherever you set yourself down, and the bed had to be moved when it rained. You send me more money every month than I used to make in a year. Your father would be proud of you, son."

"Thanks, Mom. Tune in to NBC tomorrow evening between seven and nine."

If Jake needed grounding, he could trust his mother to keep him in touch with the good earth, and later that evening he had cause to appreciate this. While still a child, Jake had learned tolerance. He'd discovered early that his size invited challenges from the tough boys in his school and even some of his teachers. The experiences had shaped his personality and taught him the wisdom of soft-spoken, nonthreatening manners. Gentleness came naturally, but it threatened to abandon him when the maître d' at Dino's rushed forward to assist Allison as though she were unescorted. He liked to know that other men found the woman in his company interesting, but when one after the other stared beagle-eyed at Allison, his temper began a rare ascent. Quickly, he clamped down on it.

She was seated at the small table for two, and he observed her closely. Jet-black hair cascaded around her shoulders, setting off her smooth ebony complexion and large dreamy eyes that promised a man everything. Her simple red dress heightened the beauty before him; and though she seemed unaware of it, she'd captured the attention of nearly every man present. He smiled to himself; at least he wasn't the guy on the outside. He was about to remark that he liked her hair down, when it hit him that it was indeed she who he had seen in Blues Alley.

Watch it, Jake. He couldn't remember the last time he'd felt the need to give himself that lecture. "You're different with your hair down, softer and—"

"Approachable?"

She had more red flags than anybody he knew. "I was going to say *vulnerable,* but you wouldn't like that either, would you? Let's be friends for tonight and leave aside the one-upmanship, shall we?" He glanced up from his menu for a look at the smoke he expected to see, but to his surprise, he caught her in an unguarded moment, her vulnerability unsheltered. He folded the menu and put it on the table. She might make him eat the words, but he had to say them.

"You're so beautiful. Lovely. I'd give anything if we'd met under more favorable circumstances."

"Thank you…I think. We're going to keep our relationship a business one, Jake. No one knows better than I the folly of doing otherwise."

He took a few seconds to ponder what she'd revealed. "Nothing's going to happen that we don't want to happen. So, there's no point in losing sleep over it."

They gave their orders and ate in silence, each aware that he'd admitted the possibility of their becoming involved emotionally and that she hadn't denied it.

Her gaze followed his hand as he brushed aside the black strands that hung over his eyes. "That's the second time you've alluded to that," she said as her soft musical lilt caressed him and he thought he heard a tone of resignation in her voice.

"Probably won't be the last time, either. But, as I said, you've nothing to fear from me." Her broad smile sent his heart into a tailspin, and he wondered, not for the first time, whether he shouldn't cancel his agreement with *The Journal.* And with her. He aimed to find a caring woman who radiated peace, and that ruled out the contentious female before him.

They finished what he considered an average meal and he fished in his pocket for a credit card. "Do you have any pets?" he heard himself ask.

She knitted her eyebrows and shrugged her left shoulder, a habit that seemed like a protective reflex. "I have a one-eyed goose that follows me around, but she's mean. When I don't give her the attention she wants, she attacks me."

He stared in disbelief. "You're kidding."

She shook her head. "Definitely not. I wear a lot of goose-inflicted scars as proof of her devotion."

He grinned at the picture floating through his mind.

"A half-blind goose that gets temperamental and turns on you. I'll be doggoned." Standing, he held out his hand to her, and after seconds of hesitation, she took it. Sensations raced from his fingertips to his armpits, and he knew he'd erred.

"What about the bill? I'm on an expense account, too, Jake."

"I was raised—"

She groaned. "Don't bother; I know the rest. And since I was taught not to draw public attention to myself, I'll let it slide. For now."

They walked toward Rockefeller Center, and he couldn't help marveling at the change in her. She exuded youthful joy, unconsciously seducing him, alerting him to the softer, gentler woman who he suspected lived somewhere inside her and whom he'd like to know better.

Here and there in the crisp, calm night, Christmas lights still twinkled from trees that had been decorated with them almost a year earlier; a horn blared its impatience and a hundred others replied; a tall man wearing a white sheet draped over his body strolled along with a python slung around his neck and a sign in his hand that proclaimed The End Has Come and Gone; This is Forever. Why had she never noticed that walking along a street could be such an exhilarating experience? Allison wanted to laugh aloud at the shocked expression on a woman's face when, thinking her a beggar, she reached into her coat pocket for one of the dollar bills that she'd put there for the beggars she met and handed it to the woman. The bizarrely dressed woman had stood with one empty hand outstretched while the woman beside her proffered a flier. When she and Jake stopped for the corner light, Allison glanced at the flier, saw an advertisement for a triple-X-rated show, and let the laughter that bubbled up in her throat have its way.

She'd barely recovered from her mistake when a painted man on stilts grinned down at her and said, "Hello, lovely thing. Come fly with me."

Caught up in the fun, she surprised herself by answering, "Sorry. I forgot to bring along my wings." She couldn't refrain from laughing as he strutted on his way.

Jake's fingers tightened almost imperceptibly around her arm, and she glanced up to see a smile aglow on his face. An intimate smile, not the studied brightness that he wore for his public. A pervasive contentment enveloped her, but when her mind warned of danger, she tried without success to push back the feeling. She'd traveled that road before, and she knew she'd better dispel the sense of rightness that being with this stranger, a business associate, gave her.

"What is it, Allison? Am I losing you already?" Jake asked her, resisting the temptation to sling his arm around her waist.

"Not…not really," she said with seeming reluctance, and he knew he'd disconcerted her; she wouldn't want him to understand her so well. Her unexpected feminine softness reached the man in him, and against his better judgment, he took her hand in his and clasped it tightly as they walked along Forty-ninth Street. At the Plaza in Rockefeller Center, they gazed at the flags of all nations, the chrysanthemums, lilies, and shrubs, and the crowds—people from all over the world—that milled around looking for something to happen.

"Oh, Jake," she said, her voice warm with enthusiasm, "this is the first time I've seen Rockefeller Plaza at night with the lights and flags. It's…like a fairyland. Gee, I wish I had my camera. Listen! That's Gershwin's 'Love Walked In.' Where's it coming from? This is wonderful."

She didn't resist when he pulled her closer. *But she'll probably go into a rage if I try this tomorrow morning,* he cautioned himself. The gaiety and childlike stars in her eyes played like tiny fingers on his heartstrings. Squeezing. Tugging. He gazed down at her, thinking of the change she'd undergone since they left the restaurant. How could a person have two such distinct personalities? "Is there anything you've always wanted to do in New York and haven't done?" he asked her.

"Ride through Central Park in a hansom," she blurted out. "I always dreamed of doing that, but…" To his amazement, she appeared shy. Was this the same woman with whom he had ridden up from Washington that morning? He could hardly believed what he saw.

"But what?" he prompted.

"I don't…" She tugged at his arm. "Say, wasn't that guy sitting diagonally across from our table back there in the restaurant?"

Jake controlled the impulse to whirl around and look at the man. "What guy?" he asked with all the nonchalance he could muster. "Where?" From the corner of his eye, he followed the direction of her gaze, but didn't see anyone he recognized.

"The one who's leaning against the railing just beside the stairs going down to the rink."

He didn't turn his head; best to let the man think he hadn't been noticed. "What makes you so sure he's the same fellow?" he asked her, knowing she'd give him the man's description.

"Same gray suit, green-and-red tie and handkerchief, and the same dark, bushy eyebrows. Also, he finds us very interesting."

He kept his voice even. "You can't blame a man for looking at a lovely woman. What else does an out-of-town guy do on a night like this after he's had a good meal? Go back to his hotel?" However, his concern far exceeded the casual interest that his voice and words suggested. She'd pegged the man correctly, and her description perfectly described a man he'd seen in the restaurant, but he didn't share his thoughts about it with her. He would have dismissed the likelihood that he was being tailed if the man hadn't fit the description of an agent. But who was he and what did he want? In the restaurant, the stranger wore glasses, though he removed them in order to read the menu, but he apparently wasn't wearing them now, out of doors, which meant they were a disguise. Their ride through Central Park would have to wait; he had to call the chief.

"Let's take a rain check on that horse-drawn carriage, Allison. I just remembered I ought to call a friend before too late, and his number's in my briefcase." A strange tightness squeezed his chest when a look of disappointment clouded her face, her expression suggesting that he was deserting her. He had the urge to put his arm around her but, as much as the effort cost him, he didn't give in to it. He put his hands in his pockets where they were less likely to get him into trouble.

To her credit, he thought, she didn't pout, nor did she insist. "Next time, maybe. But isn't it a bit late to phone anyone?"

"No. He's a night person. Shall we go?"

He walked with her to the door of her hotel room and made himself smile and appear casual, but the possibility that a man might be tailing him had dissolved the amorous feelings he'd had earlier in the evening. He held her hand for a second.

"You're a woman of many sides, and I could get used to the one I've been with tonight. Thanks for a more than pleasant evening. See you in the morning."

Her lips parted and then closed before she whispered, "Good night, Jake."

What had she left unsaid? He walked off with the feeling that unfinished business remained behind, that they hadn't dealt with something important, and from the look of disappointment that had clouded her face, he'd bet she felt the same.

He didn't use his cell phone to call the chief at his home, so he made certain that he wasn't being followed, took a taxi to the Hilton Hotel, and went straight to the bank of public telephones. He had to use a third set of codes before he could reach the chief.

"What's up?"

Jake described the man he'd thought was following him. "I can't figure out why a hit man would wear such a loud tie. And he must have had a few chances to take a shot, so why didn't he?"

"Maybe he wasn't a hit man. You haven't been hanging out with anybody's wife, have you?"

Jake snorted. "Your sense of humor's getting rusty. Are you suggesting this is a coincidence?"

"Just checking. I've yet to figure out what blows your whistle. That business about the glasses intrigues me. Was he wearing them at Rockefeller Center?"

Jake thought for a minute. "No. And if he couldn't read with them on and wasn't wearing them out of doors, they were a disguise."

"Right. I'll put a couple of men on him. But watch your back."

"Sure thing," Jake said and hung up. He left by the side door, walked up to Central Park South, hailed a taxi, and went back to the Drake Hotel. Sometime later, he stood at the window of his room and stared down Park Avenue toward St. Bartholomew's Church, almost ethereal in its solemn majesty as it stood shrouded in moonlight. The vision mocked him, dredged up his near-surface discontent over the loneliness of his existence. Did the emptiness that always haunted him account for his mistake in letting Allison accompany him on his tour? For he now saw it as a serious error, and he could only attribute it to the feelings she kindled in him. One way or another, that decision would one day haunt him. He closed the blinds and got ready for bed.

Allison stood where he'd left her, unconcerned about the ringing phone. Transfixed. Her gaze lingered on her room door long after she'd closed it. Jake had behaved correctly, precisely as she should have wanted. And she did want a strictly platonic relationship with him, didn't she? Then why did she feel as though he'd let her down, had promised her what he'd later withheld? Why did she have that big hole inside her? She had to get Jacob Covington off her mind, and for want of a better method, she telephoned Connie.

"You've got that handsome hunk all to yourself, and you're calling *me?*" Connie asked.

"How do you know he's a hunk? Have you met him?

Listen, Connie, the Kennedy Center Honors program is scheduled for next month, think you could get us some tickets?" The thought had just occurred, but she had called her friend in order to get her mind off of Jake, not to talk about him.

"The firm might be able to get us some. Say, guess who surfaced recently, all cloaked in respectability?"

For reasons Allison couldn't fathom, apprehension gripped her. "You'll tell me."

"Roland Farr. I thought he'd be in jail by now, but he was at Chasan's with Penelope Wade, Senator Wade's daughter. I wonder where he's been."

"I don't. I had hoped I'd heard the last of that man. What else is new?"

Connie's chuckles would lighten anybody's burden. "Plenty, I suspect, but nobody's given me the lowdown. Hurry back."

Allison hung up, pressed the red button on her phone, and got her message. Jenkins wanted her to call him. She looked at her watch. Ten-forty at night. Not on his life. She moved around the room, her thoughts on Connie's news of Roland Farr. She shrugged. No point in wasting time wondering where the man got money to hobnob with Penelope Wade. She turned on the television, tuned to a local station, gazed at crowds milling around the streets of New York, and flicked it off. Restless. Such a magical evening as she and Jake had enjoyed should have had a different ending. And she'd thought...

Wait a minute. Jake had said that they would ride through the park, then he'd suddenly remembered he ought to call someone. Tension began to build in her, and she dropped to the edge of the bed and sat there.

This wasn't the first time she'd sensed something mysterious, even false about him. She telephoned his room. No answer. Air seeped from her lungs. Maybe the friend of whom he'd spoken was a woman, and maybe he'd spend the night with her. Not that she cared. She had no interest in him as a man, she told herself, reached for a notebook, and began recording the events of their day. But the image of a tall man with hazel eyes, the skin color of unshelled peanuts, and a wicked, out-of-control wink danced across the pages, daring her to fall in step with him and grab hold of life. She closed the notebook, opened the bathroom door and turned on the light, and went to bed. Her fear of a darkened room was absolute. It didn't matter whether she was alone or with someone, a dark room terrified her, and she would neither enter nor remain in one.

Dozing off to sleep that night, Jake remembered their early morning program, sat up, and dialed Allison.

"Don't tell me you were already asleep. I'm sorry if I awakened you, but I wanted to remind you that I have to be at the TV station no later than six-thirty in the morning. You remember that the taping is at seven-thirty." Her soft groan—or was it a purr?—sent hot darts of sexual tension leapfrogging through his body, and he turned over on his belly. "Allison, wake up."

"Hmmm?"

"Don't forget we're meeting downstairs at six-fifteen. I'll have a taxi waiting."

"Okay. I'll…okay. Night."

"Damn!" He turned off the light and fought for sleep that wouldn't come, thanks to visions of her thrashing beneath the covers, beckoning him to her with arms outstretched. The streaks of light that at last filtered through the venetian blinds had never been more welcome.

Allison crashed into Jake as she raced into the breakfast room for her life-giving cup of coffee. "'Scuse me, sir. Uh… Oh, Jake. You've *already* had breakfast?"

Jake regained his balance, picked up his briefcase, and shook his head. "The Washington Redskins might be interested in a good linebacker like you. Lady, you're dangerous."

"I didn't expect to run into anybody this time of morning. Sorry about the pun. What's the fastest way to get some coffee?"

He looked at his watch. "We've got eight minutes. I'll get two cups while you find a table."

She couldn't believe he'd said that. Find a table? They could have any one in the dining room. Jake brought her a glass of orange juice with her coffee, and she told herself that it would be safer to hate him for causing her to get up before daybreak than to soften up and like him when he revealed this kind, thoughtful side of himself.

"Thanks, but I don't have time to drink all this, do I?"

"We'll take the time. It may be afternoon before we get anything else." He sat facing her, waiting patiently while she sipped the juice and drank the coffee. A deep, dangerous feeling welled up in her. In all her life, only her brother, Sydney, ever placed her needs before his own.

After the taping of his interview that morning, Jake conferred with his publisher, leaving Alison with free time. She went back to the Drake and returned her boss's call of the night before.

"Took your sweet time getting back to me. I wanted you to dash over to the United Nations and get an interview with the president of Ireland, who's speaking this afternoon, and find out what that dame's got going for herself. Well, it's too late now. Next time return my call, even if it's three o'clock in the morning."

"I'll do that." And he could bet she'd enjoy it.

Later that afternoon, Allison sat at a corner table in the hotel's breakfast room with a cup of hot chocolate and Jake's book and concentrated on his words. After finishing the first three chapters—remarkable for the masterful use of words and knowledge of the subject matter—she went back to her room and made her weekly call to her mother, a woman whose world was a small town named Victoria, Vermont, where Allison was born, and who prided herself on being arbiter of social life among its eleven hundred African-American inhabitants.

"You mean to tell me you plan to travel all over the United States with this writer?" Edna Wakefield asked her daughter, and in her mind's eye, Allison could see her mother's pursed lips and knitted brow.

"Mother, this writer has written a book that commands the attention of both the literati and our government's leaders," she said, hating that she sounded as stuffy as her mother. She could imagine the gleam that entered her mother's eyes when she heard *that*.

"Why, that's remarkable, dear. Has he won the Nobel Prize?"

Here we go, she thought, hating her disloyalty. She'd always been fiercely loyal to her family, had grown up proud of her parents and respectful of their views, but their outlook on most things had seemed to narrow with the years.

"Really, Mother."

Edna Wakefield cleared her throat. "Well, as long as he's not a Democrat. What does he do now?"

Allison laughed. "He's a published author, Mother, and I haven't asked him about his political views, but he sounds pretty liberal to me."

"We'd like to see you sometime soon, so come home when you can, dear." It was always the same; they had nothing in common. She loved her parents, but by the time she'd reached school age, they had missed the opportunities for genuine closeness. She and her brother, Sydney, had clung to each other as children, and the bonds remained. She called her office at *The Journal,* retrieved her messages, and returned to Jake's book, but the ringing phone interrupted her joy in it.

"You're there?"

She controlled what she realized was excitement and anticipation and infused her voice with nonchalance. "Of course I'm here. You said you'd call me, didn't you?"

If he detected coolness in her manner, he ignored it. "Allison. You may prefer watching the interview this evening on TV to accompanying me to my town hall lecture. If I were you, I'd catch the telecast, since your boss will probably see it. You saw us tape it, but it will appear very different on television." It was good advice, and she might not have thought of that angle.

"Thanks, but I've been looking forward to being at your lecture, and I hate to miss the immediacy, that live quality of your talks. Where are you now?"

"Downstairs at the desk. Care to join me for coffee or something of that order? Nothing stronger, since I have to prepare for tonight."

"I'll be right down."

She took in his lazy, disjointed stance as he leaned against the wall in front of the elevator door, waiting for her and smiling. *What a man!*

"Hi."

"Hi. How'd it go?"

He ordered coffee, and she settled for tea with milk. "Great. Did I detect a little testiness in your voice when I called a minute ago? What was that about?"

Warm blood heated her face. "I appreciate your suggestion that I watch that interview on TV, but how do I know you didn't make it because you don't want me to go to your lecture tonight?" Shivers raced through her and her nerve endings rippled, but she brazenly returned his stare.

"You heard the same lecture that night at the Library of Congress. If you think you'll miss something by not seeing me deliver it again, then *please* be my guest. The more information you get, the better your chances of turning in a thorough and accurate story."

She lowered her gaze, remorseful for having thought unkindly of him without reason. "I suppose you mean that; after all, it's to your advantage that I deliver a factual report."

His expression hardened. "Have it your way. I have to make some notes." He stood, and she wished she'd been more charitable. "I'll see you tomorrow," he said and walked away.

Allison watched Jake's taped interview, and she knew he'd been right. His suggestion brought unexpected bounty, for the camera caught what she hadn't seen: his momentary hesitations, occasional looks of disdain and flashes of annoyance at the interviewer that had been imperceptible to the naked eye. He was not a casual man. At the end of the program, she put away her notes, remembered that she'd promised to telephone her brother, and dialed his number.

"I just watched that guy," Sydney informed her when she told him why she was in New York. "I read his book, too. He's a powerhouse."

"What else is new?" She hadn't intended to sound forlorn, but Sydney could almost read her mind, so there was no point in covering up.

"Is there something between the two of you?"

"We've just met, Sydney."

"Yeah, but it only takes a moment. What do you think our mother has done to me? She's signed me up for one of her fund-raisers, and I have to stand on a platform in front of a bunch of women to be sold to the highest bidder for one evening."

She made no pretense at controlling the mirth. "Strut your stuff, Sydney. It's just a local fun thing; only people who live in Victoria participate. Otherwise, it would be unsavory."

"Sure, but I don't live here. As far as she's concerned, neither of us has left home. Her first and last question no matter how often we talk is when am I coming home?"

"I know. Are you going to participate in that rookery?"

"I don't have a choice, but I think I'll pay someone to bid high for me."

"You're crazy."

"I'm smart, and you bet I won't be the only man to do that. You might try being clever and pay attention to that guy you're following around. That's a good man."

"I'm not blind, Sydney."

"I'm glad to know that; I'd begun to wonder. You need a man who's more clever than you are and who knows it. I have a feeling this one fills that bill."

"What? How can you… Sydney, this is my call, and I'm terminating it."

His laughter rang out. "You'll never change. Get too close to your truth, and you close the door. When you come this way, bring him to see me. Bye."

She hung up. Pensive. Not much chance of that.

"What kind of audience did you have?" she asked Jake when he called an hour later. She'd told herself that she waited up to interview him about his lecture, but when she heard his voice she had to admit that her true reason had nothing to do with work.

"Wonderful. Jacked up my ego. Can you come down to the bar?"

She dressed hurriedly in a green silk jumpsuit and met him a few minutes later. As thanks for her trouble, his slow gaze made a seductive trip from her head to her feet before resting on her face. To her disgust, she looked downward, flustered and embarrassed.

"Beautiful." As though the word was for his ears alone, he barely murmured it. He gave her an account of his lecture, a list of the round-table members who discussed his talk and his work, and his views on the audience's reaction. Stunned at his thoughtfulness and kindness, she relaxed, unaware that her tough reporter's cloak had slipped a fraction.

In the bar, they talked and sipped ginger ale, and Jake didn't question his enjoyment of those companionable moments. He couldn't say why he told her about the woman he'd seen walking across Park Avenue backward, stopping traffic for at least once in her life. On the other hand, he didn't mention the stranger who he was certain had tailed him; she didn't need to know that.

Chapter 3

Jake walked the length of his hotel room, retraced his steps, and walked the same route again. He could not permit himself to fall for Allison Wakefield, beguiling though she was. Well, not all the time, he reminded himself, as when she wouldn't acknowledge common decency on his part. He had a recurring thought that Allison hadn't known much tenderness, at least not from a man, and that she didn't expect it. She bet on her intelligence, her competence as a journalist as a source of status, and didn't count on her womanliness. Fine when she was working; that was as it should be. But, hell! She wasn't prepared to let him enjoy being a man with her, not even when she softened up. He pushed strands of hair out of his face, thinking back to those moments when she'd walked with him from the restaurant on Forty-ninth Street to Rockefeller Center, sparkling with joy and gaiety.

"I don't believe her, and one day she'll prove me right," he muttered to himself as the phone rang and interrupted his musings.

"Covington."

"How are you, son?"

His antenna shot up; why was his mother calling him? "What is it, Mom?"

"Nothing to worry about. The department wanted to know where you are, because they've left messages at your hotel that you didn't answer, and they'd like you to call them soon as you can. You're not going back to that, are you, son? It was so dangerous."

"I don't do undercover work any longer, Mom, but I'm on a leave of absence, and the chief may call me whenever he needs me. I'm a policy analyst now. Remember? Stop worrying."

"Yes, but you made a lot of enemies in that other job, so you be careful. I'll be praying for you."

"Thanks. I'll try to get down to see you soon. Unless plans change, I should be back in Washington Thursday night." Just what he needed, another break in his book tour. He dialed the special code number.

"I'll check back with you later today," the chief said in response to his question. "Be prepared to spend a couple of days here, briefing a new man."

"I hear you." He hung up. With each day that passed, his lifestyle bore more heavily on him, and he became more certain that he wanted a normal life. He had quit the spy business, but he still didn't own his time.

Allison hurried down to the hotel's breakfast room the next morning, hoping to enjoy her coffee at her leisure. She glanced over her notes, searched her mind for any small thing she might have missed, and shook her head in bemusement. Not one sensational thing about Jacob Covington had she uncovered, at least not anything to which she'd sign her name. His raw sexuality wasn't material for her report. The man's skill at revealing only what he wanted known was unequaled by any other person she had interviewed. Her sigh of resignation prompted her to consider the implications of her interest in Jake. If she'd already let his sizzling masculinity put dust in her eyes and cotton in her ears, Lord help her professionalism. She had definitely better watch it.

"Hi."

Her head came up sharply at the sound of his voice. "Hi. You're early this morning."

He grinned as if he knew that was one way of disconcerting her. "My antenna said you'd be down here, so I got here as early as possible." He unzipped his briefcase and handed her a sheet of paper. "Here's the day's schedule."

He had turned off his cell phone to avoid answering it in Allison's presence, but when he opened his briefcase and saw the flashing red light, he figured his plans were about to change.

He pasted a grin on his face. "Excuse me a second," he said and headed for the men's room.

"Tonight?" he asked his chief.

"Yeah. Get here by two this afternoon. Our man is flying out from Ronald Reagan on Delta 4113 at five this afternoon, and I'd like him to have a couple of hours with you. He'll meet you in the men's room."

"Right. I'll be there."

He ambled back to Allison, let a frown on his face

give her the impression that he'd had a sudden reminder of something important. He'd use any ruse to allay her suspicions about the interruptions in his tour. His work with State was top secret, and the department took every means possible to ensure that he didn't fall into the clutches of terrorists or kidnappers.

"This is terrible," he said and meant it. "I have an appointment in Washington this afternoon." He ran his fingers through his hair in a gesture of frustration. "I'm beginning to wonder if I need a social secretary; it wouldn't do to—"

"What about your publicist?"

"Not the same thing. I'd like to take the one o'clock shuttle to Washington. Can you make that?"

She rolled her tongue around in her right cheek, and he wondered about her thoughts. A woman with her smarts and experience as a journalist had to question the sudden changes in his schedule.

"I can make it," she said at last, "but won't these interruptions prolong this tour?"

Her mind was at work all right, and he'd bet she hadn't voiced her true thoughts. Quickly, he finessed the situation. "You're probably right. See you down here at eleven, bags in hand."

Jake put his briefcase in the plane's overhead compartment and extended his hand for Allison's. She spent a few seconds, evidently making up her mind, before handing him her briefcase. He took the aisle seat and got as comfortable as a man of his height could in a business-class airplane seat.

"What would you do if I held your hand?" he asked her and primed himself for a reprimand. It suited him best to get straight to the point. Besides, he liked to let a woman know what he thought of her and where she stood with him.

She glanced at him, then looked away. "I don't know."

So she had her own moments of truth, did she? What could he lose? He folded her left hand in his right one, and when she failed to protest, his heart took off, racing like a thoroughbred out of control. Spooked. He told himself to cool it, that it was nothing, that she was testing him. But he didn't believe the lie. Unaccustomed to tripping around an issue, he gave life to his thoughts.

"You mean something to me, Allison. You could be important to me. I don't know why I'm telling you this, but—"

She interrupted him, her voice suggesting that she was afraid to hear more. "But in the end, we'll go our separate ways. More's the pity, because I have a feeling that you're an exceptional man."

Her fingers tightened around his, and she leaned back in the seat and closed her eyes. He stared down at her full, luscious mouth and sucked in his breath as frissons of heat rode roughshod over his nerves. Needing more than he'd probably ever get, he let his thumb graze over the tip of hers, rubbing gently and rhythmically until his action stunned him. He glanced down at her face—peaceful, seemingly unruffled—and wondered if she recognized the symbolism of what he'd just done. If she did, she had to be the world's best actress.

Allison locked her lips together and squeezed her eyes tight. She didn't dare utter a word, and nothing could have made her look at him, open and vulnerable to him as she was, for she knew what he'd see. His callused thumb staked a claim on her, its rhythmic friction filling her head with dreams and her body with desire. Yet she didn't stop him and didn't want him to cease. She hadn't cried in five years, but if he kept up that…

His voice penetrated the haze of her thoughts. "Are you asleep?"

She shook her head, not trusting the voice that would surely betray her.

"Then I'd like to be inside your head. You haven't moved a muscle in the last fifteen minutes."

Her eyes flew open as if of their own will, and shivers beset her as she gazed up into his face and read his thoughts and feelings. Open and unsheltered. Eyes stormy and fierce with desire. "You… You've been looking at me?"

He released a long, heavy breath and plowed his left hand through his hair. "How could I not? Nothing and no one else in this plane attracts me."

"Jake—"

He held up his free hand. "I know, I know. We must be circumspect. Heaven forbid we should admit to feeling anything."

The wheels dropped and the changed sound of the engine told him that they would soon land. He smiled his pleasure and squeezed her fingers. "I don't know when I'll wash this hand again." His left eye winked at her. "Must have magic powers. It's been snug in yours for the last forty minutes, and I enjoyed it."

She looked straight ahead. "Me, too," she said and meant it. She figured she'd knocked him off balance, but hadn't he done that to her? "What time are we meeting Monday morning?"

The plane taxied to a stop, and he stood and retrieved their briefcases. "Same time. Same spot." He stared down at her, his gaze boring into her until she looked away. How could he, with just a look, tie up her insides and invade her soul?

"Stay out of mischief, Allison." His voice, choppy and hoarse, lacked its usual sonority.

"Wouldn't think of it," she replied, groping for emotional balance.

After staring at her until someone behind them yelled "Let's go," he turned and headed for the exit.

Just before he stepped into the terminal, he glanced over his shoulder, saw that Allison was preoccupied assisting another passenger, and ducked into the men's room. He didn't feel right about slipping away from her without saying goodbye, and especially not after the warmth they'd just shared. But he had a job to do, and he meant to make it up to her if she let him.

They had been back on the tour for two days. His cell phone rang as he headed for the shower that Wednesday morning, and he dreaded answering it. Allison hadn't treated the slip he gave her in the airport the previous weekend with anything approaching generosity, and if he had to abandon the tour again so soon, she'd ask some questions. And she'd be entitled to answers.

He pushed the button. "Hello."

"We've got word that an unknown operator placed an order for a mother lode of dynamite. We don't want it delivered. I hope you can come up with a plan. I need it, pronto."

Jake leaned forward and rested his chin in his palm. This was not what he wanted to hear. "I'm in the midst of a tour." He wondered why he'd bothered to voice it since the chief knew that. First the department, and now the agency knew his every move, maybe his thoughts, too.

"We know, but this requires priority."

He canceled his Thursday morning interview and telephoned Allison. "I've postponed my remaining interviews for this week and tomorrow's twelve o'clock book signing because I have to get back to Washington tomorrow night. Unless I let you know otherwise, I should be going to Boston Monday morning as planned."

"Didn't the same thing happen last week when you suddenly remembered you had an appointment? I'd give a lot to know why your schedule is uncertain all of a sudden."

"And you'd pay too dearly, because there's no mystery involved. I hope I haven't spoiled your plans, but I'm learning that a six-week book-signing tour can be filled with glitches, changes, and disappointments. You'd better get used to it."

Dissatisfied with the idea of sitting in his old office trying to put together a plan to foil delivery of a load of explosives, Jake phoned the chief. "Give me the particulars, and I'll find a quiet place somewhere and work it out. This is a tough one."

"What sort of place?"

He could tell from the chief's tone of voice that the idea didn't please him. "Someplace where I can swim, fish, and get fresh air. Idlewild, for example."

"I'll check out the place and get back to you in a few minutes."

Jake knew his boss would do everything possible to

accommodate him. Putting together that kind of fool-proof plan would challenge the most shrewd intellect, and although he considered himself sensitive to criminal behavior, guessing a man's moves could backfire. He needed a clear head.

"No problem," the chief said when Jake answered his cell phone. "Get it to me as quickly as you can."

Jake didn't bother to tell Allison he had changed his destination; time enough for that Monday morning.

Jake phoned Morton's Hotel in Idlewild and booked a flight to Reed City. Six hours later, he stood in an anteroom off the hotel's lobby selecting a fishing rod.

"Haven't seen you around here before," the woman said as she approached his spot carrying a rod, a reel, and a tin box in which he assumed she stored bait or lures.

"I don't suppose you have," he answered, hoping to discourage conversation.

"Staying long?" She threw out her line, and he knew he was watching an expert. Few occasional fishermen could cast with such deftness.

"A couple of days."

"Not very talkative, are you?"

"I've yet to catch a fish when I was talking," he said, standing in order to cast farther from shore.

"Hmmm. Where you from?"

If the woman hadn't been at least seventy, he might have answered sharply. He told her part of the truth.

"I just came in from New York."

Within five minutes, the woman reeled in two pikes. "Well, I've got plenty for supper and some to freeze for winter. Stay as long as you like."

He told her goodbye and left after pulling in a bass, which he presented to the hotel's cook.

"It must be *him,*" Allison heard her aunt Frances say when she answered the phone that Friday night. "Who else could it be? When he stood up, he nearly knocked my eighty-year-old eyeballs out. *And he had on his clothes.* That one was a real looker. Just didn't talk much. Closemouthed as a kid in a dentist's office. Child, if he's the one—"

"I'd better start spending my weekends up there instead of down here in Washington, D.C., where you see ten women for every man, and most of those are ineligible."

A lecture was coming, and she'd brought it on herself with her thoughtless comment. Her aunt did not disappoint her.

"The older you get, the fewer men there are, Allison, and the city you're in hasn't got a thing to do with it. When you're twenty, everybody your age is single; when you're forty, you're already sifting through has-beens and never-would-have-beens. At age fifty, you're dreaming. So you watch out."

After hanging up, Allison phoned Connie. "I'm bored. Want to go to Blues Alley?"

"Did I ever say no? Where's tall, tan, and terrific tonight?"

"No idea. Meet you there ten minutes to eight."

"Would you believe this?" Connie asked her when the band assembled on the stage. "No Buddy Dee and no Mac."

The manager went to the microphone and addressed

the patrons. "We have a real treat for you tonight, folks. Mark Reddaway will show you what the blues are all about, but don't let the man fool you. Monday morning he'll be in his office on Connecticut Avenue designing skyscrapers." He put his hands over his head and applauded. "Give it up for Mark, everybody."

"They must be kidding," Connie said when the man, elegant in a gray pin-striped suit and with a twelve-string guitar strapped across his shoulders, began picking and singing "It Ain't Nobody's Business If I Do."

"Close your mouth, girl," Allison said as Connie looked as if she'd been stung by a bee. Allison didn't remember having seen the polished and self-assured woman so attentive to anything other than her work as an engineer. Tall, svelte, and fashion-conscious, Connie was a woman at the top of her field professionally and with a tight grip on the remainder of her world. Allison couldn't believe the lost look in Connie's eyes. At least she wasn't the only woman a man had poleaxed the minute she saw him.

For the remainder of Mark's performance, Connie, always talkative and with a ready quip, didn't say one word. The set ended, and Allison watched the man bowing to the prolonged applause and whistles, obviously pleased.

"What…" Connie's chair was vacant, and when Allison looked toward the stage, she saw Connie standing there shaking hands with Mark Reddaway.

"What was that about?" she asked her friend when Connie returned to the table for the beginning of the second set.

"Uh…tell you later. Do you mind leaving alone? I…

uh… I want a chance to get to know Mark. Thanks, friend."

"Sure. Go for it." In the five years that she and Connie had been friends, the woman dated frequently, but hadn't become attached to anyone. "You think this has possibilities?" she asked Connie.

Connie lowered her gaze in an uncustomary show of diffidence. "I know it has. It… Lord, I hope so."

At home later, Allison pondered her feelings for Jake and her increasing insecurity in regard to them. She had detected a mystery about the man, a puzzling demeanor that should warn her to steer clear of him, and it did. But then, he would show her how gracious, kind, and considerate he could be, or that wink of his would captivate her, and she'd forget her misgivings.

Jake completed the plan, faxed it to his chief, and was back in New York Sunday night. He imagined that Allison spent the weekend in Washington and quickly verified it. As he was about to dial her phone number, he received a call from the chief. "This is great. Congratulations on an excellent job. I'd like you here Wednesday morning for at least half a day, so we can discuss it with the secretary." In his mind's eye, he could see the chief throw up his hands, palms out, when he said, "Just half a day is all I'm asking."

He figured that, as far as Allison was concerned, he'd just banged one more nail in his coffin, but this had to do with the welfare of the United States of America. His right shoulder lifted and fell quickly, almost as if by reflex. "I'll be there."

After his book signing at Borders Bookstore Tuesday evening, Jake admitted to himself that, at his signings, lectures, and interviews, Allison was a comforting and stabilizing factor, one who always seemed immersed in what he said and did.

He'd probably regret it, but before he left the next morning, he wanted to see her. "Have dinner with me tonight?"

"What time?"

"Seven okay? And, Allison, please leave your recorder and your notebook in your room. This will be a social occasion; journalist and author will be nowhere in sight."

"You serious?"

He could imagine her brows knitted in perplexity. "I'm always serious."

"Even when you're supposed to be teasing?"

He kicked off his other shoe and stretched out on the bed, warming up to the inquisition that he knew would come. "Why not? You're so skittish that I don't dare use plain English, and if I spoke frankly, you'd accuse me of being unprofessional." He wished he could see her face, because he could imagine her dilemma as to how sharply she should zing him.

"Well, thank you for not using the word *abuse*."

He laughed. "Ah, Allison, I could—"

"You could what?"

"If I thought you wanted to know, you wouldn't have to ask."

"All right. I don't want to know, but I'm stubborn. Tell me."

He didn't believe in self-destruction and told her as much. "If the day comes when I think you can handle it, I'll tell you." She didn't have to be told, he realized, when he heard her softly seductive reply.

"And if I come to that conclusion before you do, I'll hasten the day. But don't wait for it. Meet you downstairs at seven. Oh, and, Jake, what was the name of that cologne you wore on Monday? I liked it."

So she's decided to get fresh and shove him back into his place, has she? Well, he'd show her. "I never wear cologne," he shot back, "and from what you just said, I take it nature did a decent enough job." He hung up and headed back to the shower, Seven o'clock wouldn't come fast enough.

What did he mean, he never wore cologne? She'd swear in open court that he'd been wearing a cologne so seductive that she'd been tempted to walk right up to him and sniff. She put on off-black stockings, a short red-beaded dinner dress, black silk slippers in size ten-and-a-half-B, picked up a small black silk purse, and glanced in the mirror. What she saw didn't please her, so she removed the combs from her hair and brushed it out, then applied Arpège perfume in strategic spots, threw on a light woolen stole, and went to meet him. He'd said it was a social occasion; well, when she went to dinner with a man, she dressed.

What she wouldn't have given for a camera. She'd never have expected to see his bottom lip drop, and the evidence was fleeing indeed, but drop it he did. He recovered quickly and stepped toward her as she walked out of the elevator.

"Lovely lady, have we met somewhere?"

"My dear man," she retorted, head high and shoulders back, "if I had ever seen you, *I* wouldn't have to ask that question." With half-lowered eyelids, she let her gaze travel slowly from his feet to his head, allowed a half smile to curve her bottom lip, gave the appearance of being well satisfied with what she saw, and stepped ahead of him, a queen who didn't doubt that her subject would follow. A glance in the wall mirrors revealed his wide grin and his delight in her frivolity. She swallowed a laugh when it occurred to her that she didn't know where they were going and that she'd have to stop and wait for him. She spun around. The devil. That explained his amusement.

His head went back, his eyes closed, silent laughter seemed to ripple through him, and his grin glistened as though a bright beam had settled on his mouth. "I have a car waiting. We're going to The Golden Slipper. Does that suit you?"

She nodded in appreciation of his choice. "It's a lovely place, but how did you know I'd dress?"

"Because you wouldn't pass up the chance to go one up on me. I said this would be a social occasion, and I knew you'd show me what that meant."

"I am not transparent," she grumbled as they got into the car.

"No," he agreed. "You aren't; you're consistent. You're also beautiful." His voice dropped a few decibels when he added, "Very beautiful." She hid her pleasure at his sensual, barely audible whistle.

"Up to now, I've been enjoying my social evening with you, Jake."

"But being sweet is getting the better of you. Right?"

Allison tossed her head, shrugged, and ignored his question. The limousine pulled up the curb, and the uniformed doorman opened the door and helped her out. When they reached the top of the stairs, Jake gave the maître d' his business card and followed the man to a secluded table. A bouquet of red roses adorned their table, and she was glad she'd chosen her red dress.

He didn't speak until after the maître d' lit the candles and left them. "We aren't author and journalist this evening, Allison, but we do have to deal with what those identities mean to us. Something is bubbling between you and me, just beneath the surface, and it could explode like hot lava from a live volcano. I don't like surprises. I know what I want out of life, and I long ago decided what I would and would not sacrifice in order to achieve it. That's something a person should know early on."

She settled in the chair that was upholstered in avocado-green silk damask, folded her hands in her lap, and looked at him, seeing the man, thankful that the celebrity was absent. "What wouldn't you sacrifice, Jake?"

He dipped a shrimp into its sauce, held it to her lips, and let a smile light his eyes. Surprised and pleased by his gentle gesture, she ate it, rimmed her lips with her tongue like a contented feline, and waited for his answer.

"I won't trade having a family of my own, not even if I have to go back to wearing hand-me-down clothing, splitting wood with an ax, and cleaning the floors of a canning factory as I did during my teens."

Her lower lip dropped, and she knew her eyes widened. This man had known pain, and she hurt for him. Every feminine part of her wanted, needed to soothe him. In an effort to brush it aside, shaken, she sat forward and blurted out, "If you want to see your children grow up, seems to me you should have some by now. Why haven't you married?"

He leaned toward her and placed both hands on the pristine linen cloth. "My point exactly. I'm single *because* I want a family. What about you?"

She lowered her gaze. He had a penchant for shifting the questions to her, but she'd never tell him that she had pushed aside everything in quest of fame as a journalist, even the realization of her desire for a family of her own. Oh, but she wanted that, perhaps more than he. She shifted the question back to him.

She glanced at the elegance surrounding them, thought of his facile acceptance of it, of how much a part of him it seemed, and remembered his having said he'd turn his back on it rather than sacrifice his dreams.

"I hadn't realized that you were… That, as a child, you might have had a difficult life," she said, and tried to keep the sympathy she felt out of her voice. His easy smile didn't fool her; nobody took pleasure in being poor. "How was it for you as a child?" she asked, her voice gentle, but not solicitous. His pause suggested uncertainty of her motive for asking, as if he were being careful not to reveal himself, and suddenly she wasn't certain that she could handle the answer.

He shaped his hands into a pyramid, the tips of his index fingers resting beneath his chin, and the smile that flashed across his face bespoke loving remembrance. "We were poor, Allison, but I was not underprivileged." His voice held unmistakable pride.

She hadn't known that her hands gripped the edges of the table until a numbness drifted up her fingers. "Would you mind elaborating on that? My family had material things to throw away, but I used to think all of my friends were better off than I. Sounds fanciful, I know, but as an adult I've learned that kids have a clear understanding of the relationship between them and other people."

"Weren't you close to your folks?"

She shrugged, wary of his personal questions as, once again, he turned the inquiry back to her. "To my brother mainly. I'm not sure why, but we can almost read each other's minds. We've been that close for as long as I can remember."

"But not your parents?"

"Oh, they love my brother and me, but they're so devoted to each other, to their causes and their place in the community, that they sometimes forget us."

A tenderness in him reached her when his hand covered hers, draping her in a blanket of warmth and security.

"I'm sorry," he whispered. "My parents lived for us—the whole family including me, I mean—and when my father died, my mother turned to me and said, 'It's just us now, but he left us a wonderful legacy.' She's strong, and so was he; I want what they had."

Jake didn't know the details, but he had understood what she hadn't even voiced to her beloved brother, Sydney. She looked into the stroking tenderness in his hazel eyes, warm centers of beguiling sweetness, and had to lower her gaze. She didn't want to care, didn't want to need him, but he pressed her hand, and her fingers threaded themselves through his. Immediately, she tried to remove them. They had agreed to a social evening, but she was still a reporter, and he was her assignment.

"Look at me, Allison. What we're feeling is not going to bring the world to a crashing end, and it may prove uplifting for us both."

Maybe. She wasn't so sure.

* * *

Jake walked out of the restaurant slightly behind Allison, his senses alive to her radiant beauty and carriage, his nostrils filled with her elegant scent. Something like lilacs or jasmine. He splayed his fingers at the small of her back, stifled an urge to wrap his hand around her waist and bring her body to his. How had he veered so far from his earlier thoughts, when he'd been certain— had sworn to himself that, despite her powerful attraction for him, he wouldn't get involved with her? He had never been an irresolute man; he evaluated a situation, decided his course, and stuck with it. But each time he saw the softness in her or, as happened tonight, when he learned more about the person in her that she so successfully hid, he came a little closer to needing her.

"Want to stop by The Realm for an hour or so?" he asked her. "They have a great house band. How about it?" He wondered at her hesitation.

"Well, for a little while," she agreed as their car pulled away from the curb. "I've never been there."

He noticed that she left plenty of space between them, and a smile floated over his features; old habits died hard. The band was just completing a show tune as they entered the supper club, but by the time they'd seated themselves, an alto saxophone had begun its wailing statement of unrequited love in the finest example of jazz. He stood, extended his hand to her, and with an expression of resignation covering her face, she looked from his hand to his eyes and back. Then she took his hand and went into his arms, and they joined the dancers to the provocative rhythm of "Help Me Make it Through the Night."

Her body gave itself over to the throbbing music.

He wouldn't have believed it if his eyes hadn't seen it. Voluptuous. Sensuous. "You're a fine dancer," he said, imagining what it would be like to have her in his arms on a regular basis.

"Thank you, but I'm not that great. It's simple enough to dance well when one's partner guides so smoothly," she said with not a little diffidence.

He looked down at her and grinned. "Thanks for the compliment."

Chapter 4

Allison had had as much of his mercurial personality as she could handle in a single evening. If she was going to keep passion out of their relationship, she'd have to limit the time she spent with him to their working hours.

"It's well deserved," she said, forcing herself to adopt an offhand manner, and added, "We'd better go. I've been losing too much sleep on this tour."

A smile settled on his face, and he winked, intentionally or not, she couldn't tell. "I'd never have guessed. You look good to me."

"Thanks." She inspected a spot beyond his shoulder and chewed on her bottom lip. "I'm using up energy that could be better spent otherwise." Why did he always seem to have the upper hand?

His grin broadened, and he reeked of self-assurance. "Really? I'd like to… Okay. We'll leave if that's what you want."

* * *

Allison told Jake good-night in the lobby of their hotel, grateful that he'd judged her mood correctly and hadn't insisted on seeing her to her room door. She took the ever-present flashlight from her pocketbook in case a maid had extinguished the light she'd left burning. Once inside the door, she had pangs of remorse for having left Jake so early, but quickly banished them. Her work had priority, and passion for Jake Covington, real or imagined, could only derail it.

I don't have to stick to him every minute, she told herself, deciding to interview people who had lived or worked with him. She opened her laptop computer and looked up Jake Covington on the Internet. Strange. The only entry appeared as author of *For the Sake of Diplomacy.* She couldn't locate a biography, none of the encyclopedias listed him, and he didn't have a web page. Where *did* he work? Who were his friends and acquaintances? The eerie feeling that gripped her quickly shifted into suspicion. Absence of information about such a famous man meant that he or someone deliberately withheld it.

She dialed Jake's room with the intention of leaving a message, but to her surprise he answered.

"Covington."

"Hi, Jake. I've got some errands to do tomorrow morning. Think you can get along without me?"

His long silence was evidence that she'd surprised him. "Well, sure. I…I'll catch you sometime in the afternoon. Right?"

"You will? I thought you were leaving town tomorrow morning right after your seven o'clock TV interview."

"Don't worry. It's only postponed. See you later."

"Right," she quickly answered, relieved to have the time to herself. "Have a good day."

The next morning, Allison was at the New York Public Library when it opened, but her search of the library's catalogue for information on Jake proved futile. Not even the notations about his book held a clue to the man, and he hadn't written it as a personal memoir, the catalogue noted, but as a report on the experiences of many diplomats. No help there. From the back of her mind, she recalled her promise to write only of his professional activities on the tour, but what kind of story could she write? At the moment, she could tell her readers his age, that he was born in the sticks somewhere near the Chesapeake Bay Bridge, had a commanding presence, and possessed a wink that made her blood race.

Discouraged, she stood to leave. Was that…? She sat down, certain that the man at a table nearby was the one she'd seen at the restaurant and later at Rockefeller Center. It couldn't be a coincidence. Furthermore, the man behaved suspiciously. She'd turned her head and found him peering at her over the edge of a newspaper. Furor boiled up in her. Bill Jenkins had sunk as low as a person could. How dare he hire a man to spy on her! She grabbed her briefcase and headed for a telephone.

"Jenkins speaking."

The calm of her voice belied the state of her temper. "You sent a man up here to spy on me? When I take a job, I—"

He interrupted. "Hold on there. I haven't sent anybody after you. What makes you think some guy's spying on you? And why would he? Make sense, babe. This call is costing me."

A wave of apprehension clutched at her. "You're telling me you haven't put a tail on me?"

"Hell, no. This story's costing me enough as it is. I don't care what you do as long as you bring me a first-rate story on Covington. And I mean first-rate. You got that?"

"Guess I made a mistake."

She hung up and stared at the phone, momentarily baffled. That man hadn't been there by accident. She raced up the stairs to see if he was still where she'd left him, and as she'd expected the chair he'd occupied was empty. Nor was he elsewhere in the reading room. She took the elevator to the first floor and stood in line at the exit while an employee examined everyone's bags, including women's pocketbooks. As casually as she could, she strolled down the stone steps that were flanked by the famous lions and stopped. The same man. He paused at a refuse basket, threw a newspaper in it and hurried up Fifth Avenue. Allison waited until he was half a block away, retrieved the paper, and quickly shoved it into the outside pocket of her briefcase. She walked rapidly in the opposite direction, past the vendor of imitation designer handbags, darting through the thick lunchtime crowd—an obstacle that would test an athlete—and got a taxi to the Drake Hotel. A Spanish language newspaper. No help there, but she'd keep it in case.

Allison walked into the hotel lobby, and shock reverberated through her as her gaze landed on Roland Farr. "What do you want, and how did you find me?" she asked with the barest civility, although she knew almost at once that Farr was Bill Jenkins's emissary. What had she ever seen in the man? Had he always been so lacking in character, and had his eyes always been so vacant?

"Loosen up, Allison. Your boss told me where to find you. I'm opening a new hotel, the poshest place in D.C., right on the corner of Connecticut and Kalorama, and he says he's sending you to cover the event. I want to make sure I can count on you."

"Not on your life. Find another gullible woman."

"I didn't do one thing to you, doll. What happened was your own doing. So can we sit here somewhere or go to your room so I can fill you in on my plans for the opening? The place will be crawling with celebrities."

So he wanted another cover-up, did he? "Yes, Roland. What happened was my fault with a lot of help from you. I don't need a job badly enough to cover that story, and you can tell Bill Jenkins that for me. I'm a big girl now, and I had some hard years in which to learn my lesson. If Jenkins insists I take that assignment, I'll go for the jugular, and you'll think your veins have been turned inside out."

"You've shocked me. What happened to turn my sweet Allison into such a tough woman?"

She gloried in her immunity to him, in her ability to see him for the charlatan that he was. "You amuse me. Don't you know a deflated balloon is useless? Don't waste your time." She walked over to the bellhop and asked him to escort her to the elevator.

"Any problems?"

"Not yet. I'm making certain that that man doesn't follow me."

"Don't worry. I'll see that he doesn't."

The phone rang as she walked into her room, but she didn't feel like dueling with Roland Farr, so she let it ring half a dozen times before willing herself to answer it.

"Hello!"

"Hi. Say, what's the matter? Somebody trip your trigger?"

She released a long breath and let her anxiety go with it. "Jake. Hi. I…uh. I'm fine. What about you?"

"Yeah? Well, you certainly fooled me. If I ever had an angrier greeting, I don't remember it. But as long as I'm not the bad guy on your list, how about joining me for lunch?"

"Where are you, Jake?"

"Downstairs. Coming down?"

Allison let the desk chair take her weight. She wanted to see him, to enjoy his company, but if she was going to distance herself from him socially, she'd better start now. "I'm having lunch here in my room," she said, "but thanks." She hadn't planned to do that, but the idea suddenly appealed to her.

"I asked you what's the matter, Allison, and you haven't told me. Something is wrong."

She hated lies and liars, but she couldn't tell him the truth. "I don't know why you say that. I'm fine. I'll meet you at six-thirty as planned." The dead air told its own tale; Jake didn't believe her. "You haven't canceled your YWCA lecture again, have you?"

His voice, dry and unfriendly, bore no trace of the sexy masculinity that fascinated her. "Why would I? Meet you in the lobby here at six-thirty." He hung up.

Allison ordered lunch in her room, opened her computer, and searched the Library of Congress catalogue again for information on Jake. When the last of her leads fizzled, she slumped in the chair and admitted defeat. Four hours of research had yielded nothing but the title, description, and publication date of his book. This wasn't normal. How could she write a story about a man she didn't know? An idea lurked just beyond the door of her conscious thought, but she couldn't reach it. Frustrated, she stamped her foot. It would come to her. Sooner or later she would know Jake Covington.

She telephoned Twenty-first Century Publishing Corporation, identified herself as a reporter, and asked to speak with Jake's editor.

"Mr. Covington is talented beyond measure. There doesn't seem to be anything that he can't do and do well. We consider him a treasure, the best crowd pleaser we've ever had. And his book is currently our bestseller. He's a great guy and wonderful to work with."

Allison resisted putting her hands over her ears to shut out the woman's stock answers. "Where does he write?" she asked.

Inelegant sputters greeted her ears. "Well…he's very private, so I…I can't say."

Allison cringed. She'd try again. "I'm doing a profile on him. I suppose he has a family, since he's nearing forty." It wasn't true, but perhaps the woman would correct her.

"Well…I… Why don't you send me your list of questions, and I'll forward them to him?"

So much for that. She thanked the editor and pondered her next move. As soon as she'd asked a direct question about him, the woman jettisoned the ebullience and shut down like an engine out of gas. She got out her manual on bibliography research and began looking for clues as to where she might begin.

She paced the floor, turned on the television, and tried to distract herself with *Oprah,* but to no avail. She had to write a breakthrough story on Jacob Covington, one that would catapult her into the big time, and in doing it she had to honor her agreement not to dig into his private life. She also had to put the brakes on her escalating attraction to Jake. What was it about the man that lured her? When she wasn't with him, she wanted to see him, and when they were together she didn't want to leave him. Fortunately, he didn't know how much energy she consumed just trying to resist her feelings for him!

At six-thirty, as agreed, Allison stepped out of the elevator and, as usual, there he stood, facing it. His bland expression quickly shifted into one of warmth and appreciation, and in spite of the lectures she'd given herself, her heart took off in a trot. She knew her smile communicated more to him than a casual greeting, for his eyes suddenly blazed with desire, burning her, plucking at something deep inside her. For long seconds, they stood before each other. Mute.

Finally, his hoarse words restored her presence of mind. "I have a taxi waiting. It's only a short ride to the YWCA, but we'd better hurry."

She sat through his lecture, marveling at his ability to keep it on course when his gaze continually strayed to her. After his talk, she remained seated while his fans crowded around him, asking questions and obtaining his autograph.

"You did yourself proud tonight," she told him as they waited for a taxi.

He stood uncomfortably close, his gaze roaming over her face as though seeking something. "Thanks. But you caused me plenty of trouble, lady. You took a seat in my mind and wouldn't move. How about some food? It's nine-thirty, aren't you hungry?"

She'd think about those words later. "Yes, but I don't want to make a big deal out of eating."

"Snack at the hotel?"

She agreed. At her suggestion, he got a table while she went to her room to leave her coat and handbag. They finished a light supper, and as he accompanied her to her room, the hall lights suddenly flickered. He took her plastic key card, opened the door, and stroked her cheek while gazing intently into her eyes. Then, he abruptly walked away.

As she stepped inside the room, the light she'd left burning flickered and went out. Her scream pierced the air, and almost immediately the doorbell rang. Perspiration beaded on her forehead, and she stumbled, knocking over a floor lamp, as she struggled to get to the door and out of the room. She managed to open it, and to touch Jake when he rushed to her.

"Jake! Oh, Lord!" Darkness surrounded them. "Jake, where are you?"

He grasped her hand. "Right here. Are you—"

"I…I'm scared. I hate the darkness. I—"

"Shhh. Nothing can hurt you while you're with me." He relinquished her hand and draped his arm around her waist. She squeezed her eyes shut and clung to him, and her entire being responded to his whispered words of comfort, reassuring and soothing her as they stood locked together in the darkness. His big hands lovingly stroked her back and caressed her arms, and she settled into him, secure for the first time in her memory. The stroking changed, and his arms tightened around her in an unmistakable gesture of masculine need. Tremors that she knew he felt raced through her body, and her arms crept up around his shoulders.

"Allison. Something's happening here. I... Honey, the light is back on."

Heedlessly, her right hand lifted to caress the back of his head, and her parted lips begged for his.

"Allison!"

She stared into the blaze of desire that his eyes had become. Stormy. Wild. Fierce with a masculine need to mate. Her fingers grasped his nape, pulled him toward her, and waited.

His lips met hers in a powerful claim to her whole being, firing and possessing, as the heat of desire singed her nerve ends and settled in her loins. The longing that had gripped her from the moment she first looked at him shut off her thinking and took possession of her body. She opened her mouth and he plunged into her. More. She wanted, needed more of him. All of him. Her nipples hardened, and she locked him to her. His velvet tongue danced in her mouth, possessing every nook and crevice, every centimeter, as the hot swell of desire shot through her bloodstream, weakening her limbs and turning her into a mass of raw need. His big hands gripped her hips, and she spread her legs in a symbolic quest for what she needed.

He attempted to move her from him, but she sucked his tongue into her mouth, grabbed his buttocks, and undulated wildly against him. He groaned and, capitulating, pulled her closer and rose against her. She slumped into him, shackled by the wild longing that had overcome her.

After a time, she realized that he held her away from him, and she opened her eyes to see the question that blazed in his. Sadly, she stepped away. What on earth had she done?

"I started that, Jake. I asked for it and I'm not sorry. But you know we can't… That nothing can happen between us."

He stared down at her, his desire far from dormant. "I don't know any such thing. What I do know is that we want each other, and one of these days we'll get what we want. I can wait till you're ready." He brushed a thumb beneath her chin. "Good night, Allison."

Allison closed the door slowly and softly. Then she slumped into the nearest chair, threw her head back, closed her eyes, and surrendered to the emotional turmoil that gripped her. His fingers still pressed into her hips, and his hot tongue still plunged into and out of her mouth, promising her a ride into the stratosphere by the sheer power of his loins. She moaned in frustration. She had ignored her warnings and lectures to herself. Now that she'd had a taste of him, how could she stay out of his arms? She went into her bathroom and drank several glasses of water. Calmer, she undressed and got into bed.

When she closed her eyes, the vision of Roland Farr loomed before her, and she threw back the covers and sat up. What had she done? After such a bitter lesson, how could she have been so foolish as to walk back into the same trap? Roland Farr had been her first important news assignment. "Bring me everything you can find on him," her editor at that time had said. But Roland Farr was a handsome charmer, a man of the world, and at twenty-four she'd been no match for him. He'd courted her without seeming to do so, had even pretended that he didn't want anything to develop between them. It would be unethical from her perspective, he'd said. And then he'd seduced her, taken her most precious possession with an oath of love. She'd believed him, and out of loyalty she had omitted from her story the undocumented tales of his trafficking in illegal immigrants, telling herself that if she couldn't prove it, she couldn't print it.

The day after her story broke in *The Herald, The Star* printed what she had omitted, and Roland Farr disappeared. Her editor awakened her with a phone call at two o'clock in the morning and told her she had no job. The next day he reported her dismissal on the paper's front page, but the man for whom she'd taken the risk left her to face the heat alone. Farr was never indicted or even publicly held criminally suspect, and she had sworn that she would never again find herself in such a predicament.

She believed in facing the truth, and she had to admit that her strong and growing attraction to Jake could put her in a compromising situation. The Allison whom Jake had held, loved, and aroused was not a twenty-four-year-old girl, but a woman whose clock had ticked for work and work alone over the last six years, and whose cold, drab, and lonely life he'd just heated up and torn apart. A woman who had just discovered whom and what she needed and who knew she wanted what he offered. She didn't doubt that Jake was special, a rarity among men in her circles. Intelligent, strong, gentle, and caring. Honorable. Affectionate. Yes. And common sense told her she'd be a fool to throw away such a diamond as Jake. She put the pillow on top of her head in the hope of getting to sleep, but pulled it off at once, sat up, and idly flicked her nails. No matter how great he might be, and no matter how badly she coveted him, she couldn't afford to walk back into that trap; it had taken her years to get out of the last one.

The next morning she telephoned Bill Jenkins.

"What do you mean you're not covering the opening of that hotel? The hell you say! You work for me, you'll do as I tell you."

The bile of her distaste settled in her mouth. "Put me on that story, and you will regret it."

"Don't tell me you still break out in a sweat over Farr. Well, if you do, that's your problem. Deal with it. That opening's big time. Senator Wade's sunk a bundle in it, and everybody who's anybody will be there."

"Except me, so you'd better assign somebody else. I refuse to whitewash that man."

"Oh, yes, you will. He's paying for this."

Allison couldn't help laughing as her anger dissolved. "Bill, if you don't want Farr to sue you for fraud, assign somebody else. He's a crook. That's why he's paying you for a story that makes him look good. If you force me to do it, I'll ruin him, because I know how he operates, and I'll find whatever he's hiding."

"I'll deal with you later." He hung up, but she didn't doubt that he'd give that assignment to one of his feature writers and split the fee.

She'd asked for it, she said. Jake walked into his darkened room, disoriented for the first time in his memory.

No matter what *she* said or that she assumed responsibility, *he* had wanted that kiss…and more. He'd been primed for it, and she had reached him in places that no one else had touched. She'd said she wasn't sorry, though she considered it a mistake, so he'd just as soon it had never happened. He disliked the sense that pieces of himself now lodged elsewhere, that another human being could set him aglow, fire up his engine, and immediately turn off the ignition. *She'd made a mistake.* He undressed and crawled into bed without turning on a light, fell over on his belly, and locked his hands beneath the pillow. He wouldn't swear not to touch her again, not even if doing it hurt. When something felt as good as her body in his arms and her mouth moving beneath his, he didn't doubt that he'd go back for another taste. But he'd protect his flank.

Jake had assumed that, when he met Allison that next morning, he could expect a slight chill, but she didn't look him in the eye. Shy? He hadn't thought shyness a part of her makeup, and he figured dealing openly with it would clear the air.

"Good morning, Allison. I see you're as dumbfounded about last night as I am." She nodded her greeting, but her eyebrows shot upward, and he knew he'd taken the right course. She'd been prepared to pretend that their relationship hadn't changed. "We have another four weeks on this tour," he went on, "and the more we see of each other, the more intense this is likely to become. We'll get on better if we talk about it now."

He watched as she drew her shield tighter, shrouding herself in her professional armor, and it stunned him that he wanted to give her the treasure a woman gained by letting go, to show her the wonders that awaited her in the galaxy of loving. He had no doubt, after last night, that she didn't know and wasn't ready to risk learning. Her feigned nonchalance was all the evidence he needed that she was prepared to forgo that knowledge indefinitely. He touched her shoulder and smiled inwardly when she stepped back, as he'd known she would.

He changed tactics. "I hope you slept well, because we have a crowded schedule today. I hadn't thought we'd tour this week, but we did, and I'm relieved. I'm taking the four o'clock shuttle back to Washington. How about you?"

She smiled, but he could see that she forced it. "I haven't packed, so I'll take a later flight."

His grin must have embarrassed her, because she lowered her gaze. That from a woman who looked him straight in the eye whenever she decided to give him some sass. Unrepentant, he let the grin spread into a full-faced smile. "Chicken. I won't ask whether you'll miss me this weekend, because you'd be scared to tell the truth."

Her chin poked out, and he could see that she'd squared off to defend herself. "You're just like one of our Vermont cows that gives a pail of fresh milk, swishes her tail a few times, and kicks it over. If I find myself missing you this weekend or any other, I'll give myself such a tongue-lashing that you can bet it will never happen again."

He laughed aloud at that. "If you succeed, please tell me how you do it." He touched her elbow. "Let's hurry, or we'll be late for the taping."

Allison looked down at the clean sheet of paper on her knee. After one hour during which Jake had answered the interviewer's questions, matched wits with him, and sassed him a few times, she hadn't detected one special mannerism, habit, point of view, or idea about which she wanted to write. Dismayed that he didn't seem to spring to life in the interview, she started to put the writing pad in her briefcase when she heard the interviewer say, "You're the most unique subject I've had the pleasure of interviewing. You don't project yourself, only your work."

And then she knew. Her previous days with Jake had proved interesting to such an extent that her notes had filled a writing tablet. Today, she searched for a different Jake, the private man she'd gotten to know the previous evening, the one for whom her insides had churned while his mouth seared hers and his tongue possessed her. And that Jake wasn't being interviewed. She couldn't believe that she had relaxed her professionalism to such an extent. Annoyed with herself, she zipped up her briefcase, folded her hands in her lap, and waited for the interview to end. Jake could have been right; maybe they had better talk about it. She'd make that a priority when they met on Monday.

Jake got to Washington a few minutes before five that afternoon and went directly to the agency. The chief handed him his orders.

"You've got time for a couple of phone calls. We want you to leave right now." Jake walked down the hall to the nearest telephone booth and placed a call. His disappointment in not finding Allison at the Drake Hotel in New York stunned him. He didn't leave a message.

"If I'm not back here Sunday night," he told the man,

"call Allison Wakefield and give her my regrets and a sound excuse."

"What's her number?" Jake's eyebrow rose slowly as though he didn't believe what he'd heard. "All right," the man said, "I'll call her."

Jake headed for the basement and the chauffeured car that would take him to the airport. He used the car phone to call his mother, but not Allison, because he didn't particularly want the official to know what he had to say to her. He sat back in the heavily tufted leather seat and began to plan his strategy. The agency had a plan, but if it went awry and he got into trouble he'd have to rely on his own wits, and he was prepared to do that.

Three days and six hours later, his plane touched down on United States soil, and he walked through the Ronald Reagan National Airport in Washington a greatly relieved man. As usual, he reported immediately to his superiors, but ten hours after that, refreshed and with his guitar under his arm, he headed for Blues Alley.

That Saturday afternoon, Allison left Mother's Rest around four o'clock, tired but exhilarated after two hours with eight-month-old twin girls. As soon as she walked into her house, she telephoned Connie. "Let's go to Blues Alley tonight."

"I was going to call you," Connie said. "Mac will be there tonight, and you know I don't want to miss him. Oh, and Carly Thompson just called me. She's always liked jazz, so why don't we ask her to come with us tonight?"

"Great idea," Allison said. "Where's she staying?"

"Mayflower. You know Carly. She's here doing business and that means the best address, even if it breaks her. She's on the way, though. We always knew she'd make it."

"Yeah. Desiree used to say Carl had it all together," Allison said as her mind traveled back to her college days. "She was the youngest of the bunch, but no one would have guessed it. A den mother, if there ever was one."

Nostalgia eclipsed Allison as she thought back to those carefree years and the dreams she had shared with her Alpha Delta X sorority buddies, Carly, Connie, Desiree, and Rachel. The gang of five, as they were known on campus.

"I'd better get dressed," she told Connie. "See you shortly."

"Let's meet for dinner. Carly said she has an engagement, so I'm going to tell her to join us at Blues Alley."

"Works for me. See you at Basel's. Seven-thirty." She changed into a green woolen pantsuit and dark camel-hair coat and went to meet Connie.

"You'll be sick gulping your food down like that, Allison," Connie warned. "Mac will be at Blue Alley until two o'clock in the morning, and we have a reservation, so what's the hurry?"

"I'm not rushing to see Mac; I'm curious about him. Do you think he's blind and that's the reason why he wears those black glasses, and we always see him sitting?"

"Could be. Not everybody who has a handicap wants to broadcast that fact. Give the man a break, and stop chasing him."

The hamburger remained suspended between Allison's plate and her mouth. "Sometimes I think you have a serious mental problem, Connie," she complained. "I am not chasing Mac Connelly; I have a peculiar feeling about him is all."

Connie sipped her Coke, swallowed, and waved the air in a gesture of dismissal. "Of course you do, and I'll bet you have to cross your knees very time you try to figure out what it is."

"Connie, for heaven's sake! Wait till you eat those words."

"You don't scare me, girl," Connie boasted. "We engineers don't fear you journalists, because we're so dull and uninteresting you'd never consider writing about us."

"My next freelance piece will be about our undervalued engineers, and you can watch out. By the way, when will you see Mark what's-his name?"

Connie's eyes took on a dreamy look. "I've seen him every night since we met. Let's go; it's almost time for the first show." When Allison's lower lip dropped, Connie released a deep-throated, lusty laugh. "I hope I haven't given you the impression that I'm slow, girlfriend. When I see what I want, I go after it."

"And you didn't tell me you were seeing him?"

"I didn't want to jinx it. I'm still scared to talk about it. He's what I've been looking for."

Perplexed at her friend's odd behavior, Allison said, "But you've only known him ten days. How can you be so sure?"

"I trust my instincts. I'm thirty, and I haven't known anyone else like him or felt what I feel when I'm with him. I've dated a lot of guys, but I've not one taken one of them seriously. Mark is it."

Allison stared at her friend. The cool, unassuming woman who didn't allow herself to get excited about anything was as susceptible as she. And far more self-assured about the man she wanted.

The maître d' led them to their table, and Carly jumped up and rushed to meet them. "Hey, you gals. You look fantastic," she said.

"You're the one," Connie replied and Allison concurred.

After they hugged each other, Carly spoke in a wistful tone. "I wish we did this more often. You don't know how much I miss you guys. I haven't seen Desiree in ages, and I hear she just lost her art gallery in a fire. Kaput. Everything."

"Oh, no!" Allison said.

"That's a terrible thing," Connie said, rubbing her hands together. "We ought to do something to cheer her up."

"I'm all for it. Let's talk it over after the show," Allison said, her attention already on the stage as the lights dimmed and Buddy Dee's downbeat floated over the room. The music began, and Allison's heart skipped a beat as the lights went up and Mac Connelly's fingers sped over the guitar strings.

She hated that their table was so far from the stage that she couldn't see Mac's facial expressions. She hoped she hadn't gotten a fixation on the man, but the more she watched him, the more curious she became about him. He didn't slump in his chair, and he didn't have the lost, faraway manner that stamped the persona of his fellow musicians. He sat upright, in control, alert to everything around him. And he could pick that guitar! Quickly, she scribbled a note, asking him for an interview, and handed it to a waiter. He read it, put it in his pocket, and tipped the waiter, but didn't send a reply. The band finished the chorus of "Round Midnight," acknowledged the long, boisterous ovation, and the stage lights dimmed. Allison rushed toward the stage, but by the time she darted through the crowd and around the tables, she'd missed him. She ran to the side door and out on the street and stopped. He had deliberately escaped her; she knew it. All the other musicians stood in a group getting that long-needed cigarette, because smoking was not permitted in the club.

"He doesn't want me to interview him," she grumbled to Connie.

Her friend's shoulder moved upward with the laziness of one disinterested. "Next time, tell him you're Barbara Walters; he'll break his neck getting to you."

"Very funny." Allison didn't like being bested. She had a nose for news, and she'd never known her suspicions to be unfounded. She stopped walking and regarded Connie intently, though her mind roamed elsewhere. "Have you ever seen a blind person move that fast?"

She continued to muse over it after she got home, and the idea hit her with the suddenness of a thunderclap. He reminded her of someone. But who?

Jake looked in every direction before getting out of the cab. His numerous and dangerous stints for the government had taught him the value of caution. Deciding that he hadn't been followed, he got out of the taxi, went into his house, stored his guitar and musician's clothes in his closet, and wondered what to do about Allison. She was either a fickle woman or a reporter who smelled a story. In either case, he had better walk carefully.

He couldn't rid himself of his unease about her interest in Mac Connelly. The black glasses assured him anonymity only so long as his thick, black wavy hair was covered and he didn't reveal his height. He had the management's agreement that he needn't stand, and his fellow musicians would go to great lengths to make certain he played with them. Not even jail mates had a stricter code of loyalty.

He'd managed to follow his vocation and to enjoy his hobby without having his career wrecked by reporters bent on ensuring the public's right to know. The journey to his present status as an acclaimed author had been a rough one. He had left the security of his home, arrived at the university a freshman wearing patched jeans, the first sweater his mother had ever knitted, and his deceased father's army overcoat. And his height had made his impoverished condition doubly conspicuous. He'd gotten to the school on a hard-won scholarship, and he had refused to be ashamed of the contrast in wealth and status between himself and most of his schoolmates, none of whom eased his way.

Jake didn't fool himself. He wanted the last laugh, and he worked hard to get it. He wanted to show all of them that superior intellect counted for more than classy cars or the latest fashions. Writing national bestsellers wouldn't do it, but being appointed scholar-in-residence at his alma mater would. The university had one such chair, which it awarded to the former student who won wide national acclaim in his field of study, and he wanted that chair. The supercilious fathers who bestowed the honor would pass over any alumnus whose character had the slightest blemish. And in their view, playing in a jazz band and associating with jazz musicians did not befit their august scholars. Yet, his music was his life; he could bear anything, so long as he had that.

The department had never liked his nocturnal activities, reckoning that one of the enemies he'd made when he was an undercover agent would eventually trace him to Blues Alley, where he was any gunman's easy target. The agency liked it even less. He'd told the chief that he disguised himself as best he could, that he'd be careful, but that he had to take the chance. He needed his music. No matter where he went, what he did, or how many plaudits he received, a restlessness pervaded him until he sat down with the band and raced his fingers over those guitar strings. He'd take the risk.

Chapter 5

He hadn't been with her in four days, and he had to force himself to walk, not run, to the Delta Airlines ticket counter, where he knew he'd find her waiting. And what a sight she was! Exotic and lovely in a knee-length beige silk suit, high-heeled brown leather boots, and matching briefcase, and her jet-black hair pulled away from her face in what he now knew would be an elegant chignon. She had slung her raincoat over her left arm. When he saw her, it seemed that he walked faster, but he knew he'd stopped. Stunned.

"Come on," she said. "They're just about to board."

Her smile returned his senses to him, and he took the last few steps, stopping inches from her. "Hi. If you tell me you didn't miss me this past weekend, I'll mark you down as a liar." He let a big grin soften his words.

She turned away and faced the ticket agent, letting

her words find their way over her shoulder. "What do I say to that?"

"My parents taught me that if you tell the truth, you have nothing to remember, nothing to fear, and nothing to haunt you later. So how about it?" He gave the ticket agent his ID and credit card. "Did you or didn't you?"

Her fingers rubbed the side of her face as if to suggest she couldn't remember. "It'll come to me."

He put his ticket in the inside pocket of his coat, stacked her carry-on on top of his bag, and took her hand. "One of these days, you'll tell me the truth, and I won't have to ask."

"You're so sure of yourself."

"No, but I'm sure of this: our story hasn't even begun. When it really gets started, it will be riveting. I can hardly wait."

As had become their pattern, he stored their bags overhead, she took the window seat, and he settled in the aisle seat, glad that he could stretch out at least one leg. He needed so much from her, to know which of the women she showed him from time to time was her real self or if, indeed, any one of them was the real Allison. He wanted to talk with her, tell her how he longed to have his alma mater recognize him with its scholar-in-residence honor. But this was not the time. He couldn't tell her, either, how he had hated avoiding her at Blues Alley and how much he wanted to question her about her interest in Mac Connelly. He contented himself with squeezing her fingers and then holding her hand.

"Coffee, sir?" the flight attendant asked, blessing him with a warm smile. He thanked her, and she put the coffee along with a half pint of milk and several packages of sugar on the table in front of him. Then the flight attendant looked at Allison.

"What would you like?"

"Coffee with milk, if it wouldn't trouble you too much," Allison said evenly, her tone just short of sharp.

His head snapped around. He'd never seen such a stormy expression on Allison's face, and he had certainly provoked her often enough. A glance at the flight attendant, and he settled farther down in his seat; those two sisters definitely understood each other.

With a face the color of crimson, the flight attendant passed Allison a napkin and a cup of coffee, to which she had added a bit of milk.

"Thank you," Allison said with such frostiness that he scratched his head, perplexed.

"What did she do to you?" he asked her, and when she looked at him he wished he'd kept his mouth shut.

"Just like a man," he heard her say under her breath. To him, she said, "I'm on the inside. Take a look around. She serves the inside first. But Miss Moonbeam was so busy trying to impress you that she ignored me. She also gave you a pint of milk to put in a six-ounce cup of coffee, but she hardly put enough milk in mine to change the color. Do women always fall all over you?"

So that was it. He wanted to laugh, but he didn't dare risk making her angrier than she was. He opened the box of milk and poured some into her coffee. "Come on, Allison, you can afford to be generous. I'm leaving her with you."

She turned fully to face him then, and he thought she would pop. Try as he would to stop it, the laughter began as a rumble deep in his chest and bubbled up slowly like a volcano threatening to expel its lava. He braced his arms against the back of the seat in front of his and shook with laughter, and the more he laughed the happier he felt. Relieved, as it were, of every burden he'd ever had. It hit him forcibly then, that something had just happened to him, something of great import. He sat up and looked at her. Awed, it seemed, by his laughing fit, her anger had dissipated, and what he saw humbled him. He took her hand.

"I have no doubt that if we were alone right now, I'd take you in my arms, hold you, and kiss you thoroughly."

Her lower lip dropped. "I…you'd need my cooperation."

He squeezed her fingers. "And I would get it." It didn't surprise him that she remained silent, for he had learned that she preferred not to lie.

"I'm still holding your hand," he said, as the plane neared Logan Airport in Boston.

"I know, I know."

They walked into the Ritz-Carlton Hotel facing the Boston Commons, and she had to stifle a gasp. "Who picked this palace? My boss will stand on his head when he gets the bill for this place."

"My publisher takes care of this. Wait till you see these suites."

Her reply was a withering look. "I'm taking a room. Bill would hang me if I gave him a bill for a suite."

The change in his demeanor didn't escape her, for she had learned that mention of her boss's name served as a kind of reality check for Jake, making him cautious and ill at ease.

"It isn't Bill who's writing this story, Jake. I'm writing it. So come back from wherever you went."

His response, a half sad, half questioning facial expression, unsettled her. She had relaxed her guard, and for all she knew she'd made the biggest error of her life.

"I have a noontime signing at Black Library. After that, we're free until five-thirty. I didn't have a decent breakfast. What do you say we unpack and meet down here in twenty minutes?"

"Suits me. See you shortly." Minutes later she looked out of the window at the famous and historical Commons, feeling as if she'd been thrown back in time. As her gaze traveled from the old State House, to the George Middleton House, the Somerset Club, and Fisher College, she couldn't help wondering about the minds of the framers of the Constitution. Brilliant men who thought only to gain and preserve their own freedom, without thought as to the rights of women, Native Americans, and the enslaved human beings who toiled for them in the land of the free and the home of the brave.

Better shake this mood before I get back to Jake, she told herself, knowing that her reflections stemmed in part from her running battle with her boss, a man who didn't esteem women and most men. Her gaze drifted toward the park, and she imagined that in spring the Public Garden, as it was known, was a beautiful and restful place. She glanced at her watch. Ten minutes left, and she hadn't unpacked. Quickly, she hung up the two dresses and two suits, stored the remainder of her things in drawers, and left the room.

By then, Allison expected that she'd see Jake lounging against the wall facing the elevator when the door opened, and he didn't disappoint her.

"Your respect for time is one of the things I like about you. How's your room?"

"Rich. Even for my blood," she said without thinking of the impact those words might have on Jake.

"Come again. What was that?"

"It's elegant, and the view is wonderful."

As soon as the waiter took their order and left them, he said, "When you told me about your relationship with your parents, I realized you were well off, at least until you left home. But what you said back there... Are your folks rich?"

"They have a lot of money from real estate, inheritance, and the stock market, but people who don't share themselves with their children are definitely not rich."

She heard the bitterness in her voice and wished she had spoken differently. With his ability to discern the slightest nuance, he would probably pigeonhole her as "poor little rich Allison," and he would be wrong.

"Jake, I got my first job three weeks after I graduated from Howard University, got a degree in journalism from Columbia, and my first paycheck three weeks later. I've never taken another cent from my parents, and believe me, there've been times when I was flat broke."

"I believe that. Everything about your personality says you overcame a lot of hurdles to get where you are. Don't you want to know about my suite?" he asked, changing the tenor of the conversation. And surprising her.

"Uh, yes. I would love to see it."

She wouldn't call the change in his eyes from hazel to nearly black in seconds a sign of heightened sexual desire, though it could be, but the rest of his face suggested she'd shocked him.

"I mean, as luxurious as my room is, your suite must be the epitome of posh." He grinned, and she quickly added, "That's all I meant. And stop grinning, you hear?"

He didn't look toward the waiter who filled their coffee cups. "Be thankful for that waiter. That's what I meant, too, but I see you've thought past that. Welcome to the club. Allison, my mind spends a lot of time on you, so you may imagine it occasionally conjures up some intimate scenes with you. If your mind has never done the same, I don't mean much to you."

She put the coffee cup back into its saucer without taking that first precious sip, folded her hands in her lap, and considered her words. He waited. At last she told him, "Jake, you don't want me to mean anything to you, and you have showed me that in many ways. I also don't want your importance to me to extend beyond the information from you that I need for this story."

She could almost see his patience snap. "It's too damned late for that."

She agreed with that, but she'd never tell him. "How far is the Black Library from here?"

"It's on Huntington Avenue, wherever that is. We'll get a taxi. Boston is not a huge city, so half an hour ought to be plenty of time."

As if he knew that a crowd awaited him, a smile claimed his face as the taxi drove up to 325 Huntington Avenue. He stepped out and extended his hand to her. For once, she welcomed his assistance, for she wouldn't have noticed the street's sunken slope at the place where the taxi stopped.

"Thanks."

His grin caught the curve of his bottom lip and gave him a roguish appearance. "You see? I'm good for something."

The proprietor gave her a comfortable chair a few feet from the table at which Jake was to sign books, and she took out her pad and tape recorder in the hope of capturing something personal about him.

He'd signed about thirty books when she noticed what seemed to her a familiar figure approach the table. It couldn't be. It wasn't… But it was.

"Sydney! Sydney!" Forgetting professionalism, she sprang from the chair and raced around the table. "Sydney!"

Jake's pen screeched across the page and he closed the book, put it on the floor, and reached for another. His aplomb restored, he signed Heather Wilkinson's book and gave her a bookmark for good measure. Who the devil was Sydney that he should excite Allison to the extent that she forgot where she was? He made himself smile at the teenage boy who stood before him with a worshipful expression on his young face.

"I'm Matthew Hill, sir, and I want to be a spy just like you used to be."

He extended his hand, and the boy grasped it, albeit reluctantly. "I'm sure you'll be a good one, young man, but I was never a spy," he said as he signed the book.

"Oh, I know that, sir, but if nobody knew what you were doing, that's the same as spying."

It wasn't, but he didn't have time to explain it. "I expect you'll be the best at whatever you do," he said, wished the boy good luck, and looked around for Allison. At last his gaze captured her as she leaned against a section of books, holding both hands of the man called Sydney. After that, he greeted his fans with forced enthusiasm, signed books automatically, and smiled mechanically, for neither his heart nor his mind was in it.

After nearly two hours, during which his fingers almost lost their feeling, he signed the last book. If she didn't come back within the next two minutes, she'd see his TV taping on the television in her hotel room, provided she remembered it and was interested enough to watch.

He gathered his fliers, bookmarks, and the pens he gave to each buyer, and as he stood he saw her walking toward him holding Sydney's hand, her face adorned with a happier smile than he'd ever seen on her. And pride seemed to suffuse her. *What the hell?* he said to himself.

"Jake, this is my brother, Sydney. He really surprised me. I hadn't seen him in months. Sydney, this is Jacob Covington."

Sydney held out his hand. "I'm glad to meet you. Your signing was advertized on fliers, radio, television, and a blimp. I wouldn't have missed meeting you and getting a chance to touch base with my sister."

As best he could, Jake camouflaged the deep breath of relief that seeped out of him. "It's a pleasure to meet you, Sydney. Allison speaks highly of you." Now why had he said that? He had to get a grip on himself. That lapse into jealousy had him in shock.

"She's biased," Sydney said, "and I'm starved. How about lunch?"

Of course they would be expected to have lunch with Allison's brother, and Jake was anxious to see more of the man and get better insight into Allison.

"I'd love it," he said. "My publicist gave me a list of recommended restaurants. I can do without the clam chowder and baked beans. What about you two?"

"I vote for Italian," they said in unison, and he suppressed a smile.

"What's the difference in your ages?" Jake asked after they seated themselves in the Ristorante Vivola at a table overlooking the Commons.

"I'm two years older," Sydney said, "and since she probably didn't tell you her age, having said that, I'd better not tell you mine."

"Oh, she won't mind. Allison is a liberated, independent woman. Besides, a beautiful woman doesn't have to hide her age."

"Whew," Sydney said, wiping his brow. "I walked into that one."

Sydney leaned forward, and his voice held a note of urgency. "This story is important to my sister, and I'm getting the sense that you are also important to her. She acts tough, Covington, but she isn't. Please bear that in mind."

He glanced at Allison, whose gaze centered on the she-crab soup that the waiter placed before her, and he wondered at her silence. Where was the feisty, contentious woman who bedeviled him at every opportunity?

"Have no fear, man. I was brought up to respect women. Allison calls the shots."

Sydney nodded his head. "Yes, but the day will come when you should call them. She—"

"Will you two please not speak about me as if I'm not sitting here listening to you? Sydney's thirty-two, Jake."

He had to laugh at that. She let him get her age by deduction.

"Hmm, this soup is great. As I was saying, Jacob, it isn't easy to find the cracks in that armor of hers, but if you're discerning, you'll see them. Those are my last words on the subject."

Jake savored the veal marsala, contemplating his next words. "Tell me, Sydney, when the two of you are alone later, will Allison chew you out about this conversation?"

Sydney's arm slid around his sister's shoulder, and she leaned toward him. "Hardly. She might be a little miffed, but... Jake, from my earliest memory, it was Allison and me against the world. That sounds foolish now that we're adults, but no, I can't imagine her chewing me out."

After lunch, they walked through the Public Garden draped in its midsummer beauty, with the fragrance of roses perfuming the air. The visual evidence of summer maturity reminded Jake of the ticking of his own biological clock. Thirty-five years old, and his dreams were still dreams. He didn't have the family that he longed for or the woman who would give him that family, and he had yet to achieve the honor that his alma mater bestowed. He also couldn't stand up before the world as Jacob Covington and play the music he loved.

People who read books knew the name of Jacob Covington, and those concerned with government security knew what he had accomplished as an undercover agent, but his goals didn't center on fame.

"I'm an only child," he said at last, "and I always wanted a brother, but I can see that having a sister could also have been nice."

He had lowered the ring of his cell phone, as he always did when in Allison's company, but he heard it nonetheless. "I've got to get back to the hotel and prepare for my TV appearance, Sydney. I hope to see you again." To Allison, he said, "I'll be in the lobby at four-thirty."

As soon as he stepped out of the park, he called the chief. "You call me?"

"Yeah. Get to a pay phone, use a secure number, and call me."

"Ten minutes." He hung up, hoping that he wouldn't have to break the tour again and further arouse Allison's suspicions. If she didn't have some, she wasn't much of a reporter. He headed for the bank of pay phones off the lobby and dialed the number.

"Have you seen that agent again? We have information that he's on the general's payroll. My Lord, man. It's been almost five years since you broke up that cocaine ring."

"I haven't seen him. Maybe he changed his disguise."

"That's possible. Watch your back. I'm thinking of giving you a bodyguard."

A bodyguard? That might save his back, but he'd have some explaining to do for Allison. "Hold off on that, chief. I'll keep a lookout."

"If you spot him, we'll put a tail on *him*. All for now."

He'd forgotten about the man, which meant he'd slipped. One of the reasons he'd been so effective as an undercover agent was his lack of emotional ties. His preoccupation with Allison Wakefield had taken his mind off his own safety. He went up to his suite, looked at the sunken tub and Jacuzzi, and resisted the impulse to relax and let the interview take care of itself. But when he sat down to review the section of his book that he planned to talk about, Allison pushed all else from his thoughts.

Her soft, feminine, and delicate manners with her protective brother told him that he didn't truly know her. It told him also that he could have with her what he needed, that she could be the woman he had longed for, the sympathetic, warm, and understanding woman he needed for his life partner. He closed the book. How could he encourage that side of her without making her feel that she wasn't his equal as a person, without challenging her independence?

He answered the phone on the first ring. "Covington."

"Hi. Hope I'm not disturbing you. I didn't get anything on you during the signing except that huge crowd. Seems they get bigger with each stop on the tour. Uh... can I come up and see your suite? Sydney's with me, so nothing can...you know—"

Laughter shook him. "Now you listen here, lady. Sydney's big, but I'm bigger, and if I get any lascivious notions, I'll pitch him out of here and have my way with you."

Did he hear giggles? Allison didn't giggle. Nonetheless, the sound that floated to him through the wire was precisely that.

"I'll tell him what to expect, but I'd better warn you. Sydney doesn't take down for anybody except our mother. We'll be right up."

He kicked off his bedroom slippers, put on his shoes, and waited. He wanted to stand in the open door and watch her sashay toward him, but he'd implicated himself enough for one afternoon. He draped his right foot over his left knee. When had the notion of Allison and himself as a permanent couple settled in his head?

"Why do you want me to go up to the guy's suite with you? He'll think you need a chaperon."

"I don't want him to get the wrong idea. That's why. And I want to see what these suites look like. Considering the elegance of my room, the suites must be palatial."

"Quit fooling yourself. You're nuts about the guy, so why can't you go up there by yourself? The man's a gentleman, and nothing will happen unless you want it."

The elevator stopped, they got out, and he began to laugh. "Please let me in on what's funny," she said, showing mild irritation.

"Sis, the funny is that you trust Covington, but you don't trust yourself. If you're at that stage, go for it."

"Tsk-tsk. Suppose our mother heard you say that."

"It would be damned good for what ails her," he replied and pushed the bell at suite 14R.

The door opened. "Hi. Come on in."

But she stood there transfixed until Sydney nudged her in the back. "Hi." She had never seen him without his suit jacket, and had gaped at the sight of him in that open-collared, short-sleeved T-shirt that stretched tight over his pectorals and exposed his rippling biceps. She had always been conscious of his sexuality, but as she gazed at him, she saw a different, more earthy man, one who reached something primal inside her.

"You want to look around?" he asked her, breaking the silence and reminding her that the two of them were not alone.

"Sure thing," Sydney said so quickly that she knew

he sensed the tension reverberating between Jake and herself. She followed the two men into the living room, the writing room, and then to the bedroom.

"The bath is really something," Jake said. "Have a look."

"I wouldn't have guessed that you're so neat, Jake," she said, after peeping in the bathroom and ducking out quickly as if reluctant to invade his privacy. She looked out of the living room window and said, "You have the same view that I have." He didn't comment, and she didn't expect him to; he disdained small talk.

"We'd better let you get back to work." Sydney cleared his throat. "Unless you two have some business to discuss."

She let her eyes censor him. "He's preparing for his TV interview, so you're right. We ought to leave now."

Jake kicked at the beige broadloom carpet. Then he looked directly into her eyes. "I wasn't having any success, so I closed the book. You've got a lot to account for."

Stunned at that admission in her brother's presence, she managed to say, "Yes. Well, I'll see you downstairs at four-thirty. Let's go, Sydney."

"When are you leaving?" Jake asked Sydney.

"I'm getting a six-fifteen train to New Haven this evening. This has been a pleasure."

They shook hands, but Jake barely shifted his gaze from her face. "See you later." His voice caressed her, and she looked at Sydney in time to see his raised eyebrow.

"You needn't bother pretending," he told her as they walked to the elevator. "You two are ready to explode so be honest with yourself and with him. He's laid his cards on the table, but you're still behaving as if you're uncertain or you don't want to get involved. Girl, that man is worth any woman's time. Wake up."

"Sydney, I've been there—"

"Clean that out of your head. Farr was a scamp. This man is first-rate. Besides, you care a lot for him, sis. I'd hate to see this thing fizzle." When she would have responded, he held up both hands, palms out. "All right, all right. My last words. But he'd make a great brother-in-law."

"When did you get to be so fanciful? I'm not as stupid as you seem to think. Besides, what I'm feeling will take care of it one way or another."

"You know him better than I do, but it's my hunch that if you don't play it straight with him, he'll be out of your life like smoke in a windstorm. I'll call you."

His hug gave her a feeling of security as it had for as long as she could remember. "Thanks for coming."

She closed the door and because she knew she wouldn't work, she telephoned Jake. "What have you got to say for yourself, mister? What made you say those things in my brother's presence?"

"If this is a reprimand, it doesn't sound like one. If it isn't, surely you don't want to talk about it over the phone. Which is it?"

She had called him because she wanted assurance that he meant what he said, wanted to hear him repeat it. His reaction said he knew that, and she wanted to give herself a good kick. She attempted to finesse it. "Sydney is very dear to me, and I don't mislead him."

"Too bad I didn't see you when you said that. You may not mislead him, but you didn't volunteer to tell him the truth, at least not in my presence. I meant every word I said. If you need more information on the subject, be more forthcoming yourself."

She tried to think of a way to end the conversation without seeming uninterested, rude, or abrupt. Finally, she said, "Could we talk about this another time? I'm at a disadvantage right now."

"All right."

She inspected her shoes, cleaned and polished them, and was about to check her dress for wrinkles when she heard the chimes of her door. She lifted the peephole latch, and her heartbeat accelerated. Jake!

He had her in his arms before the door closed. "Jake. This isn't... I mean—"

"You called me because you needed me, and for once admit that you're as human as I am, and that you know it's only a matter of time before you welcome me into your body."

"Jake. Please. I don't want to start anything with you. We have to work together, and I have to do my job. I... Help me, Jake."

"I agree it would have been better if we'd met under different circumstances, but we didn't, and the more I see of you, the more I want you."

She should move out of his arms, away from his strength, his magnetism, but she couldn't; every cell in her body wanted to be closer to him, to know him as a man. "We shouldn't be having this conversation," she managed to say.

"No, we shouldn't. By now, we ought to have an understanding. Do you realize that you're holding on to me and that your hand is stroking my face?"

He tipped up her chin with his left index finger, forcing her to look into the impassioned turbulence of his eyes. "Say that, if you feel you have to, but tell me straight right here and now. Do you feel anything for me?"

"You…you know I do," she whispered.

She couldn't stop the sudden quivering of her lips, and when her breath shortened, lost in an emotional fog, she closed her eyes and gripped his shirt. He didn't hesitate. His big hands gripped her waist and tightened, drawing her so close to him that she inhaled his breath, and rivulets of heat cascaded through her body. He seemed to possess her, and his masculine aura besotted her as his scent—the odor of aroused man—filled her nostrils. She tried to shift her glance, but with his gaze he held her captive as surely as if he'd been a stranger with a gun.

"Open your mouth and kiss me. Let me taste you, feel myself inside you. Sweetheart, open up to me."

She didn't know that she obeyed or when she did it. She only knew the heaven of his tongue in her mouth, and his lips, hungry and searching, moving over hers. She sucked him deeper into her, and he sampled every crevice, every centimeter of the sweetness she offered him, taking possession of her senses, destroying her willpower. A tide of frustration welled up in her, emboldening her, and she rubbed her chest against him in an unspoken plea. Immediately his hand went to her breast and began to stroke her nipple. She wanted more, needed it, for she thought she'd die if she couldn't feel his mouth on her, tugging at her aching nipple.

"Jake. Oh, Jake." She heard her moans and wondered at their origin. And then, he no longer held and kissed her, but had set her from him and stood staring at her, his nostrils flared and his breathing short and deep.

"I have to be at the studio in one hour and twenty-seven minutes, and that means I don't have anywhere near the time I'd like to spend with you. If this happens again, we'll make love. You know that. Is there a man anywhere who means more to you than I do?"

Half-numb from what she had just experienced with him, she managed to shake her head. "There's no one, and you don't know what an effort I've made these past four years to be able to say that. Is there a special woman in your life?" She remembered that she had never asked Roland that question. If she had, she might have saved herself a lot of pain.

"You are the only woman in my life." He thought for a minute. "Other than my mother, of course." A half smile moved across his lips. "Thanks for not telling me you're sorry it happened. I'm not. It's what I came down here for."

"I...I guess that's why I called you."

His eyes sparkled. "I knew that, but I appreciate your telling me. See you downstairs at four-thirty."

She couldn't imagine what kind of expression he saw on her face, for he grinned and said, "Oops. Almost made a big boo-boo," clasped her shoulders, kissed her quickly, and left.

She closed the door and leaned against it, contemplating the last twenty minutes, maybe the most important twenty minutes of her life, for she had admitted to Jacob Covington that she cared for him, wanted him, and would someday probably be his lover. Somehow, he had changed his mind about a personal relationship with her, and she'd give anything to know the reason for it.

Her cell phone rang, and she dashed across the room

to get it. She glanced at the caller ID, saw her boss's name and phone number, and dropped the phone back into her purse without answering it. She was in no shape to speak with Bill Jenkins and certainly not to ward off his innuendos. Jake had possessed her head, heart, and body, and she couldn't think straight. Only the Lord knew where that tour would lead them.

Jake was in no such quandary, however. The day had been one in which the pieces of his life puzzle began moving into place, slowly perhaps, but surely. Back in his suite, he stripped and headed for the shower. He didn't remember when he had last sat in a bathtub, but that elegant marble fixture tempted him. He hoped the water would cool his passion, so he turned it on full blast and let it punish his still-hungry libido.

"It would be best if we waited until I finish the tour and she turns in that article," he told himself, "but if that happens, we'll both deserve medals. I'm taking it as it comes."

He rushed to get down to the lobby before she did, but she joined him when the elevator stopped at the fourth floor.

When she saw him, both of her eyebrows lifted, and a smile broke out on her face. He moved over to where she stood, past the rotund man who emphasized his girth by wearing a red plaid sports jacket.

"I tried to get down there before you did, but I'm moving slow. Still staggering under that wallop you gave me," he said, speaking in a muffled voice. "Lady, you pack a wallop."

She moved closer to him, maybe only an inch, but in doing so she gave him the confirmation he needed:

they had experienced a communion of hearts as well as of minds.

"You're pretty good at that, too."

An unfamiliar feeling of contentment pervaded him. It wasn't the way he felt when he sat down to eat his mother's buttermilk biscuits, fried corn, string beans, crab cakes, Virginia ham with redeye gravy, and peach cobbler—that peace you only found in your mother's presence. No, he thought, as they left the elevator, it was an indefinable something that took pounds from his shoulders, put a spring in his steps, and brightened everything around him.

"Want to have dinner someplace nice this evening?" he asked her, almost impulsively, while the doorman signaled for a taxi.

"Sounds good to me," she said, her tone airy, an indication that she was still rattled. "It doesn't have to be fancy, Jake. Let's…just have a nice evening."

The doorman opened the door of the taxi and stood aside waiting for his tip. Jake did the unexpected and accepted the man's thanks with a smile, for he knew well the lowly life and the humiliation it could bring.

"We'll work that out when we get to it. My problem right now is getting into the right frame of mind for that interview. I don't know what kind of smart-ass of an interviewer I'll get. If it's a guy bucking for a promotion, I'll need all my wits." As usual, she'd taken a seat in the far corner of the taxi, so he had to lean toward her in order to touch her. "And you stay out of my head, lady."

Later, as they ate supper in a small bistro on a side street just off the Commons, she surprised him with an observation about his interview that he had already made.

"When you were talking with the interviewer, you were so much more personable, charming, and far less businesslike than during your previous TV interviews," she told him. "I can't wait to see the tape. You smiled and appeared so relaxed. Was it the interviewer who made the difference?"

"You're right, I suppose. I certainly enjoyed this one more. I didn't feel as if I were on trial. It could have been the interviewer who made the difference, but I'm not sure."

She was perceptive, and he'd do well to remember that and not loosen up to the extent that he forgot to protect his flank. He didn't like keeping secrets from her, but he didn't see an alternative.

As if she read his mind, she stopping eating the New England clam chowder and leaned toward him. "I want to know all kinds of things about you, but I can't ask them, because the reporter promised to report only on your daytime activities, interviews, and book signings. But the woman wants to know everything about you. But if the woman knows, the reporter will also know, and I'm not sure I can separate it."

He stiffened, and he knew she saw it, a complication he had not thought through. He didn't see how an intimate relationship could thrive in a climate of secrecy, but she had just given him another reason to withhold particulars about his job, not to speak of his moonlighting as Mac Connelly.

"The more we're together, the more we'll learn about each other," he said, as if he didn't understand what she meant. "That's inescapable. You'll sort it out."

She toyed with her napkin, twirling it around her finger, absentmindedly, he knew. "I guess. It's as if fate is hounding my steps, dangling diamonds in front of me and daring me to steal them."

He dabbed his own napkin at the corners of his mouth. "What do you mean by that? All you have to do is write the truth about what I do from nine to five and at interviews Monday through Friday. Shouldn't be such a stretch."

She leaned back in the booth and looked at him as one would a recalcitrant toddler. "Then it's all right to describe the way you kiss a woman, the way you can spin a woman's world off its axis. Should I include that? It happened well before five."

So the contentious Allison was emerging, and he had summoned her. "I trust your integrity, Allison." At the first sip, the espresso nearly burned his lip. He put the cup in its saucer and thought about what she said. "Tell me. Am I really that good? Hmm? I'd have thought I'd gotten rusty. Ouch! That's my bad toe you kicked."

"Sorry. Why would you be rusty? I can't believe the women you meet are that imperceptive. You surprise me."

He let a grin crawl over his face, once more enjoying the fencing at which she was so expert. "If you want to know, you'll have to ask me a direct question."

Her fingers caressed her neck, and for the first time he noticed how long and delicate it was and began to imagine the pleasure of tracing it with his lips until she begged him to move farther down. His thoughts must have been mirrored in his eyes for she sucked in her breath and rimmed her lips with her tongue. *I'd better get myself in hand,* he admonished himself. To her, he said, "What's the matter, don't you want to know? Chicken?"

She spread her hands, palms out. "I'm chicken. Can

we leave soon? I have to pack, and I'm getting an early flight to Washington."

"Why so early? Tired of my company?"

She didn't take the bait, merely shook her head. "I have a one o'clock appointment, and prior to that I want to go home, unpack, and get my goose out of the pet shop."

"Mind if I call you tomorrow morning?" They lived in the same city, and if he didn't contact her for the entire weekend, she'd have a right to be both suspicious and angry.

"Of course not, Jake. I'll be at home all morning."

They held hands as they strolled the short block back to the hotel. An idyllic moonlit night with crisp air, a mild breeze, and a single star shooting through a blanket of twinkling little planets. Sniffing the salty scent of the distant ocean, he wondered if paradise could give him more peace.

"Did you see that?" he asked her of the shooting star. "Fantastic."

"It's lovely," she said. "Too bad things can't always be so perfect."

In the lobby, she said, "I want to tell you good night right here. I haven't decided how far I'm going with you, but if you go with me to my room, it won't be a question of deciding. You understand?"

He did and said as much. "We'll speak tomorrow." Then, for reasons he couldn't fathom, there in the lobby, he pulled her into his embrace, and brushed her lips with his own. "Night, sweetheart," he said and headed for the elevators. But remembering to check his cell phone before going to his suite, he found a message from the chief that said, "Call Me."

Jake walked around to the pay phones and dialed him.

"Your Rockefeller Center pal is keeping close tabs on you, but you haven't noticed. I told you to watch your back, but instead you're focusing on AW. So as of now, you have a guard."

"A what? I don't need—"

"But until we find out what this goon wants from you, you'll have one. Incidentally, you're taking a cruise next week, as part of your book-signing tour, and Miss Wakefield will accompany you. Be on your P's and Q's."

"I'm doing *what?* How do you know she'll go?"

"You know the answer to that. She'll go."

Jake hung up and allowed himself a laugh, harsh and bitter. What would they think up next? He was supposed to lecture, sign books, court Allison, and find somebody or something that the government wanted found. Good that his superiors thought well of his abilities, but there was a limit to what he could achieve in an unfamiliar environment with Allison at his elbow. He telephoned his mother, spoke briefly with her, and went to bed.

By eleven the next morning, Allison had arrived home, unpacked, taken her clothes to the cleaner's, picked up her goose from the pet shop, and begun to dress for her appointment. As her mind traveled back over the previous week with Jake, their time with Sydney, and the few precious moments in Jake's arms, the ringing of the telephone interrupted her musings.

"Hello." She hadn't meant to sound seductive, but her voice had dropped to a lower register and softened, for she hoped to hear Jake's voice.

"What's the matter, child? Did I wake you?"

Her aunt seldom called, and she was immediately

alert and on edge. "No, Auntie. I just got back from Boston this morning, and I'm catching up on a few things. Uh…everything all right?"

"Fine. I just wanted to know if you're coming for the annual barbecue feast this year. Everything going on nowadays is a fund-raiser; we're trying to restore Idlewild to its former glory. The barbecue is always fun."

"I don't know, Auntie. I have to write a report, and everything depends on it." She gulped, stricken with a sense of horror. She had forgotten to call her boss. Though she hadn't taken the call, he'd left a message. Maybe Idlewild would be the perfect place for escape while she worked on the story. "Maybe I will. When is it?"

"August third. You be sure and come now."

"I'm going to try, Auntie." She hung up. A quiet place out of the reach of both Bill and Jake might be just what she needed.

She waited until a quarter of twelve, then got into her green Mercury Sable—her mother thought Allison should drive a Mercedes or a BMW, but that would mean accepting money from her parents—and headed for Mother's Rest. She hadn't been surrogate mother to any of the precious little children nearly as often as she would have liked since beginning the tour with Jake and, anticipating the joy of loving one of the little girls or boys for two hours, she realized how much she missed being with them.

"We're short today," Zena Carter, the head nurse, said when she opened the door and greeted Allison. "Go to your locker and get ready. I've got a very needy one for you today."

Allison knew that meant the child was fretful and refused nourishment. She changed into the white gown and cap, and put a mask over her mouth.

"This is Freddy," the nurse told her and placed the crying child in her arms.

Allison took him to the window and talked to him about the trees, the passing automobiles, and anything else that she saw. He stopping crying, and she noticed that he paid attention to everything she said. She snuggled him closer, caressing him and enjoying his sweet, baby scent. Then he startled her when he clapped his hands and said, "Car, car," as a white sports car passed. Surmising that he was about fourteen months old, was bored and ready to talk, she began counting his fingers, and he soon joined her in the game.

"I think his problem is boredom," she told Zena at the end of her two-hour visit, and explained how she discerned it.

"You may be right. He's fifteen months old, and we don't have time to talk to him and teach him things that a child that age can easily learn. I'll pass the information to the next volunteer who gets him."

On the way home, she bought a supply of gingersnaps and munched them as Freddy and Jake played games with her mind. Teasing her into believing they were a family. She slowed down to the speed limit. Maybe Jake called her and maybe he didn't; she would neither ask him nor worry about it.

Little did Allison know of Jake's frustration when his phone calls to her that morning went unanswered. He prided himself in being a man of his word, and he also didn't want Allison to lose confidence in him. He spent several hours in the library working out a scenario for his next book before going to see his boss.

"Why do you think she'll go with me on the cruise?" he asked the chief for the second time.

"Because you're still on tour, and she doesn't want to miss anything."

He ran his hand through his hair, fingered his chin, and finally got up and began to walk from one of the chief's office windows to the other. He was supposed to keep his job secret, and now the chief wanted him to carry out an assignment with Allison Wakefield—a reporter and a woman with whom he was rapidly becoming involved—in his company.

"But her boss might refuse to pay the bill. Maybe he won't want the story that badly. And another thing: if she's in danger, what do you think I'll do first?"

"She'll go. Jenkins wants her to dig up as much dirt on you as she can find. What better place for you to shed your exalted image than on a huge cruise ship? He'll send her, trust me. And if she gets into any trouble, I expect you to protect her."

Jake stared at the man. "That goes without saying. What about my publisher?"

"That's taken care of. He doesn't care where you sell books as long as you sell them. Cruise ship's the ideal place, and he doesn't even have to pay the freight."

The chief had ways of getting what he wanted and did it with integrity whenever possible. But he'd been known to use less than honorable means. So Jake knew that some time within the next two weeks, he would find himself aboard a cruise ship with Allison Wakefield. In such a romantic setting… Shaking his head in exasperation that fate seemed to be running his life, he picked up his guitar and banished thoughts of his book, the chief and the cruise as his fingers danced over the strings. All of it escaped to the archives of his mind… all except Allison Wakefield. Allison and the seat she'd taken in his heart.

Chapter 6

"So you didn't bother to call me," Bill Jenkins said when Allison answered her cell phone. She had just returned home after her visit to Mother's Rest, and his voice dissipated her euphoria the minute she heard it.

"I just walked into my house, Bill. When did you call?" She knew he was referring to his call to her in Boston, the one she deliberately ignored.

"I phoned you at that posh place you stayed at in Boston. Who does that guy think he is, the Prince of Wales? I get ill when I think how much that place costs per night."

"Come on, Bill," she teased, "he draws such a crowd, his publisher should be glad to pay it."

"Really?"

In her mind's eye she could see his pudgy face break into a grin with a glint of victory in his watery gray eyes.

"Women? I'll bet they're all women. You get everything, babe. Everything. Check the inside of his shoes. There isn't a man on this earth who's perfect, and especially not one with crowds of females hanging around him."

His laugh sent shivers through her.

"He's like the rest of us; he can be had."

The anger that she immediately felt disappeared as fast as it came, and she let out a laugh. "I've never seen him without his shoes, Bill, and as big as he is, I definitely can't take them off him. I expect we'll be winding this down in about ten days, at least according to the schedule he originally gave me."

"Uh...well..."

She sat down, on edge, wondering as to his hesitation. She'd have thought he'd be glad for an end to that tour, considering what it cost him.

"What's up, Bill?"

"Well, the guy's publisher called to tell me he's booked Covington on a cruise, and he'd appreciate it if you could include that in your story. I thought he was a decent fellow to acknowledge that I'm doing him a good turn by having you report on the tour. Not many publishers bother to recognize a thing like this. So... uh...I told him we'd cover it."

She jumped up, almost jerking the phone from its socket. "How could you tell that man I'd go on a cruise without first finding out whether I could go or wanted to go?"

"Look, babe, don't get out of joint. I'm paying you to get this story, and if it means getting on a ship, you get on a ship. Maybe you'll come off your lofty high and mighty and have some fun."

Her sigh of exasperation sprang not from the idea

of spending more time with Jake, but from the recognition that she wasn't in control of her life, that somewhere, somehow a course had been charted for her and she seemed powerless to move in a different direction.

"When is this cruise scheduled?"

"They'll let me know, but get ready to spend three or four days, and see that your passport's in order. You may want to go ashore when the ship docks in some of those countries."

"Which countries?"

"Damned if I know, but with September coming up, you can bet you won't be going to Alaska."

She hung up, took a shower, and lay down for a nap. But as soon as she stretched out, groaning with the pleasure of it, the telephone rang.

"Hey, girl," Connie said when Allison answered. "Want to go out this evening? According to *The Post,* Buddy Dee will be at Blues Alley, and Mac will be with him. I've had one awful week, and some good jazz is what I need to unwind. Besides, Carly's in town, and I told her we'd get together and do the old Gamma Delta *rah-rah.*"

"I'd love to see Carly," Allison said, "since I'm not going to Howard's homecoming this year, but, Connie, I've been dreaming of this bed I'm lying in. This tour has been tiring. How about tomorrow night?"

"Can't. I'm flying to Seattle Sunday morning, and I can't be up late Saturday night. Please. Anyhow, Carly's leaving for New York tomorrow morning."

"You're not seeing Mark the night before you go away?"

"Can't. He's at a conference in Los Angeles."

"All right, but I can't meet you for dinner. I'll meet you there at eight. Get a table."

"Great. See you later."

Somewhere, someone or something had decreed that she wouldn't get a nap that afternoon, she decided, answering the telephone on the second ring.

"Hello." It didn't sound as if she welcomed the caller, because she didn't.

"This is Jake. I called several times this morning. Sorry I missed you."

"Me, too. I was doing errands."

"Did you get your goose?"

"Yes, but she hasn't been very friendly. She didn't even bite me."

His chuckle, warm and exciting, reached her through the wire. "She'll come around."

"I don't think so, at least not soon. She's mad at me." Allison stretched, uncurling her frame and wiggling her toes. "Hmmm," she said, enjoying the release.

"Are you in bed, for heaven's sake?" he asked in a tone that was half accusing and half wistful. "Be careful, Allison. I'm not that far from Alexandria."

"I don't have the slightest idea what you're talking about."

"No? If I go over there, you will. I never heard a more suggestive sound in my life."

"Oh, pooh. I was just releasing a little bottled-up stress."

"Really?"

She imagined that his eyebrows shot up when he said it.

"I can think of a far more enjoyable way to get rid of stress."

"I'll bet you can," she said, "but I'm not going to ask you what that is."

"Chicken. Are you in bed because you're feeling bad?"

"I'm fine. I need to unwind. Then, I'm going with my two girlfriends to Blues Alley tonight. My favorite jazz band will be there. Do you like jazz?"

It took him a while to answer, and she wondered at the long silence. "Don't tell me you're one of those intellectuals who thinks it isn't music if it's not Beethoven?" she chided.

"On the contrary, I love jazz, spirituals, and even some country music if it's well played. Have a good time tonight. What're you doing Sunday afternoon and evening?"

"Nothing special. Why?"

"How about picnicking with me in Rock Creek Park? I'll bring everything."

"Sounds great," she said. "Want us to take my car?"

"I'll rent a car. Let's see, you're at Eleven Monroe Avenue? I'll be there at eleven-thirty."

"Can't I bring anything?"

"Just your beautiful self."

She sat up in bed with her knees up and her arms wrapped around them. If she'd had any doubts that he intended to pursue a relationship with her beyond the duration of his tour, he had just dispelled them. If only she could decelerate the pace of their growing attraction for each other, cool it off until she finished her story on him, she could respond to him as she longed to. She turned over on her belly, weary of fighting what she needed and wanted so badly. Maybe he didn't have any skeletons lurking in his background, waiting to entrap her.

"Oh, Lord, this time let it be. Please let it be," she whispered, dabbing her teary eyes with the corner of the pillowcase. "I promised myself that if I got another chance, I wouldn't withhold one thing, not even if I was writing about Sydney. I can't suffer again the way I did when I protected Roland." She sniffed to keep from crying. "I can't. I won't."

Jake stood at the chrome sink in his kitchen, not seeing the yellow curtain that billowed before him, or the expensive double-lined copper pots and pans hanging beside his head, or the blue-tiled floor, blue brick walls, and vaulted ceiling that told him he'd arrived, that poverty was well behind him. He peeled the navel orange mechanically as he pondered his conversation with Allison.

How much had she guessed about Mac Connelly? Had she associated him with the guitar player at Blues alley, and if she hadn't, why had she told him she'd be there that night? Was she trying to get a reaction from him?

He ate the orange, went to the refrigerator, and got a handful of grapes. How long before she recognized him in Mac Connelly? As he tripped up the stairs, it occurred to him that he didn't have to play that night. He had looked forward to it all week, but if he didn't play, it wouldn't be his first disappointment.

He phoned Buddy. "I have to disappoint you tonight, man, and you know it hurts me to miss a gig with you."

"I understand, Mac. Let me know when you'll be back in town. Keep it close to the chest."

"Right. See you."

With the letdown came a feeling of hostility. "Damn right I like jazz," he muttered in reference to Allison's question. "My life revolves around it. She likes it, but I *love* it, and she's the one who's going to hear Buddy play it tonight."

He looked around for something to do. He didn't have a lot of friends with whom he could spend an odd hour or two. When he was an undercover agent, he couldn't have friends, and after leaving that job, his work was so highly sensitive that he stayed to himself, deeming that the one way to ensure that he didn't slip up and reveal a secret. Friends asked questions, and they deserved answers. It wouldn't surprise him if Allison began questioning the abrupt changes in his schedule, to say nothing of the fact that he didn't make dates with her for Friday and Saturday nights when they were at home.

He took out his guitar, tuned it, and began work on a guitar concerto, something he had postponed for a long time. Thoughts of Allison roamed through his mind, conjuring up the way she reminded him of late spring and the sweet perfume of a flower garden in the moonlight, and the notes came to him so fast that he could hardly write them down. Humming and playing as he composed, the grandfather clock in his foyer chimed twelve times, and he remembered that he hadn't eaten dinner.

She's good for me, he said to himself. *If I needed proof, this evening confirmed it.*

Dressed in jeans, a yellow cotton turtleneck sweater, leather jacket, and ankle-top leather boots, Allison paced the floor of her living room. Maybe she should have told him that she was busy. After her disappointment the night before when Buddy Dee announced that Mac Connelly was indisposed, she should have realized that it would be a weekend of disappointments. Thirty-three minutes late. Where was he? When the telephone rang, she walked to it as slowly as she could without losing her balance.

"Yes?"

"Hello, Allison. I see you're annoyed. I've been standing in this one spot on the Shirley Highway for the last forty-one minutes. There are ambulances and squad cars inching past, so I presume there's been an accident. Please be patient. I'll get there as soon as I can."

"Thanks for letting me know. I...I was—"

"Don't tell me you thought I'd stood you up? I've never done such a thing as that in my life. How was the music last night?"

"So-so. I was disappointed because Mac Connelly didn't appear, and he's the star of the show."

"I'm sorry."

"How did you spend the evening, if you don't mind me asking?"

"I was home all evening. It isn't often that I get to do that. The traffic is beginning to move, so I ought to be with you soon. Bye for now."

Home all evening? She mused over that. So he really didn't have a special woman friend. "See you soon," she said.

The doorbell rang in much less time than she thought it would take, so she peeped out the window and relaxed when she saw his long silhouette.

When she swung the door open, his face broke into a smile, warm and...yes, lovable. "Hi," they said simultaneously.

"Want to come in?" she asked him, realizing at that moment that she hadn't planned for that to happen.

He moved across the threshold and gazed down into her face. "I don't know what I expected, but I'm looking at... Well, I like what I see."

"And it's a good thing," she said, tugged at his hand, and closed the door behind him.

"You live here alone?" he asked.

"Yes. It's tiny, really. Two bedrooms and two baths upstairs and a living room, plus a combination kitchen and dining room, and a powder room down here. Most apartments are probably bigger. I have a real nice patio out back."

She noticed the way his gaze roamed over everything, slowly and carefully. "I'd like to see it sometime. Upstairs, too."

Her eyes narrowed, not because she did that deliberately, but out of habit when she became defensive. "Now, look—"

He stepped close to her. "No, Allison, you look. If you don't trust me, if I have to weigh every word I say to you, we'd better forget this. You're old enough to know from other things I've said to you, and from the way we are in each other's arms, that I not only want to see your bedroom, I want to be in your bed with you in my arms."

He tipped up her chin and held her captive with the passion that raged in his eyes. "Is it wrong for a man to want to make love with the woman he cares for? Is it?"

More than his words, she responded to the softness, the tenderness in his voice, and the longing in his eyes, and wordlessly, she raised her arms to him.

"Allison. Sweetheart. I'm—"

He was all she could see, feel, think of. She could smell and taste the man in him as his aura tantalized her, capturing her senses, and her fingers gripped his nape. "Kiss me," she whispered. "Hold me and kiss me."

She heard the yearning and the need that her voice projected, but she cared for nothing but that second when he would once more grip her to the warmth of his body.

He lifted her until she fit him breast to chest and center to center. "Jake. Oh, Jake."

With a groan, his lips sent frissons of heat plowing through her body, and she opened her mouth to take him into her warmth. His big hands clasped her buttocks tightly as his tongue dueled with hers. Frantic for more of him, her hips undulated against him, giving him unmistakable evidence of her need to have him buried deep inside her body. He squeezed her to him until her nipples ached and she thought she would die for want of release.

Not until he pushed her abruptly from him did she realize how close they had come to making love on her living room floor. Embarrassed and annoyed at herself for not using better judgment, she couldn't look him in the face but he hugged her to him and stroked her back.

"I told you the next time this happened we'd make love, but I spent all morning making those shish kebabs and hamburgers, and by damn, we're going to eat them."

Lord. It felt so good to laugh, and she let it out. "Am I ever going to find something about you that I don't like?" she asked him, knowing it was a backhanded compliment.

"Not if I can help it. Let's go, woman. I'm hungry."

* * *

"Those are the Moses Hepburn home and town houses," Allison pointed out to Jake as they passed 206-212 North Pitt Street in Alexandria. "Moses built them in 1850 with money he inherited from his white father. Seems Moses's mother was enslaved to this man, and he provided in his will for the children she bore him. That made Moses the wealthiest black man in Alexandria. Quite a story behind it."

"I can imagine. What did he do with the money?"

"He went to Pennsylvania, got an education, invested his money, and increased his wealth, none of which sat well with the local whites, and when Moses subsequently educated his son, Alexandria authorities threatened reprisals. The boy had to leave the state of Virginia."

He shook his head as if mystified. "No other people now living have scratched, scrambled, and fought their way so far up from so far down as we have. When I think of what our forebears endured and the great legacy they left us, I'm humbled."

He glanced toward her when she patted his hand. She couldn't resist touching him, for she wanted him to know she thought him the best example of what that legacy produced. But she only said, "I'm glad I know you."

A grin crawled lazily over his face. "If you aren't, I may be headed for trouble."

He found the spot in Rock Creek Park near a stream—a place where he liked to relax and, sometimes, to write. He put kindling and charcoal in the hibachi, lit the fire, and began fanning to make it burn more quickly. From her seat on a nearby boulder, she watched him nurse the coals to readiness, spread a blanket, and place a picnic basket on it. After putting the shish kebabs and hamburgers on the grill, he opened a cooler.

"Madam, I can offer you beer, wine, ginger ale, and coffee." He bowed from the waist. "What is your pleasure?"

"I'd like a beer, but it will fill me up, and I won't be able to eat all the other goodies. I'll take wine."

He poured some into a long-stemmed glass. "I want beer, and since I'm driving, I can have only one. So I'll wait till we're eating."

The more I see you, the stronger my feelings for you, she thought, as she watched him place a big pillow on the blanket and beckon her to sit on it. He had thought of everything, and she told him as much.

"It isn't much, and I enjoyed doing it. I want you to be happy when you're with me. I seem to recall your saying that you studied at Howard?"

"Yes. I graduated with a bachelor's degree in social sciences from Howard University, and I got a degree in journalism at Columbia University."

"I did my undergraduate work at my state university and graduate work at Georgetown. Seems like a million years ago," he said and jumped up from his perch beside her. "The food's ready." He put rolls on the grill to warm, took plates and utensils from the basket, and served them.

"You can take me picnicking any day," she said, savoring the meat, rolls, potato salad, and coleslaw. "I suppose this means you're a good cook."

"I can hold my own. Say, what's your reaction to going on a cruise with me? My publisher has added a lecture and book-signing date on a cruise ship to my tour."

From her lack of surprise, he realized she already knew about the cruise and was waiting for him to mention it. "My boss told me about it yesterday. He's ordered me to go."

He swung toward her. "Didn't you want to?"

"I wanted to be asked, to have a choice, but he put it to me as an order. Right now, he thinks I'm going with reluctance."

"And are you?"

She seemed to think for a minute, to ponder her next words. "Of course not. I'll be with you and I'll get more material for this story. Besides, I may shake that guy I think is following me."

He nearly dropped his plate of food. Thank God she wasn't looking toward him when she said it.

"What guy?"

"The one we saw at Rockefeller Center in New York. He was at Blues Alley last night. That's the third time I've seen him since we were watching the crowds that night."

Heaven was surely watching over him. Who knew what the man had intended to do last night or who accompanied him? "Why do you think he's following you?"

"Come now, Jake. I was in the New York Public Library reading room, looked up, and saw him peeping at me above his newspaper, a Spanish-language newspaper, incidentally. He disappeared as soon as he realized I saw him. I got a glimpse of him when Sydney and I were crossing the Commons in Boston and again last night. That's too much of a coincidence. Next time, I'm going up to him and shake my fist in his face."

He grabbed her wrist a little too firmly, shocking

her. "Don't you do that. Don't ever do a thing like that. Try not to get close to him. Ever heard of kidnapping?"

"What would he want with me?"

"I wish I knew. Maybe I should get you a body-guard."

"Quit joking."

He let her see what he was feeling and thinking, allowed it all to mirror on his face. "I was never more serious in my life."

He hoped it wouldn't come to that, but he meant to see that she was protected if the chief didn't find a way to get rid of the man.

"I'd hoped we'd have a longer afternoon, and we would have except for that traffic jam. I love to spend long hours practically in this spot. I wrote parts of my book sitting right on that boulder." He took some roasting chestnuts from the grill, slipped on his grilling glove, shelled them. She opened her mouth and he fed them to her, thinking it one of the most sensuous things he'd ever done. She didn't shift her gaze from his as she chewed, her eyes flaming with passion. He sat back on his haunches, staring at her. What was it about that one woman that could make him think such foolish things? His libido had begun enticing him to lay her on that blanket and...

"I don't want darkness to catch us here," he said, partly as an excuse to break the tension, but also because he didn't think the park safe after dark. And he had to call the chief.

They packed the remains of their picnic and stored them in the trunk of the rented Mercury. When he opened the front passenger door for her, her arms went around him, and she rested her head on his chest.

Stunned at her soft, feminine gesture, he clasped her to him and waited for the words that would explain.

"I…I just want to enjoy being with you like this, because I know it won't last. It can't. Nothing this wonderful ever does."

Taken aback by her candor and her open need to have him cherish her, he hugged her to him. "It will be what you and I make it." He couldn't say more, but he wasn't ready to commit himself beyond their present level of understanding.

"I need to stop at a gas station," he said, thinking that would be the fastest way to get the privacy he needed in order to call the chief.

"Didn't the rental agency give you a full tank?" she asked, demonstrating her alert and inquisitive mind.

"Yeah, but if I return it with a full tank, I'm paying for gas at a lower rate." He hoped that made sense; he hadn't previously considered the matter.

"Fill it up," he told the attendant when they had stopped. Then he got out and headed for the restroom.

"Sorry to bother you on your day off," he told the chief, although he wasn't sorry at all and the chief knew it. "I just learned that our man is the third person on this tour. He was at Blues Alley last night, but I wasn't."

"I know. That was too close to home, so I had him booked for harassment. You picked the perfect time to stay away. No one will know which cruise you're taking. We'll get Ms. Wakefield's tickets and give them to you."

"What about her boss?"

"He's in the publisher's pocket. The guy is anxious to whitewash himself and be important. As far as he

knows, the publisher is so appreciative of his cooperation that he's paying for Ms. Wakefield's cruise ticket."

"Suppose whoever is paying that snoop puts somebody else on the job. At least we recognize that one."

"Good point, but I expect we'll find out from him
who's paying him."

"Hope so."

"Glad you had a nice picnic."

"A what? Oh. I forgot you have eyes in the back of
your head."

He hung up and went back to Allison, knowing she'd
think he went to the men's room.

However, Allison was not taken in by Jake's ruse.
Frequent glances at her watch made her suspicious at
his ten-minute absence. And the attendant confirmed
for her that Jake hadn't needed gas when he told her, "I
couldn't get more than three gallons in there."

"He wants to return the car with the tank full," she
said.

The man made a slovenly attempt at cleaning the
windshield. "What for? He's already paid the rental
agency for it."

"Sorry. That took longer than I expected," Jake said,
getting into the car and starting the motor. "How would
you like us to spend the evening? We could see an early
movie and then have a late supper. What do you say?"

"I'd have to change."

"Then I'll wait while you do that, after which you
can wait while I do the same."

"Jake," she said, phrasing her words carefully, "if
you're serious about a movie and supper afterward,
think up a different plan for us to go home and change.

I suggest you drop me at my house and I'll meet you at the movie."

This man is a rogue, she said to herself, when a grin began around his mouth and escalated into full-blown laughter. "What's the matter, sweetheart? Is there some-body in this car that you don't trust?"

"Very funny. Maybe there is. Tell me which movie, and I'll meet you there."

"I'll call you when I get home."

At home, she showered and dressed in an avocado-green rayon dress that clung to her body, brown lizard accessories, and gold hoop earrings. Then, she combed her hair down to her shoulders, dabbed Callèche perfume behind her ears and at her wrists. When he rang the bell, she was opening the closet in her foyer to get her beige raincoat.

"Hi," he said, his gaze seeming to photograph her. "What a change! Woman, you make me proud to be a man."

His words sent a flush of heat through her body. She wanted to tell him that he made her feel good, wom-anly, and feminine. Instead, she said, "You made cer-tain that all the women will envy me." Flirting was a lot less dangerous than revealing her true feelings. She handed him her coat. "Ready when you are."

She couldn't remember having watched a movie with one hand in the hand of a man she cared about and the other free to dig into a bag of buttered popcorn. He'd bought two bags, admonishing her not to expect any of his after she ate her own. So conscious was she of the man beside her that she saw little of *The Red Shoes,* an old, World War II-era film.

"I like the ballet," he said as they left. "As a child, I didn't go to the theater or the opera; we had to deal with the basics of life. When I went to college, I discovered that most of my classmates had seen paintings by Rembrandt, Picasso, and other great artists; I had seen pictures of their works in books that my father occasionally borrowed from the library. Occasionally, because we lived a good forty miles from a library. Music was the one thing I had in abundance, because we had a radio. I listened to the opera on the Texaco program Saturday afternoons. I loved it. On that program, Milton Cross taught me stories of the opera and about the great opera composers. Often, I listened with pencil and paper in hand, taking notes. Enthralled."

Growing up, she hadn't dreamed people lived that way. "Didn't you have a television?"

"We had one, but the signal was so poor that we rarely watched anything."

At Togi's they ate crab cakes, French fries, and mixed-green salads. "You planning to play it safe when I take you home?" he asked her, not bothering to smile.

"You care to explain that?" she asked him, although she knew he referred to her suggestion earlier that waiting in each other's homes would ensure that they neither saw a movie nor ate supper.

"Absolutely." But he didn't explain it, just signaled for the waiter. "This place has the best crab cakes in town."

He walked with her to her front door, holding her hand. She handed him her key, and he opened the door, stepped behind her into the foyer, and stared into her face.

"Thanks for the day. I don't want to leave you. Understand? But I won't ask to stay, because tomorrow morning we have to meet at Delta Airlines and head for New Orleans. When we spend the night together, I want to be able to sleep late. Very late."

She imagined that her eyes widened, and she heard herself suck in her breath. "That's right," he said. "We need to find out about each other, and that will take time."

Before she could think of a reply, he clasped her face in his hands, smiled—his contrary wink adding to his charisma—and pressed his lips to hers. She parted her lips, but he hugged her and moved away.

"See you in the morning."

I'm getting in deeper and deeper with this man, she told herself, walking up the stairs to her bedroom. *But no matter what I learn about him, it's going in my story. I can't be a fool twice.*

As the taxi headed for Reagan National Airport the following morning, Monday, she telephoned her boss. "Just wanted you to know we're headed for New Orleans," she told him. "This is a short trip; we'll be there for two days and three nights."

"Yeah. I'd like to see your face in this office when you get back."

"I may need to spend some time in the library, getting background information." She didn't want to write the story in the office, because Bill Jenkins would read over her shoulder, then take her copy before she finished it.

"Do what you have to do. Just bring me something that sizzles."

The taxi drove up to the gleaming new airport and stopped at the curb. "I'll be in touch," she said, glad to hang up.

For the first time, Jake waited for her at the check-in counter. "Thought I'd surprise you," he said, his grin wide and welcoming.

"You did." How was it that the man looked better every time she saw him? Unable to stay awake, she slept for most of the three-hour trip to New Orleans.

After his signing at the Community Bookstore on Broad Street that evening, Vera, the proprietor, treated them to a soul-food dinner—fried catfish, stewed collards, baked corn bread, and candied sweet potatoes.

"Now, *this* is food," Jake said. "I love gourmet cooking, but this stuff nourishes the soul. You Yankees don't know what good *is*."

Facing her in the hotel lobby later, he said, "It's been a long day, and I imagine you want to rest. My television interview is at eleven, and I have to be at Michelle's African-American Book Stop at one. We'd better eat a substantial breakfast, so I suggest we meet in the restaurant around eight-thirty. Okay?"

Stunned at his blunt announcement that he wanted the evening to himself, she said, "Thanks. I wouldn't mind some personal time."

His left eyebrow shot up, and his face seemed to darken. "If you want to join me for breakfast, I'll be in that café around there at eight-thirty. Good night."

He hated to desert her, but he couldn't come to New Orleans and not visit his favorite jazz haunts. Taking her with him would be tantamount to telling her he was Mac Connelly, for the jazzmen at his favorite saloons knew him well and would invite him to sit in with them and play the guitar. He had never been devious and certainly not deceptive, but he couldn't share that part of his life with her. She cared for him, but she was a journalist, and he couldn't risk her reporting it, for if she did he would surely lose the chance to become scholar-in-residence at his undergraduate university.

He waited in his room for a reasonable time, then left the hotel by a side door and headed for Snug Harbor, where he knew he'd find some of the best jazz in New Orleans.

"Hey, man, it's been centuries," the maître d' said when Jake walked in.

"Smell's the same," Jake said, sniffing the odor of fried mushrooms, crab cakes, and fried catfish. "Who's on tonight?"

"Ellis."

Jake let the music roll over him, absorbing it into his mind, his heart, and the pores of his body. The waiter brought a plate of fried mushrooms, and Jake nibbled at it, sipped beer, and thought about Allison. He needed time alone with her, time to find out if she was the woman for him, as he had begun to suspect. And he had to figure out how to appease her, because right then she was either mad, suspicious of him, or both.

After a performance by one of the best jazz singers he'd heard in a while, the manager took the mike. "Ladies and gentlemen, we have a rare treat for you tonight. Mac Connelly is in town, and he's here. What do you say I give him a guitar?"

Any performer would have been gratified by that audience's roar of approval, and Jake was moved to humility. The lights dimmed and he ducked in back of the stage where the maître d' gave him a broad-brimmed hunter's hat, a pair of dark glasses, and a Chet Atkins guitar.

For the next twenty minutes, he lived in the world that his fingers created, a world of consummate jazz. At last, he played "Back Home in Indiana," his signature piece, which was guaranteed to set the audience roaring, clapping, and stomping. Then he bowed, the lights dimmed, and he left the stage and headed back to the hotel.

Playing renewed him as spring rain renewed and nourished flowers. If only he could share it with Allison, tell her what it meant to him! He showered, slipped into bed, and began his now familiar wrestle with the sheets. He turned over on his belly and gazed at the telephone, knowing that if he dared dial her room, it would bring the sound of her voice. Disgusted, he released a sharp expletive and turned out the light. At daybreak, he still ached for her.

As they boarded the cruise ship *Saint Marie,* Allison began to question her senses. "How far is your room from mine?" she asked him, remembering her distrust of long narrow corridors, public stairwells, and unattended elevators.

He didn't look at her. "We share a wall."

"Don't tell me we have connecting doors."

"We don't, and I won't. How long will it take you to learn to trust me? We share a small deck, or at least I agreed to that."

After standing in a long line for a security check, room keys, and reboarding passes, they could at last see their rooms. "Mine's a knockout," she said to Jake after joining him on the deck.

"Mine, too. Even has a chintz-covered chaise lounge.

Trouble is, I don't like chintz." He opened the door. "Come on in and have a look."

"It's lovely. Don't like chintz? You're acting just like a man."

Both hands went to his hips. "What would you expect me to act like? A child?"

She punctuated her irreverence with a shrug. "Why not? Most men manage that on a regular basis."

He grasped her shoulders, gazing into her eyes as he did so. "Are you asking me for a demonstration of my manhood? If you are, don't expect me to disappoint you. I'm itching for the opportunity."

His facial expression told her it wasn't a time to smart-mouth him, so she said, "I didn't mean to provoke you. I was merely stating a fact. If you don't fall into that category—"

He cut her off. "Stop while you are ahead, Allison. Nothing would please me more than to show you what I'm made of, but I am not going to let you goad me into it. If you want us to make love, create the environment for it." He waved his hand around the room. "You can't say the opportunity isn't here. A man will take sex where he finds it, but that's not the same as making love, and especially not with a woman he cares for."

"I wasn't goading you, at least not intentionally. Thanks for showing me your room; except for the colors, it's just like mine."

"Now wait a second. You have no right to be angry. I put my cards on the table. What was wrong with that?"

"Nothing. I'm going to unpack, have a nap, and get dressed for dinner. Go read your notes."

"Right. I'll phone you at seven. We have an eight-thirty seating."

He wasn't anxious to spend the afternoon with me. If he's planning the nights for himself as he did in New Orleans, he can kiss a relationship with me goodbye. I'm not holding still for that. In her stateroom, she unpacked, showered, and stretched out on the chaise lounge to watch television. After a few minutes, she switched it off. So far, she had no reason to distrust Jake. If only she could wash that experience with Farr out of her mind. *Was she going to let it rule her life forever?* She jumped up. "I'm wasting precious time. I should be scouting out this boat for background information."

She dressed in a yellow T-shirt, white shorts, and sneakers and headed for the main deck. "Everybody on the main deck for life raft and safety drill. Bring your life vest with you," a voice over the loudspeaker admonished the passengers. She retraced her steps and reached her stateroom at the same time as Jake.

After the drill, he suggested they watch the ship pull away from shore. "You should see the seabirds out there."

She had thought seagulls and water fowl only hung around northern waters, but they covered the Florida pier. As the *Saint Marie* coughed out its booming signal, she stood on deck with Jacob Covington's arms wrapped around her—a pair of lovers to the eyes of all who saw them.

Jake gave her his lecture and book-signing schedule. "I'll be busy a part of the time gathering information for my next book, which will have several scenes on a ship. Hope you won't mind."

She gazed at him, reading him and refusing to flinch beneath his appraisal. "In that case, I'll work on my introduction to this story on you. Bill told me it will take up four full pages of the weekend 'Living Section.' That's a lot of writing for a journalistic account of a man's daily activities."

The fingers of his left hand rubbed his chain. She'd seen him do that several times and had yet to discern the meaning of it.

"As long as you keep your promise, I don't care what you write."

She hoped he didn't notice how she flinched at that remark. *Don't surprise me, and I won't surprise you.* Knowing she could never be callous about anything relating to Jake, she said a silent prayer that she wouldn't uncover anything he didn't want known.

Jake went to the head porter's officer and introduced himself as a writer. "I'm thinking of setting my next story on this ship," he told the man. "How many passengers did you check in?"

"Twelve hundred thirty."

"Quite a crowd. How do you manage to get all that luggage to the right passengers?"

The man beamed with pride, as Jake knew he would. "Most women bring two pieces of luggage plus hand luggage, and men bring one piece. We have five hundred males and 730 females, all ages included. We screen every piece."

Jake made himself seem impressed. "What a job. Do you screen when passengers reboard after doing ashore?"

"Well, we haven't been doing that. Maybe we should. I'm going to speak with the captain about it. It's a great idea, what with terrorism and all."

"Yeah," Jake said. "That's what I was thinking about. A guy likes to know he's safe."

He headed for the kitchen to make friends with the chef and scrutinize his crew. If packages and passengers weren't screened at reboarding, anybody could smuggle anything on board, perhaps even illegal aliens. And ship stowaways needed food and water, for which they had to have the help of the kitchen staff.

After Jake introduced himself as a writer who hoped to use the cruise ship as the setting for his next novel, the chef gave him free access to the kitchen and permission to interview the staff. The only man to refuse him an interview—a United States citizen of slight build and shifty eyes—aroused his suspicion at once. He returned to his stateroom, satisfied with what he had accomplished, and phoned the chief.

"Get me what you can on this guy. The kitchen help called him 'Ring.'"

"You'll get an email tomorrow morning. Good job."

It amazed him that about two hundred people jammed the lecture hall for his first talk at ten the next morning. He had planned to read from his book, but instead he told them a story about a young man who pulled himself up from poverty and anonymity to national fame. Frequent glances to Allison verified her amazement. She didn't write, but listened with her gaze glued to him and hardly moving a muscle, as if spellbound.

Following his thirty-minute talk, his listeners crowded around him, wanting to shake his hand and clamoring for his autograph. He couldn't believe the reception they gave him.

"On a cruise where people come to be frivolous, I'm surprised that they appreciated anything that serious. It's amazing," he told Allison when they were at last alone. "I didn't plan that, but once I started talking, I went with it."

"I'm not surprised that the people enjoyed it," she said. "I knew some of your life story, but this morning...well, you were riveting."

"They'll bring our lunch to our deck, if we ask for it," he said. "Shall we?"

She nodded. "What haven't you done that you have always wanted to do, or that you long for?" she asked him.

He draped his right foot over his left knee, leaned back, and locked his hands behind his head. "I want to be scholar-in-residence at my alma mater, settle down there, write, and teach our youth."

"You've mentioned that before. Is there a real chance?"

"I think so, provided I maintain a squeaky-clean reputation. I've been nominated, but the university has only one such chair. We'll see."

"You would certainly get my vote."

"Thanks. The boat docks Thursday morning. What're you doing over the weekend?"

"My aunt wants me to visit her in Idlewild for the annual barbecue picnic, the second biggest community function of the year. Want to come?"

"I'd love to, but I'm not sure I can. I promised my mother I'd get to see her before I took this trip, but like you, I got almost no notice of the departure date, and I had to disappoint her. We'll see."

They ordered lunch, and two waiters appeared with

large round trays and racks upon which to rest them. The order of shrimp scampi teased her nostrils before she saw the food. They ate with relish as the boat glided over the Caribbean waters and a soft breeze brushed their faces.

"I could live like this forever," she said.

"You really could?" he asked her, savoring a crab-and-shrimp cannelloni.

"Not really, I guess. It's not domestic enough. But it sure is wonderful being out of my boss's reach," she said, moving the conversation away from her.

"If you dislike him so much, why don't you quit and get another job?"

She wasn't yet prepared to tell him about Roland Farr and what the liaison with him had cost her. "It's a long story, Jake. I hope that one of these days I can tell you about it."

"Is it too painful, or are you sworn to secrecy?"

"Painful."

His arm encircled her shoulder. "I'm a big guy, and not just in size. If it gets too heavy, let me help you carry it."

As a child, she had leaned on her brother, Sydney, but from the day she'd graduated from college, she had fought her own battles. She didn't want to lean on Jake, but she gloried in the knowledge that he was there for her.

Leaning toward him, she asked, "How many ways can you endear yourself to me?"

His lips brushed hers, and then he let the back of his hand graze her cheek, making her wonder how such a big man could be so tender.

"As many as you will permit. Want to walk around

and see some of the boat? I understand there's a movie in the theater, but I wouldn't like to spend my time here sitting in the dark."

With her hand in his, they strolled through the lounges, past the gaming rooms, closed until the boat was once again on the open sea. "Will you get off at the next port?" she asked him. "I wouldn't mind seeing Martinique."

"You bet. I'm anxious to…see it," Jake said.

She wondered why he stopped in midsentence, but when she followed his gaze, she saw nothing unusual.

"I'm going in there and get some frozen yogurt," she told him when they passed one of the restaurants. "Want some?"

"Thanks. And while you're getting that, I'll duck in here." He pointed to the men's room.

She got a cup of black cherry for Jake and raspberry for herself and walked back to meet him. She waited fifteen minutes, threw the yogurt into a refuse basket, went back to her stateroom, turned off the telephone, and tried with little success to work on her story.

If she could, she'd box his ears. Unless he was deathly ill, spending twenty minutes in a public bathroom made no sense. It occurred to her that Jake might have secrets that he didn't want to share with her. Well, if he thought she was going to pout, he'd get a surprise. When she met him for dinner, she meant to smile if it killed her.

Chapter 7

Only the Lord knew what she'd think of him now, leaving her standing by the men's room with two cups of frozen yogurt. But he had to move. That shifty little cook bumped into him, looked as if he'd seen a ghost, and slipped around the corner. Jake took out his government-issue cell phone, hoping to find an email from the chief. With unsteady fingers he opened it.

Ring may not be your man, but he served eighteen months in a Missouri prison for accessory to a crime. He didn't have any drugs on him, but his partner did, and he was driving the car. Word is that when he's lying low, he gets a job on a boat. We haven't yet been able to get "Mr. Harasser" to talk, but he will. 312.

He followed the cook to the laundry room, where the man spoke at length with a passenger, but the cook neither gave the passenger anything nor received anything from him. That wasn't grounds for indictment, only for suspicion. Jake started for the elevator and tripped over a couple making out in a corner.

"What the…" His gaze went immediately to the woman's left hand; he saw the rings there and said nothing more, pitying her poor husband. A call to Allison in her room yielded no response, but he knew she was there. He also knew he was in trouble. He passed the florist shop and ordered a bouquet of lavender calla lilies and pink orchids.

"Deliver them to Ms. Wakefield, 303 Deck, please."

"Yes, sir." The man handed him a white card. "If you wish to include a message."

I'd rather hurt myself than you, he wrote. *It couldn't be helped. Love, Jake.* He put the card in the envelope, addressed it, and hoped for the best. That cook was up to something, but what? If Jake encountered drug smuggling on the ship, he would of course report it, but his assignment was to identify smugglers of human beings, and he had to focus on that. He'd watch the shifty little man, but he didn't believe that man was his quarry.

On the way back to his stateroom, he encountered the delivery boy who had obviously just delivered his flowers to Allison. He waited until he thought she'd had time to read the note, then, fearing that she wouldn't answer the telephone, he knocked on her door.

To his amazement, she opened it and stood in the open door, looking up at him with watery eyes. Wordless. He waited for her reprimand or even for her to slam the door shut. She did neither. Only stood there looking at him.

"I'm more sorry than you can imagine," he said. "May I…come in?"

She stepped back, giving him access. If only she'd say something. He looked first at the vase of flowers on the table beside her bed and then at her. Never had he seen her so fragile or so vulnerable, and as badly as he wanted to hold her, he didn't dare touch her, for she still hadn't said a word to him.

"It couldn't be helped," he said, unfamiliar with the desperation he felt. "Are you going to... Allison, can you forgive me?"

She held out the card that she had obviously been holding in her hand, but which he hadn't noticed. "Did you write this?"

"Yes. I wrote it."

Her lips quivered, and she seemed to battle with herself. "Did you mean what you wrote?"

He took a step closer to her, and when she didn't move he shortened the distance between them until he stood inches from her. "I meant it. I didn't ask for it. I didn't want it, and I tried to avoid it. Yes, I still have reservations. There's a hot fire burning here, but we haven't tended it properly, at least not to my satisfaction. And it may blow up in our faces, but it is what it is. I've never lied to you."

Her eyes finally released the tears that had glistened there, shimmering through her smile, brilliant and forgiving. He didn't know when she opened her arms or how he got into them, but he was there, and he was home. Yes, home.

Holding her away so that he could see into her eyes, with his heart in his mouth, he asked her, "Do you... How do you feel about me?"

"You're right in here," she whispered, pointing to her heart. "Deep in here. And I'm scared of what it might do to us both. First time I ever saw your face, I knew I would never forget you. I hope fate has collected all the pain it plans to get from me."

He'd better not question that statement. That and other things he didn't know about her, not to speak of his own secrets, prevented his wholehearted acceptance of his feelings for her.

"Thanks for the flowers, Jake. They're the most beautiful ones I've ever received or seen."

"I've got good taste," he teased. "After all, look who's in my arms."

She brushed the tips of her fingers over his cheek, stroking and caressing until he tipped up her chin to look into her face. Her dreamy, passion-filled eyes sent his blood racing, and he locked her to him and bent to her mouth.

"Open, baby, and let me in."

She parted her lips, and when he thrust his tongue deep into her mouth, her moans sent desire plowing through him with stunning force. He wanted her at a gut-searing level, but he knew her well enough then to back off; if they made love, she would question his motives and perhaps destroy the progress he'd made with her. Besides, he hadn't checked their rooms for hidden cameras.

As if she was second-guessing him, a rueful smile played around her lips when she said, "I guess we have to learn how to kiss without creating an explosion. Every time we've kissed, it's like pouring gasoline on a fire."

"Yeah, and one of these times... Sweetheart, it will beat landing on the moon. If I can, I'll join you at Idlewild this weekend, but I won't stay with you at your aunt's house. Come to think of it, we ought to go someplace where we can have privacy."

"We have privacy here."

"I'm not so sure. I didn't choose these staterooms." Making a quick recovery from that faux pas, he said, "My publisher may not like paying for a tryst. I keep my personal life separate from business."

He looked at his watch. "This is the only day on open sea; the ship docks tomorrow morning in Martinique. My last lecture and book signing is at four this afternoon. After that, I'll be checking out the place, getting information for my book. The lecture's in the theater. Can you be ready in half an hour?"

"Sure. But I would like a course in how to shift gears as fast as you do."

At the end of the lecture, Allison stood, looked around, and gasped; the crowd filled the aisles and the hallway outside the door. "If I wait till you sign all these books," she told Jake, "I won't have time to dress for dinner. I'll be ready at six-thirty. You were fantastic."

"Thanks." As he looked at her, his eyes sparkled with affection and a frank admission of his feelings for her. "I hope I've finished here by that time. This is some crowd."

She had to save one gown for the gala—the last night on the ship—but for this night she wanted to look special. She inspected a pale yellow strapless chiffon gown and, satisfied, laid it on her bed. After showering, she refreshed her manicure and pedicure, donned a silk robe, and stretched out on the chaise lounge to read and correct her notes. A knock on the door awakened her.

Allison jumped up with a start. "Who... Oh, my

goodness. Jake?" she called through the door. "What time is it?"

"Six-thirty. Why?"

"Give me fifteen minutes. I just woke up."

"Need any help? I'm great with zippers."

"Yeah, I'll bet you are."

"I can slip things on as well as off. Sure you don't need me?"

"Not for this, I don't. Now go away and come back in fifteen minutes."

She twisted her hair into a French knot and secured it with a sequined comb, slipped on the gown that made her think of waltzing, put the diamond studs—her father's gift on her twenty-first birthday—in her ears, dabbed Arpège perfume behind her ears, at her cleavage and wrists, grabbed her gold lamé evening bag that matched her shoes, and walked out of her room.

"Whew," Jake said, leaning against the rail with his back to the water. "All this and one minute to spare. Beautiful. I wish I had a corsage for you."

"You've already given me flowers today. Better not spoil me; I could get to liking it." Her gaze swept over him. "What a figure you are in this white tux!" His wide grin told her that her comment pleased him.

"I knew you'd look great, so I had to live up to you. Let's get a drink before dinner."

At dinner, Allison looked around the table at their companions—three couples of differing ages. After determining that their mother tongues were not English, she attempted to guess their nationalities. The older woman, about sixty, Allison surmised, introduced herself as Marion Russell and said that she was Greek and her husband, English. The cruise was a part of their first trip to the United States. Ava Nagy and her husband were newlywed Hungarians on their honeymoon, and the third couple introduced themselves as Lena and Ned, though it amazed Allison that people with English first names spoke with such thick accents. She was about to whisper that to Jake, but didn't when she noticed that he was busy scribbling something on a small notepad.

"Want to dance?" Jake asked her after dinner.

"Sure I do. After that meal, I need some exercise." When his eyebrow shot up, she said, "I don't mean *that* kind, so don't even go there."

She loved the grin that played around his mouth, signaling a playful mood. "Guilty as charged, but I don't like seeming so transparent that you can read my mind."

"When it comes to food and sex, your mind is an open book."

A saxophone began a haunting melody, and she moved into Jake's open arms, catching his rhythm and swaying with him as if they had always danced. His hand rested lightly on her back, made almost completely bare by her low-cut gown.

"If you think my mind is an open book," he said, "I must have been doing one hell of a piece of acting. I always let you see the truth, Allison, but only as much of it as I want you to see. I'm just careful not to lie."

"But I was right, wasn't I?" she asked.

For an answer, he pulled her close, so close that air couldn't get between them, and slowed down his movement. "I'm not in the mood for a serious discussion, and I'm hurt that you want to talk serious when I'm holding you like this in such a romantic setting, with that sax wailing out the most seductive blues I ever heard. You've wounded me."

She resisted resting her head on his chest. "Poor baby. I'll make up for it. I promise."

He missed a step. "You want to clarify that right now?"

"Uh-uh. I can't think straight when I'm with you like this."

"You devil. You'll clarify it. If not now, definitely later. Want to walk through the gaming room?" he asked when the music stopped. "I don't play games of chance, but it's enlightening to watch others do it. What about you?"

"I have played the slot machines, but five dollars of my own money is as much as I allow myself to lose. I'm not much of a gambler."

As they strolled through the room, she watched in awe at the singular expression that characterized the face of nearly every slot machine player. The intensity, the hope, and then the disappointment and, for many, despair. *I've played my last slot machine,* she told herself. *I hate to think I was ever like this.*

"Making notes for your novel?" she asked Jake when she realized he was writing.

"What better opportunity to get information than when people don't know they're being observed?"

"Sometimes, Jake, you speak in cryptograms, but not to worry; I like to exercise my mind."

He stared down at her. "Good, because you certainly keep *my* mind busy." Taking her hand, he said, "Let's go out on deck."

They walked with their arms around each other

until he stopped. "This setting is making a romantic out of me."

The moon shone brightly, seeming to hang low over the sea, and his arm encircled her, shielding her from the suddenly brisk breeze. "You're a natural romantic," she said, trying to shake her sudden sense of disquiet. "I didn't realize the Caribbean Sea could get rough, but—"

"Depends on the weather. Are you cool?" He had been leaning against the rail, but he stood upright then and opened his arms. "You'd be surprised how good it feels just holding you."

"I used to dream of idyllic moments like this with someone I cared for. It's almost unreal, Jake."

"Why?"

"Because it's so perfect, and I'm…I'm not used to… to this. I'm used to problems and…and turmoil."

"I told you that my shoulders are broad, and that I'm here for you. Do you understand that I'm willing to pick up your burdens if you give me a chance?"

"Yes, I do. And if that times comes, I'll be a happy woman."

"If? Did you say *if?* This isn't the first time you've alluded to your uncertainty about yourself and about us. And yet, you can't tell me what it's about."

"After I finish the story, we'll talk, Jake—that is, if you're still interested."

He looked across the sea at the steadily darkening sky. "I don't think I want to examine that too closely. For now, I have to take it on face value." He paused as if in deep thought. "Let's go in. This water is getting a little rough."

As they reentered the lounge, she heard a voice speaking over the public address system say, "If you're on deck, please come inside. We're expecting strong winds for the next few hours." She clutched the hand that held hers.

"I'd better go to the room and get my wristband. I've never been seasick, but you never can tell."

"How do you feel now?"

"Fine."

As they walked to their quarters, only their hands communicated. Every woman they passed looked at Jake with appreciation, some with blatant lust. She glanced up at him. The man was oblivious to it, glancing neither left nor right, as if the two of them were alone.

"We'd better not sit on the deck," he said when they reached their quarters. His right hand went to the back of his head, and his fingers crawled through his hair. "But it seems a shame to end this evening so early. Back there when we were dancing, I really connected with you."

"Me too, Jake. Come in, and I'll order us some drinks and some snacks or something."

He stared down into her eyes, saying nothing, and shivers raced through her, rattling her nerves.

"Well, if you'd rather not," she said, wondering at his reticence, "I can use some sleep."

He extended his hand for her key, took it, and opened the door.

Inside Allison's stateroom, Jake went to the phone, ordered a bottle of Veuve Clicquot champagne, an assortment of canapés and fruits, and charged it to his credit card. The ship seemed to rock a little, and he had a feeling that they were in for a storm. He didn't know why he did it, but when he turned to face Allison—

seemingly more fragile than he would have imagined possible—he said, "I love seeing your hair down. I like it as it is, but when it's down, there's a softness about you that appeals to me."

Without taking her gaze from his, she removed the comb, released the twist, ran the comb through her hair, and let it fall to her shoulders. He sucked in his breath. Without saying a word, she let him know that she enjoyed pleasing him. He knew he'd better watch his step.

"I'll be right back. Have a seat," she said, and went into the combination dressing room and bathroom.

He sat in the chintz-covered chair, comfortable even if it wasn't to his taste, took the opportunity to make a few notes on observations he had made while in the gaming room, and jotted down a reminder to ask the chief if he had anything on Lena and Ned. Allison opened the door and he hurriedly slipped the little notepad into his pocket.

"Is this ship rocking?" she asked him, and he could see that she wore the wristband that was said to prevent seasickness.

"Slightly. You okay?"

She nodded. "What will we do in Martinique?"

"You name it. Swim, snorkel, horseback riding, tennis, dancing, enjoy the breathtaking scenery, a lot of things. And I've heard the food is great. If you like, we can find a restaurant that has a veranda, sit out there in the breeze, and enjoy each other's company."

She answered the door, and the waiter set the champagne service on a table beside the window and opened the champagne. Jake tipped the man, but always mindful of the dignity of people who rendered him a service, he detained the man with brief conversation.

"How's the wind out there?"

"Not so good, sir, but we'll be out of it in a few hours. Sometimes it gets pretty rough this time of year. Hurricane warnings up in the West Indies, but we're well south of the storm."

"Glad to hear it," Jake said. "Thanks for bringing this."

"My pleasure, sir."

After the waiter left them, Jake poured each of them a glass of the wine. "Come closer to me." He patted the chair beside the one in which he sat. "Are you glad you came?"

"In a way, yes."

He didn't like the sound of that. After musing over it a bit, he clicked her glass with his own and sipped the champagne. "In what way no?"

She leaned back in the chair and covered his free hand with her own. "It's like having a great ride that would be exhilarating if your seat belt wasn't broken, or like taking a wonderful trip and not knowing where the plane is headed."

"Yes, I know." And indeed he did. "It's the uncertainty. Doesn't sit well with me, either. Not knowing important things about my life—I don't mean the future; I mean the *now*—goes against everything I stand for." He glanced at her. "Did you feel that?"

"Yes, indeed. This thing is rocking."

He couldn't help grinning. A little danger had always revved up his engine, but he wondered whether she would be so serene if she were alone.

"Where's the fun? If this thing gets out of hand, I'm not letting you leave this room."

The laughter that he had smothered rolled out of

him. He couldn't control it. "Allison, sweetheart, if you think getting me to stay here with you will be a problem, you're out of your mind. Your problem may be getting me to leave."

She sipped her wine and tossed her head, dismissing his words. "Oh, pooh. You're a gentleman." She crossed her knees and began swinging her foot.

His sense of the absurd left him as quickly as it came, and he looked at her with as stern a face as he'd ever worn. "That is not a means of controlling me, Allison. A gentleman has needs, and when he's with a woman he wants on a stormy night at sea, his needs can rise up like a stallion on hind legs and throw him."

"I didn't mean to suggest that you don't have feelings, just as I do," she said, letting her gaze slowly scan the room.

Something in him jumped to life, for at that minute he realized she was scanning her room for cameras that he'd said might be hidden there.

"What are you looking for?" he growled, forgetting that he might frighten her.

"I, uh… I was…"

He jumped to his feet and stood facing her. With his right hand outstretched, he waited as she sat there gazing up at him, swinging the leg that hung from her knee. When her eyes darkened and her tongue rimmed her bottom lip, he smiled, held out both hands, and then opened his arms to her. She sprang from her chair, and with a moan that he knew signaled complete capitulation, she locked her arms around him.

Was she certain this time? He hesitated, doubting his ability to pull back. "Do you want me? Do you?" He had to be sure, because he couldn't let himself embarrass her and certainly not hurt her in any way. Her large, almond-shaped eyes gazed up at him, questioning. Yes, and inviting. But he had to be sure.

"Do you?" he repeated.

Her lids dropped over those luminous eyes, and her bottom lip trembled. "Don't ask me questions," she whispered. "Just…just love me. Love me, Jake, like you mean it. Like I'm the only woman on earth. I need you."

The sensation of her thumb rubbing his bottom lip stunned him, and when she sucked the thumb into her mouth, he felt a rush of blood, a swift tightening of his groin, and jumped to full readiness.

"Allison!"

When she locked her hands behind his head and opened her mouth, desire sliced through him, and he plunged into her. Her rhythmic sucking on his tongue sent his blood racing, as she feasted like a woman starved. He wanted to tell her to slow down, but her hand went to his buttocks, tightening him to her, and he nearly lost his composure, as she moved against him, letting him know that she enjoyed the feel of his erection, that her body was primed for his entry. He told himself to think about popcorn, *Gone With the Wind,* shoelaces, Italy, anything but the woman in his arms as she tortured him with her woman's scent, the softness of her body, and the loving she gave his tongue.

Allison didn't think of the past, nor did she worry about the future. Her reservations about Jake and herself disappeared like a puff of smoke in a windstorm, when he stood before her, open and vulnerable, and spread his arms to her. Nearly six years of loneliness and pain heightened her need of him. His arms went around her and blotted out everything that existed or ever had been, except him. When at last she felt his tongue in her mouth, her world spun off its axis.

She felt him hard against her and grabbed his buttocks, the better to feel him, as his heat touched her through their clothing. He broke the kiss, and his lips began to tease her ears and throat. She heard the moans that escaped her, and didn't care. His tongue bathed her neck, and she thought she'd die if she could feel her nipple in his mouth.

"Jake. Honey."

"What is it? Tell me what you need." For an answer, she grabbed his hand and rubbed her left breast with it. "Tell me," he whispered in a voice she hardly recognized.

"Kiss me. Please ki—"

His big hand went inside the bodice of her dress and freed her breast. Then, he bent to her hardened nipple, and lathed it gently.

"Please. Please. I want to feel your mouth on me." She felt his warm breath seconds before he pulled her nipple into his mouth. "Oh, Lord," she cried. "Jake, honey, I can't stand this." She rocked against him, finally throwing one leg around his hip. He lifted her, and she straddled him, feeling all of him. Greedy for more, she began to unbuckle his belt.

"Not yet, sweetheart," he said, setting her on her feet. "May I unzip this?" he asked her, his voice thick with desire.

"Yes. Yes."

He unzipped her evening gown, caught the dress before it landed on the floor, and threw it across a chair. As if stunned, he stared at her until she covered her bare breasts with her hands.

"No. Don't. Sweetheart, you're so beautiful. So... Let me look at you."

He lifted her, threw back the bed covering, and placed her on the bed, where she lay bare to him except for the inch-wide yellow bikini panties. As he stared down at her, her breathing shortened to a pant, moisture accumulated in her mouth, and she had to control the urge to spread her legs wide as desire washed through her. Without taking his gaze from her face, he shed his clothing, hurriedly as if racing ahead of a fire. And then she saw him, full and masculine. Her legs shifted apart as she reached for him. When he stepped to the edge of the bed, she tugged at his G-string, released him, and let him spill into her waiting hands.

He threw his head back and groaned as she fondled and caressed him. Then he joined her at last and wrapped her to his hard body.

"May I?" he asked, with his fingers on her bikini. She raised her hips to him, and thought she would break out of her skin when his hands skimmed slowly from her belly to her nest and down the inside of her thighs. She reached for him, but he moved from her.

"Be patient, love. This is too important, too precious to rush."

He took both of her hands and held them over her head, then her cheeks, ears, nose, and forehead sparkled beneath the heat of his mouth. "Jake, I want you inside me. I'm going crazy."

"Don't rush it, love. It will find us." The feel of his lips on her neck, then her chest, teasing, promising, and denying, excited and frustrated her until in desperation she slapped his buttocks, then rubbed them as moans spilled from her throat. When he kissed the top of her breast, she cupped it in a lover's offering. Finally his mouth covered her nipple, bringing a keening cry from her lips as he suckled her, nourishing himself as if he'd been starving for years. She reached down for him, but he moved away.

"Not there, baby. Not yet."

With one nipple snug between his lips and one of his hands on her breast, her senses began to reel as his other hand moved slowly down her body, stroking her belly, caressing the inside of her thighs. Unable to restrain herself, her hips undulated, but he stilled them, poised at her center, and when she wanted to scream, his fingers parted her folds and began their talented dance.

"Please. Jake. Get in me. Get in me."

For an answer, he lifted her knees over his shoulders, kissed her, and then claimed her with his tongue, rubbing, circling, and probing until her moans filled the room. Slowly, he kissed his way up her neck, reached on the floor beside the bed for the condom he'd placed there, and handed it to her as he covered her body with his own.

"Raise your knees a little, love."

She took him in her hands and brought him to her love portal. And then she felt him, iron-hot, velvety smooth, and big. Her body stiffened. "We'll go slowly," he said, but if she didn't feel him moving inside her, she'd go crazy. She swung her body up to meet his gentle thrust, wrapped her legs around his hips, and pressed his buttocks to her.

"Allison, baby. I don't want to hurt you."

"You aren't. You can't. I just want to… Honey…" She pushed upward, ignoring the initial pain, and took him in. All of him.

He raised himself up and gazed down into her face. "Are you all right?"

"Yes. Perfect."

Slowly, he began to move, then suddenly he flipped her over on top of him, and as she leaned forward, he pulled her right nipple into his mouth. She didn't know where she was. He suckled her, all the while thrusting upward, until sensations plowed through her that she hadn't dreamed possible.

"I'm going to put you on your back now," he said, and in seconds he let her know the power of his hard thrust. The pumping and squeezing accelerated in her vagina as he increased the pace, heat seared the bottom of her feet, and then he was in her, over her, beneath her, and all around her, claiming her and scattering her senses, robbing her of herself. She was his, every atom and every molecule of her body knew him and capitulated as the swelling gripped her. She threw her arms wide, gave herself to him, and sank into a vortex of ecstasy.

"Oh, Jake. I love you. I love you."

"You're mine. Mine. All mine," he whispered in barely audible tones as if he hadn't the strength to speak louder. He gripped her to him, moaned her name, and shattered in her arms.

For a long while, they didn't speak. Then he braced himself on his forearms, looked down at her, and smiled. "Did you have an orgasm?

She couldn't help grinning, for joy suffused her. "Yes, I did, thank you."

"Sure?"

"Yes. Couldn't you tell?"

"Actually, I wondered, because you started swelling around me the minute I entered."

"Believe me, I never felt anything like that in my life. What about you?" she asked, half fearing the answer.

"Me? You are perfect for me, Allison. Perfect from beginning to end. You fit me like a glove in more ways than one."

"Are you going to spend the night with me?"

"You bet, sweetheart. I like honey for breakfast."

She pinched his buttocks, and he retaliated with ten minutes of loving that took them both on a whirlwind trip to paradise.

Afterward, he stretched out on his back and hooked her to his left side.

"I just realized something," she told him. "The first time I saw you was not at your lecture, but on the beach in Idlewild early one morning a couple of days before we met. You came out of the lake and walked toward me on the beach, barefooted, wearing a tiny red bikini, hardly more than a G-string, and water from the lake dripped from your body. You didn't look my way."

"How do you know it was me?"

"There isn't a warm-bloodied woman anywhere who could see you dressed that way and forget what your body looked like. I confess I ogled you, and I was glad you didn't look my way."

"Wait a minute. You say that was a couple of days before you came to my lecture at Howard?"

She nodded. "Right."

"Hmm. Did you have on a straw hat and dark glasses, and were you sitting in a beach chair?"

She sat up. "Yes."

"I saw you long before I got to you, which is why I didn't look your way when I passed. Well, I'll be damned."

"Yes," she said. "When fate gets busy, it really does its thing."

"Excuse me." He slipped out of bed and filled two glasses with champagne. "I feel like drinking to this." He sat on the side of the bed, handed her a glass, eased his arm through hers, and with his gaze locked on her, drank every drop of it.

"What's the matter?" he asked her when she sipped slowly, barely tasting the champagne. "What is it?"

Her heart swelled with love at the caring his voice conveyed.

She didn't want to put a damper on the most important, the most precious hour of her life, but common sense told her she was in for a trial. "We have almost another two weeks on this tour, Jake. I could easily slip into an affair with you, and as much as I know I will want to be with you, I want to…to hold off till I get this story out of the way. I…uh…don't want what I write to reflect my feelings for you. If I wrote it right now, it could be a chronicle of what a wonderful man you are."

"I see your point, but after what I just felt with you, I can't swear I'll be with you day and evening for two weeks and not put my hands on you." He got back into bed and stretched out beside her. "Damned if I want that much willpower."

He switched off the light, tucked her to him spoon-fashion, and kissed the back of her neck. "Night, love."

"Good night," she whispered and went to sleep in the arms of the man she loved.

"I should be as concerned as she, maybe more so," Jake said to himself the next morning after slipping out of her bed. He went to his room, showered, put on a pair of swim trunks, and phoned the dining room.

"Coffee, orange juice, country sausage, scrambled eggs, grits, and biscuits. Oh yes, melon and whatever goes with all that. No, man. For two. Room 302. And put a nice flower on the tray, please. Thanks."

He waited in his room until the waiter brought the food. Jake tipped him, and took the tray next door to Allison's room. For long minutes, he gazed down at the sleeping woman, remembering how his heart constricted when she tightened around him and told him she loved him. Not once, but twice. He sat on the side of the bed. He had always been able to withhold himself at the moment of release, to keep something of himself. But she wrung from him the essence of his being. Everything in him poured itself into her, leaving him as vulnerable as a newborn child. He'd been unprepared for it, though he always knew that making love to her would test his manhood.

Nothing in her demeanor could have prepared a man for what he experienced with her. Thoughts of what it was like to move within her sent shudders through his body and heat to his loins. He leaned over her and kissed her eyelids.

"Wake up. The ship docks in an hour."

"Hi. What are you…" A grin crawled over her face. "Goodness. I forgot."

"You *what?* Woman, you wound me. I expected you to dream about me all night."

"Maybe I did. I usually don't remember my dreams. Did you sleep with me? You promised."

"I did, and it was a pleasure. Sit up. You're getting breakfast in bed."

"Really? Would you go to my closet and hand me a green robe?"

She slipped her arms into the robe, wrapped the garment around her body, and slid out of bed. He appreciated her modesty, but wouldn't have minded getting another look at her full, high breasts. Perfect for his hands and his mouth.

She came back to him wearing a gown and with her hair combed. "What a meal!"

"You have to get back in bed. You're being pampered. I want to give my woman her breakfast in bed."

The giggles that came from her surprised him, until he remembered that she giggled when she was with her brother and realized it meant joy.

"Are you going to tell Sydney about us?"

She savored the coffee, her eyes sparkling the way a gold digger lights up when he pans his first gold. "Hmm, this is heaven. Sydney? Probably. He'll ask me, and I can't imagine lying to Sydney. Why? Would it bother you?"

"Not at all. Eat up."

"If I had a cook, I'd eat this kind of breakfast every morning, but I don't go to this trouble for myself."

"Suppose you had a husband."

She laughed, and he reached for her hand. He had to touch her. "If I had a husband and he couldn't cook, we'd be wise to hire a cook."

"You mean you can't cook?"

"Of course I can, but I imagine working and keeping house at the same time is a daunting task."

"You bet it is. I saw it wearing my mother down, but thank God she no longer has to work unless she wants to."

She removed the pink orchid and handed him her tray. "That was wonderful, and thanks for the flower," she said, drained her coffee cup, and licked her lips. "Yummy."

He stared at her, eased his tray to the floor, and got into the bed. "Kiss me, sweetheart."

Her lips, warm and eager, parted for his tongue, and he thrust into her. "Take this stuff off me, please," she said, and he pulled the robe and gown from her body. She came back to him with open arms and swaying hips.

"If you don't slow down, baby, this will be over before it starts."

Heedless to his words, she leaned over him and reached down to remove his bikini, nudged him to roll on to his back, and ran her tongue around his pectorals, sucking and teasing while her hand pressed his belly. Realizing that she wanted to make love to him, he tried to turn off his raging libido to let her have her way. When she kissed his belly, he stiffened, knowing what was to come, wanting it as he wanted air and scared of the consequences.

The feel of her fingers skimming his thighs and playing around his testicles without touching them made him want to take over, but he resisted the temptation.

"*Allison, don't do that!* Oh, Lord," he groaned as her warm lips closed over him. His hands gripped the sheet and he prayed for control while she loved him. She had no skill at it, but the love she put into it almost sent him over. She pulled him deeper into her mouth, and he stopped her, reached down, and pulled her up to him.

"Did I do something wrong?"

"No, sweetheart. It was almost more than I could

bear." He leaned over her and kissed her eyes, her lips, and her cheek while his left hand toyed with her nipple. When her body began to shift, restless and begging, he bent to her nipple and sucked it into his mouth, enjoying her moans. His hand traveled to her delicate folds, and teased until the liquid of love flowed over his fingers. She reached for him, and he let her have her way as she sheathed him and brought him into her warm, welcoming body.

Her legs went around his hips, and within minutes after he began to move, he felt her begin to swell around him. He knew her needs, now, found the spot that guaranteed her complete release, and stroked her with all the skill and power he possessed.

"Honey, I…I want to burst. Oh, Lord."

He stroked faster and harder, and she moved with his rhythm until he felt her tighten around him, sending sensations through him until he bared his teeth and shouted his release.

Shaken at his complete loss of control, he looked down at her, saw the smile on her face, and asked her, "Did you get straightened out? Woman, you tied me in a knot; I can't believe I didn't wait for you."

"I was right with you. It was wonderful."

He put his head on her breast, still stunned. "It certainly was *that*."

Allison sat in Paris Now, at a thatch-roof-covered table for two, looking out at the azure sea. She leaned back in the chair, drinking fruit punch in the company of the man who besotted her, light-years away from the woman who she had known herself to be. Contented. Serene. Then, sudden thoughts of what she had found in Jake and of what she could lose enveloped her in sadness.

Jake reached for her hand and held it. "What's the matter?" he asked her, and she marveled at his sensitivity. "A second ago, you were as tranquil as a saint. Unruffled. I would even say happy. Now you're sad. Why? What happened?"

"I suppose it's realizing I can't stay here with you in this idyllic place forever. Day after tomorrow, Bill will be on the warpath, and life will return to normal. The way it was before—"

He sat forward, expectancy clouding his face. "Before what? Tell me. Let me understand you."

She didn't hesitate. "Before you loved me."

His eyes darkened, and he didn't have to tell her where his thoughts lay. "When didn't I?" As was his wont, his mind went immediately to the next issue of importance. "Unless we want to spend more time on this island than we'd planned, we'd better head for the *Saint Marie.*"

The taxi driver drove them through the upscale sections of Fort de France, Martinique's modern capital city, boasting of the beauty of the colonial homes and estates. "How can he be so oblivious of the fact that the wealth he seems so proud of was accumulated at the expense of his own people?" Jake muttered, adding that most of them still struggled to eke out a living.

"Aren't we getting on now?" she asked him when they reached the ship. She had expected to see a crowd lined up to get on, but only she and Jake were at the pier. She looked at her watch. Five after four. Almost an hour early. Her left shoulder lifted and quickly fell. Maybe he misread the time.

He leaned against the pier, relaxed and unconcerned. "Looks like we're the first ones back. Let's do some people-watching."

He didn't answer her question, and she had an urge to tell him she noticed that, but pushed the thought aside. "You must really enjoy this," she said, observing that he talked with her without moving his gaze from the crowd that had begun surging toward the ship.

"People-watching is an author's favorite pastime. Didn't you know that?"

She didn't. Feeling bereft of his attentiveness, she moved closer to him, but he didn't take her hand, and she began to question what she regarded as his fixation on a gang of strangers.

"Let's go," he said suddenly, grabbed her hand, crashed the line, and boarded the ship. "You go on to your stateroom; I'll be up shortly."

No apologies, and no explanations. She found it difficult to digest his often odd behavior, wondering whether he had seen a woman friend or someone else he knew, or if he was avoiding someone.

He's so mysterious, she mused, *and this isn't the first time he's done something strange on this ship, something that he either couldn't or wouldn't explain.*

Believing she should pull back, she went to her stateroom and began organizing her notes, knowing that focusing on her work would bring her out of the clouds and down to earth. *Innocent until proved guilty,* her conscience cautioned her. "Yes," she said, letting herself remember how his white teeth sparkled against the olive velvet of the face she loved to touch and the way her body responded to the feel of his strong tapered fingers. She leaned back in the chair, lost in the world that he alone had created for her, as her mind replayed the wonder of his holding her, loving her, and then coming apart in her arms. She didn't know when her annoyance at him evaporated as she sat with her arms folded across her chest and let herself dream.

The ringing telephone shocked her out of her ruminations. "Hi. Did you get some rest?" Jake asked when she answered. "How about going for a snack? It's another three and a half hours before dinner."

"I thought I'd organize my notes and maybe order tea and a light sandwich here in the room."

"Then, I'll see you at seven-thirty. I'm going for a swim and then a light snack."

He seemed glad to have the time to himself, she thought. She didn't understand men, she decided, and she'd give a lot to know what wound their clocks. She worked until six-thirty, showered, and dressed in the red silk sheath that she brought for the evening's dinner and the gala. Then she combed out her hair, applied a very light layer of rouge to her cheeks, dabbed Arpège perfume in strategic places, sat down, and waited for whatever the evening would bring.

Chapter 8

"No telling what she's thinking now," Jake said to himself as he sped down the long corridor toward the laundry room, certain that he would find Ned, Lena, or both of them there or, if not them, a couple dressed like them. When Ring met him in the corridor, Jake sensed he was on the right track. The man wearing the straw hat and the red plaid shirt seemed to him a bit older than the Ned he had met the previous evening and didn't walk with the jauntiness of a young man. Finding no one in the laundry room, he headed for the kitchen.

"Hi." He addressed the chief. "The food's been spectacular. Any chance of getting a recipe for that great rock-shrimp rémoulade you had on the self-serve counter yesterday afternoon?"

The chef preened at the compliment, as Jake knew he would. "For you, my friend? Of course."

While the chef went for his book, pen, and paper, Jake let his gaze roam around the kitchen. On his previous visits there, he had counted sixteen men in cooks' uniforms. When the chef handed him the recipe, he thanked the man and, having guessed which cook was absent, asked, "Where's Ring?"

"Should be over there in the salads. If he's not there, he may be getting a smoke. Smoking's not allowed in the kitchens."

"Where'd he get that name? Is it a nickname?"

"The fellow comes from one of those classy families, but he's the youngest and a ne'er-do-well, so they've disowned him, and he changed his name from Harderin to Ring. Kids don't appreciate what you do for 'em these days."

Jake walked around to the salad and vegetable section in time to see Ring rush in and grab his apron and cook's hat. He got out of the way before Ring saw him. He ran up the E staircase until he reached the first deck, above the water, took out his cell phone, and dialed the chief. He got more information in those few minutes with the chief than he had all day.

"Ring is the youngest son of the Cambridge Harderins, and the chef says the family has disowned him. Another thing. Have somebody at the dock to pick up Lena and Ned. I have a feeling the guy who got on in Martinique posing as Ned may be his father or brother or who knows who, but it isn't Ned. And check to see if a man reports a lost passport in Martinique."

"If your hunch is right, we may be on to something. Good show, man."

"Yeah. I hope you'll be around to repair my relationship with my friend, when it comes to that."

"Hold on. By now, you should have crowned her queen. Didn't I make it easy for you? How do you like your staterooms?"

"Great," Jake said in a voice that amounted to little more than a snarl. "When I grow up, I want to be as smart as you."

If he'd ever seen or heard the chief laugh before, he didn't remember it, and the heavy rumble that came over the phone like the sound of someone gargling a sore throat momentarily stunned him.

"You just made my day, sir," he said when he recognized the sound as a laugh.

"Hmm, and you've certainly made mine," the chief replied, sobriety having returned. "Think you can get off first, stand at the pier, and point those three out to my men?"

"Do my best. If I can, I'll get pictures of Lena and Ned and email them to you tonight. It'll be late, thought."

"Great. Expect a promotion when you return to work full-time."

"Thanks. I think." He hung up with the rumble of the chief's laughter teasing his ear. He had a difficult job ahead, and he had to figure out how to do it without ruining his relationship with Allison. But first, he wanted a swim and something to eat. He phoned Allison, uneasy about the reception he would get.

"Hello," he heard, surprised at the merriment in her voice, for he knew she suspected he was her caller.

Relief flooded his whole being. "Hi, sweetheart. Did you get some rest? How about going for a snack?" When she told him she planned to work and have a snack in her room, her manner let him know that it wasn't a brush-off. "Then I'll see you at seven-thirty."

After three laps in the Olympic-size pool, he got out, threw on the white terry-cloth robe provided there for the swimmers, stuck his feet in a pair of sandals, and went to the snack bar. He put rock-shrimp salad, a roll, and a glass of lemonade on a tray, got a table on deck, and let the sun and soft sea breeze tranquilize him.

He had expected to hate the tour, because he had low tolerance for small talk, and what else could one expect of a one-minute conversation with a stranger? The complications he had expected as a result of Allison's presence on the tour had not materialized. Instead, he'd found a woman who suited him socially, psychologically, and physically. He liked an intelligent goal-oriented woman who stood up for her rights. And she was that, the kind of woman who kept a man on his toes and his engine revved.

By the time he left the deck an hour and a half later, he had a plan for delivering Lena and her cohorts to the feds. Deciding not to risk a nap, he prowled around the *Saint Marie,* seeking evidence of stowaways, but found none. At seven-thirty he knocked on Allison's door.

Allison opened the door and stared at Jake, resplendent in a gray tuxedo, red cummerbund and handkerchief, and black patent shoes. She knew her face mirrored her pleasure in seeing him, and she didn't try to hide the fact. How glad she was that she wore the red silk sheath she'd purchased especially for the gala evening, for his eyes shone with delight as he nodded his head, appreciating what his eyes beheld.

"Beautiful." He breathed the word. "How did I get to be so fortunate? Lovely," he said, bending to kiss her cheek. "Everyone will think we planned to dress this way."

"I was thinking the same thing. You look wonderful."

"Thank you, ma'am. I tried."

She couldn't get used to the diffidence in him. "It's not much of a stretch," she said in what she meant as a mild reprimand. The man had to know that he could knock a woman's socks off just by showing up.

After the reception for first- and veranda-class passengers, they took their places at the table assigned to them. "This is my next to last chance to observe the people and how they behave," he told her, "so I may seem a little inattentive. I've noticed two people who fit a character I've got in my head."

"I'll forgive you, if you promise to make it up to me."

He did for her what a magnet does for nails as he smiled down at her, his wink reinforcing his magnetism. When her breath quickened, his nostrils flared and his eyes possessed her. She lowered her gaze, wondering where her passion for him would lead, but for the first time, thinking about the possibilities did not distress her. He reached for the hand she'd placed in her lap, gazed down at her, and grinned. "There's not a woman in this room who can hold a candle to you."

She tried to smile, praying that he would still feel that way when he read her story of him in *The Journal*.

However, although from his smile and the lights in his eyes he seemed the ardent lover, Jake's mind was not focused on Allison, but on the two empty seats at their table. He had been careful to cover his every move, and he knew that no one on that ship could identify him as an agent. So where were Lena and Ned? They had boarded; he knew that much. He resisted checking the breakfast room, also referred to as the cafeteria; but not going there cost him a lot in anxiety.

The waiters began to serve the first course, and he accepted that "Ned" might forego the meal so as not to show his face. But shortly after they began eating, Lena and Ned arrived, took their seats, and apologized for their tardiness.

Jake's heartbeat accelerated when "Ned" smiled, for the Ned who sat with them the night before did not have a left gold incisor and a vacant piece of a crown on the right side of his mouth. Satisfied that he had his man, Jake turned his attention to Allison.

"Did you say you wanted us to go to Idlewild next weekend?"

She nodded. "I thought you had forgotten it."

"Not a chance. Unless circumstances are beyond my control, I make good on my word. Did you say something special is going on up there next weekend?"

"The annual barbecue feast, and my aunt is one of the prime movers, so she'll have a fit if I don't go. Left to her, the place would be crawling with people every day of the year."

The possibility occurred to him that a jazz band might have been engaged for the festivities. He had to be sure.

"What kind of entertainment do they usually have?"

"Gee, I don't know. The barbecue starts Saturday around noon and continues through Sunday."

"I can go up with you Friday evening, but I need to get back home late Saturday. And don't forget we're scheduled to leave for San Antonio Monday afternoon."

She looked down at the table, folded and unfolded

her hands. "I have to be circumspect around my aunt, so we—"

He interrupted her. "Honey, what do you take me for? I'd never compromise you. Besides, I'll stay at the inn."

"But my aunt would be mortified if you did that. She lives alone in a big house. It's just that…that you can't walk in your sleep."

"Huh?" He threw his head back and laughed. He couldn't help it. "Lady, if I ever walked in my sleep, I didn't hear about it. You be sure you don't do that."

"I'll give myself a good talking-to before I go to bed."

The dinner feast went on for nearly two hours, and then the entertainment began with the waiters in a conga line singing "Roll Out the Barrel." Waiters passed a microphone around to patrons, asking them to sing a few bars of their favorite song. He nearly jumped out of his chair when Allison begin singing "Summertime," her beautiful soprano lovelier than the voices of all the singers who sang before her.

"You could have had a successful career as a singer," he told her.

"I wanted to be a singer, but my mother wouldn't hear of it; she looks down on entertaining as a profession. Says it's demeaning."

"What? Is she serious?"

"Yes, she certainly is. When I told her you were a writer, her next question was, 'Did he win the Noble Prize?' We have nothing in common, and there are times when thinking about it makes me so sad."

"That's a pity."

The meal over, the waiters announced the traditional midnight supper, when the cooks would display their artistic skills, presenting elegant and intricate aspic-encased meats, poultry, and wild game, as well as salads and prize-winning desserts. The waiters asked the guests at that table how they enjoyed the food, and, after receiving a chorus of approval, passed the hat, which returned to them full of twenty-dollar bills.

As Jake had hoped, wine, and plenty of it, had the passenger in a mellow mood. He took his cell phone from the inside breast pocket of his jacket, stood, and looked at Allison.

"Smile. I want a picture of you as a reminder of one of the most wonderful three days of my life." Her slight frown told him she questioned his saying that loud enough for everyone at their table to hear it. "Smile, sweetheart." She did and he clicked the camera built into his phone.

Quickly, he turned to the other guests, said, "Everybody smile," and photographed Lena and her Ned just as a loud gasp escape the woman. Pretending not to have heard it, he grinned displaying a pleasure more genuine that any of them could have realized.

"Thank you all. I'll keep this little memento forever."

"I'm not up to midnight supper," he told Allison later as they strolled on deck. "After that dinner, I don't see how I can begin another meal two hours from now, but if you want to, of course, I'll go with you."

"It's a beautiful night," she said. "Let's play it by ear."

How unlike her! he thought. *She usually wants everything cut-and-dried, but she chooses to be uncertain at a time when I need to account for very minute.*

Well, it was the chief's idea, and he had to deal with her presence as best he could.

Making certain that he understood her, he stopped walking, took her hand, and asked, "Are you telling me you want us to…to be together tonight?"

"No…I… What do you mean?"

"I mean it's the last night on the ship. Do you want to spend the night with me?"

When she didn't look at him, he had his answer. "I… Don't *you* want to?" she asked him, and he had a feeling she was about to give him a display of temper.

He put both arms around her and brought her close to him. "Shame on you. How could you doubt it? You like to know you are desired, that I want you. Well, I need the same assurance."

They went inside, and when the music to "Boot Scootin' Boogie" came over the loudspeaker, Allison looked at him. "Come on, don't you line dance?"

He shook his head. "You go ahead and enjoy it. I'll wait right here."

He liked to line dance occasionally, though he didn't think it went well with ball gowns and tuxedos, but he wanted to send the chief the photo of Lena and "Ned." After emailing it along with directions for the department's man the following morning, he found a chair and watched the dancers.

A sweet and terrible hunger stirred in him as he watched her move to the music, her lithe body supple and enticing in that red guided-missile that hugged her frame. If it pleased her to have his company, he would eat a midnight supper, though he didn't want it, and he would dance all night, although he wasn't in the mood.

That foot-stomping country tune ended and the

sound of "Diane," one of his favorites, filled the air. He reached Allison just as a man who had been dancing beside her turned to ask for a dance.

"Sorry, buddy," he said, putting an arm around Allison's waist, "she's my date."

The man looked up at Jake as if to measure his chances, smiled, and said, "Some guys have all the luck."

He moved with her in three-quarter time and sang the first words of the romantic tune softly for her ears alone. "I'm in heaven when I see you smile" were the words he sang to her, and she closed her eyes and stepped closer to him.

Life had never been easy for him, and he neither wanted nor expected it to be. He had always welcomed a challenge as an opportunity to succeed, even to excel, but for the first time he resented the hurdle facing him, hated the mountain of secrets and unexplainable actions on his part that could tear her from him for all time. She had her secrets, too, and he suspected that they loomed equally large in her life. For the first time, too, he admitted to himself that he didn't know what he would do if he lost her.

"Do you still want a late night supper," he whispered, "or would some champagne, hors d'oeuvres, and petit fours in your room do just as well?"

"That will be perfect so long as you're there."

He squeezed her gently. "Let's go."

He went first to his room, ordered the food and champagne to be sent to Allison's stateroom, took off his jacket, and went out on the deck. She didn't want an affair with him, she'd said, but hadn't they already begun one? He turned from the railing and knocked on her door.

She opened it, reached up, and kissed his cheek. He noticed at once that she had combed her hair down to her shoulders and knew she'd done it to please him.

"Am I welcome without my jacket?"

She grinned, bowed, and stepped aside. "It isn't the jacket that makes the man; it's the other way around."

"This has been a long, and very full day. Are you tired?"

"A little, but I'm mostly sorry this is ending."

"Sorry we won't be together like this, or sorry the ship is docking tomorrow morning?"

Her left eyebrow shot up, and he wondered why a right-handed person didn't raise the right eyebrow. "Jake, I remember you said you need assurance just as I do. Last night, I gave you that assurance."

She was right, of course, and he didn't know why he kept pressing for more. "Yes, you did, but somehow it's too good to believe," he said and got up to answer the door. "Our food is here.

"I suppose I can't believe that, after thirty-five years, this is happening to me," he told her as he set the food on the table, "that my life is shaping up as I hoped it would. There's just one more thing, and it's just as important."

"You mean recognition at your university?"

He handed her a glass of champagne, sat beside her on the tufted, velvet-covered love seat, and nodded. "Yes, and it may be the one thing I miss out on."

"But you're a household name. Isn't that enough?"

"I never wanted to be a household name. I still don't, and I'm not sure I am; authors are rarely that popular unless they become famous first. What about you? What do you want? We've been together for weeks, and I still feel sometimes that I hardly know you." She seemed to tense at those words, and his antenna shot up.

"I'm what you see, Jake. If you can wait until this tour is over, I'll feel free to…to open myself fully to you."

"Why then?"

She shifted in her seat so that he could see her face. "Because these two roles I'm playing in your life are in conflict. I…I care so deeply for you, but if you lose your temper tomorrow and flatten a man with your fists, I have to report it in my story. You won't do that, but the possibility is there, and until I'm out of this situation I can't give the way I want to."

He put an arm around her and rested her head on his shoulder. "It won't be easy, but I'll do my best to reduce the strain on you. Let's not let this good stuff go to waste," he said, reaching for a tiny crab cake and, at the same moment, deciding to sleep in his own bed. "I've ordered breakfast for us here at seven. The ship docks at eight, and we have to be down in the luggage room by eight-fifteen. Our bags must be beside our doors by midnight."

"Eight-fifteen? I thought we disembarked at nine-thirty."

He'd been expecting that. "Some do, but not us. I wanted to spend the night with you, but if I do, we won't get up in time. Will you be hurt if I leave you now?"

Her smile, rueful and a little sad, tugged at his heart. "I'll miss you, but if you stay here, my suitcases won't be at that door come midnight. Thanks for ordering breakfast. Imagine dealing with that crowd and getting out of here by eight-fifteen." She stood. "Kiss me and scoot."

She was never more dear to him than at that moment. If she was disappointed, she didn't emphasize it, and she didn't pout or try to detain him. She went into his arms willingly, caressed his face with the back of her hand the way she seemed to enjoy doing, raised her hands to his nape, and parted her lips. He had an urge to plunge into her as heat flooded his body, but he brought himself under control and pressed the tip of his tongue between her lips. When she would have pulled him in, he stroked her back and kissed her softly, her eyes, cheeks, and neck, adoring her and cherishing her.

He tasted the briny moisture, tipped up her face, and looked at her. "You're crying. What's the matter?"

She shook her head, denying his words. "Am I? I'm…Jake, I'm so happy."

He took the handkerchief from his pocket and wiped the teardrops. "I am, too," he said, "and if I don't leave this minute, I may be here when the boat docks."

She reached up and pressed her lips to his. "Good night, my darling."

He stared down at her for a second. *Get out of here, man. You're not made of iron.* "Good night, love. Sleep well." He closed her door and, as if propelled by some inner force, managed to get into his stateroom. He stood beside the closed door for a long time as his mind traveled back again and again over the last hour.

"There's no denying it," he said aloud as he prepared for bed. "I love her, and I've got to do what I can to preserve this relationship."

"I'm not going to second-guess him," Allison said to herself as she locked and tagged her bags. "He hasn't said it, but he loves me. No man could cherish a woman as he did me tonight if she wasn't deep in his heart."

He didn't tell her his reason for wanting to get off the boat as soon as it docked, but she couldn't ask of him what she wasn't prepared to give, so she didn't pry. Another ten days; she didn't see how she could endure them. At a quarter of twelve, she set her bags outside at her door and went to bed. Except for the few minutes Sydney had spent with them, she and Jake were never with people who knew them, and maybe that was one of their problems.

"First chance I get, I'm going to take him to meet Connie, and I want to meet some of his friends. That should give us a better take on each other." She wrapped her arms around her pillow, said her prayers, and drifted off to sleep.

She had dressed when Jake knocked on her door the next morning, bringing in their breakfast tray. He greeted her with a kiss on her lips.

"I hope you slept well. I noticed you got your bags out on time."

Why was he... She realized that he was making an effort to be less intimate, to give her the emotional space she had implied she needed.

"I slept like a log. You weren't here to rock me to sleep, but the ship did a reasonable job of it. At one time, I wondered if we were headed into another storm."

"Maybe it shifted course or something. Want some more coffee?" he asked her. "Better eat all of that. Our plane doesn't leave till three. I'll have a car waiting for us, but the traffic to the airport can be horrendous, so I don't know when we'll see food again."

"You don't have to urge me. This food speaks for it-self." He looked at his watch for the third time in five minutes and, sensing an unusual urgency about him, she finished her meal and checked the stateroom to see if she had missed packing anything.

"I'm ready," she said.

"Good." He hugged her and then took her hand. "Let's go."

So far, so good, Jake thought as they entered the baggage room to claim their luggage. When the clerk appeared ready to question their arrival before the scheduled time, Jake handed him a twenty-dollar bill.

"Thanks, friend. I've got a plane to catch."

"Yes, sir. You want the lady's bag, too?"

Jake handed the bags to a porter, and they were off the boat with time to spare. He saw the agents at once, and shook his head to indicate that he didn't want contact with them.

"What are we waiting for?" Allison asked him when the porter placed their bags beside them.

"The car isn't here." He didn't lie; he knew it was parked well away from the pier.

Shortly after nine, the first passengers walked off the plank. He had positioned himself where he could see each one, for they had to walk off single file. After a few minutes, Ned walked off. To his stunned disbelief, Jake knew he was looking at the real Ned. He held out three fingers, to indicate that the agents should expect four people, and pointed one finger to Ned.

"What time do you have?" he asked Allison, diverting her attention while an agent walked away with Ned.

"Nine-twenty. What time was the car due here?"

"Not to worry, love," he said, keeping his gaze on the disembarking passengers, "my publisher has yet to disappoint me."

Suddenly, his heart began thumping in his chest and his adrenaline stirred as it had at critical times when he was on a dangerous mission. Moisture accumulated in his mouth and his blood raced through his veins. The agent wasn't looking his way, so knowing he had no choice, he stepped up to Lena and Ned II, detaining them. Lena's worried and impatient facial expression confirmed his opinion of her as a smuggler.

"Hi. I was hoping I'd get a chance to tell you good-bye." With his left hand, the one in the direction of the agent, he held out two fingers. "All the best to you," he said when, from the corner of his eye, he saw the agent moving toward them. He ducked out of the way and almost bumped into Allison.

"Look," she said. "Where is that man taking them?"

He lifted his shoulder in a shrug. "Beats me." But he knew that one of the ringleaders was about to escape.

"I'd better call or email," he said to her, knowing she would think he referred to the driver of their car.

He rang the agents' cell phones to get their attention, hung up, and emailed them to expect Ring, who would probably leave the ship late. *If not,* he added in the email, *go on board the ship and pick him up. He'll be in the kitchen.*

Having completed his mission, he phoned the driver of their car. "We're at the pier," he said. "Right beside the sign that says 'Welcome aboard the *Saint Marie*.'"

After the driver stored their bags in the trunk of the stretched-out Lincoln Town Car and they seated themselves, Jake opened the bar. "Want a soda or some lemonade?" he asked Allison.

"Later, maybe. Thanks."

"You'll find coffee, snacks, and sandwiches to your right, sir," the driver said. "Sit back and enjoy the ride. We should be there around noon."

They checked their luggage, and when they finally boarded the plane, he took in a long and deep breath. One more job well done, and he hoped it would be the last the chief asked of him. What he couldn't get out of his mind was the question of how the real Ned got back on that ship. He'd bet anything that the man reported his passport lost, and got a new one from the U.S. consulate in Martinique in time to get back on the ship. He couldn't even guess why the man risked exposure by sending an illegal alien to the dining room in his place.

"Excuse me for a couple of minutes," he said to Allison. "If I don't write this down, it might slip me." He made rough notes on a small pad, and put the pad in his shirt pocket. He wanted food, but more than that, he wanted to sleep. He had spent a good deal of the night before looking for Ring and hadn't gotten to bed until after three.

The steward soon brought sandwiches, a salad, and drinks. He nibbled at the sandwiches. "Do you mind if I go to sleep?" he asked Allison.

"Of course not," she said. "This is a good time for me to work."

He reclined the back of his seat, put the pillow beneath his neck, and, for reasons he didn't question, laid his head against Allison's shoulder and went to sleep.

* * *

Allison eased her left arm beneath Jake's back, and he snuggled as close to her as their seats would allow. She didn't try to work. *It may be the only time he is ever truly mine,* she told herself and fought to stay awake to enjoy those moments. In spite of her efforts, she awoke as the wheels of the big plane touched down at the Ronald Reagan National Airport.

The following day, Friday, they arrived in Idlewild around three in the afternoon, and with instructions from her, he drove the rented car to 30 Michigan Boulevard.

Almost before the car came to a full halt, her aunt rushed out to greet her. *Now what?* Allison thought. *I didn't tell her he was coming or anything about him, and she'll give him the third degree.*

Jake got out of the car and went around to the passenger door, as he always did, to assist her, and she knew he wondered why she sat there and let him open the door. She never did that, but right then she focused on gathering the wits she would need to deal with her aunt and didn't think to open the door and get out.

"Well now, sakes alive. Who've we got here? Why, you're the same one I was fishing with. You don't know my…" She clapped her hands together and looked toward heaven. "Lord, you have taken matters into your own hand.

"Allison," she called, "come here, child, and introduce me to your friend. You didn't tell me you found him. Well, do tell!"

Allison walked around to where her aunt Frances stood beaming at Jake and stole a glance at the perplexed man. "Auntie, this is Jacob Covington, he's—"

"Not the writer!" She held out her hand. "I never expected to run into you again. Do you talk more'n you did when we were fishing?"

He looked down at the five-foot-three-inch woman and grinned. "Well, ma'am, I do when I get a chance."

Laughter rolled out of Frances Upshaw, and Allison noticed that her aunt still held Jake's hand. "I'll talk you to death if you let me," she said. "How long you staying?"

"Jake has to leave around noon Saturday, but I'll stay till about that time Sunday. Think you can drive me over to Reed City?"

"I'll be busy with the barbecue, but some of the girls over at the club will be glad to do it. Come on in."

"How do you like your food?" she asked Jake. "Southern style or messed up the way the Yankees do it? I'm good for either one."

Allison could see that Jake was taken with her aunt, and when a grin spread over his face, she knew that the weekend would go well.

"I take it you were born in the South. I'll eat whatever you cook, but I kinda love soul food."

She looked at Allison. "Go on upstairs and show him where he's going to sleep. I think I'll drop my line and see if I can pull up a few catfish for supper. There's a big bowl of homemade potato salad in the refrigerator, and I baked a ham last weekend. Good thing, too. Eat whatever you want. Just make yourselves at home."

Jake followed Allison up the stairs carrying their bags. At the top, he cradled her face in his hands. "I thought you said your aunt would expect you to be circumspect. She practically told you I could sleep wherever you want me to sleep." He pinched her nose. "You're the one with the rules; she couldn't care less."

"But you don't expect me to—"

"No, I definitely do not. I have a hunch she's more modern than either of us. It's still fairly warm. I'd like a swim. How about you?"

"I'm not in the mood, but I'll go with you. If you're going to wear those bathing trunks I saw you in, you should have a chaperon. Those things were three inches short of decent."

He looked at her, a grin lighting his face and his twinkle hard at work. "Got your attention, didn't it?"

She winked right back at him. "And then some." She put on a bathing suit and a long beach robe, her straw hat, and sandals.

He met her at the top of the stairs. She gulped and made no apologies for it. *I'm human,* she thought, *so why shouldn't I react to him this way?* She got a beach towel from the linen closet, folded it, and threw it across her arm.

"Ready to go?" he asked. She nodded, but if she told him the truth, she would shock him. His face creased into a smile and quickly dissolved into a laugh. "To the beach, I mean."

Caught ogling him, she put on a stern face. "Clever. I should swat you for going out in public like this."

He doubled up with laughter, and although she tried to resist, she joined him, laughing with him until they were both nearly breathless.

Sobriety took over, and his eyes blazed with passion. "If we made love right now, we'd get on a high and stay there indefinitely. See what kind of notions you put in my head? Let's go."

"If I put notions in *your* head, it wasn't until after you filled *my* head with them. What do you think crosses a healthy woman's mind when she sees you in that getup?"

With her hand snug in his, they strolled along Michigan Boulevard. "Probably the same thing men think about when they see you in *that* thing." He pointed toward her uncovered waist and hips.

"I'm wearing a robe."

"You weren't wearing one the morning I saw you out there, and let me tell you the view was just as nice as if you'd been Aphrodite rising from the sea."

She squeezed his fingers in place of the hug she wanted to give him. "What a lovely metaphor. To be likened to Aphrodite makes me feel like beating my chest."

His arm encircled her and brought her closer to him. "Believe me, I can do better than that. A lot better."

They reached the beach and he handed her his watch. "I'll be out there ten or fifteen minutes. The wind's rising. If it gets much stronger, shout. It's almost too windy now."

"All right." She spread the beach towel on the sand, put on her sunglasses, and stretched out.

"I thought I asked you to… Say, are you asleep?" he asked sometime later.

She opened her eyes, barely aware of her surroundings until he leaned over her and kissed her lips. She patted the place on the blanket beside her. "Let's stay for a few minutes. It's so quiet and peaceful here by ourselves."

He lay on his side, resting his elbow on the towel. "I've always loved the water. I can sit by the ocean, a river or a lake and know a peace, a kind of tranquility that doesn't come to me anywhere else. I wish we had more time out here, but it's getting too breezy and too cool, and I do not want to suffer the consequences. Let's go back."

But she couldn't bear to end the moment there with him. "Can't we stay a little longer? It's so pleasant and… Let's sit over there under that maple tree. We can shake out the beach towel and wrap it around you."

"After I dry off. Not that this towel is big enough to cover me."

They sat beneath the maple, an old and gnarled arbor that looked as if it had stood guard in that spot for centuries. She locked the fingers of her right hand through his left ones and leaned against the back of the bench.

"Aunt Frances said they're expecting a huge crowd tomorrow. The barbecue is a part of the plan to restore Idlewild to its former eminence as a resort. So many people are coming that the residents are offering their homes to those who have to spend the night."

"From what I've seen, I expect they welcome the income. Didn't your aunt plan to take any?"

"Auntie? Much as she loves Idlewild and as hard as she's worked to make the barbecue feast successful, she wouldn't think of it. Auntie likes her solitude and her privacy."

"I could use a little of your warmth. Move closer," he said, holding her in his arms and resting her head against his chest. "I can't imagine a more comforting setting."

She kissed his bare chest, reveling in the moment. "Me, neither. It's idyllic." She nuzzled his chest, her cheek brazing his left pectoral.

"Hey!" he said. "You're circumspect, and you're

sleeping by yourself. Remember? So go easy on that."
He hugged her when she kissed him again. "Why wasn't
your aunt surprised to meet me?"

"Beats me. If she opened her door and found a uni-
corn standing there, she'd probably say, 'Hi. Where'd
you come from?' You can't get more laid-back than my
aunt Frances."

"That's not quite the answer I want."

"Well…I described you to her after I saw you on the
beach that morning, and after the two of you fished together she told me that the man she fished with had to
be the same man I saw on the beach. She said you were
as tight-lipped as a kid in a dentist's chair."

"I don't make a habit of giving strangers my life his-
tory. Look!"

She sat up and followed his gaze. "What a sight!" she
said of the large round red disc that was the setting sun.

"Yeah." He held her closer. "Whenever I see anything in nature as striking as this, I have to thank God
for my eyes."

That was a message she never expected to receive
from him, and in spite of herself the reporter replaced
the woman. "I had no idea you were religious."

He raised his right hand as if acknowledging the
absurd, a gesture she had observed at his lectures.
"Considering where I came from and where I am, why
wouldn't I be religious? I certainly don't consider myself
all-powerful, so I expect I've had a good deal of help."

She turned to get a good look at his face while he
spoke as if he talked about himself that way all the time,
as if she should have known that about him.

*I love him, but I don't know important things about
him, just as he has no knowledge of the crucial things in*

*my past. If only I could level with him, but I'm scared.
If he knew about Roland Farr, if he knew why this job
is so important to me, he wouldn't let me finish the tour.*

"Surprise you?" he asked her when she didn't respond.

She couldn't tell him she hadn't answered because
she didn't know what to say. She thought for a minute
longer. "In a way, but I would have been much more
surprised if you told me something about yourself that
wasn't positive."

"Woman, you're good for my ego," he said, hugging her.

"It's just about to slip away from us," she said of
the setting sun, its red image across the lake growing
shorter and shorter.

"What's slipping away from... Oh! You mean the
sun. I hope those words don't prove prophetic."

He stood, folded the towel, draped it across his left
shoulder, and extended his right hand to her. "If your
aunt will lend me her fishing gear, I can still fish for
half an hour or so."

"Course you can borrow it," Frances told him when
they returned to the house. "They're biting right good,
too. I got four catfish and a pike, but I've been fishing
in these lakes so long I know where to go and how to
do it. What did you catch when you were here a few
weeks ago?"

"A four- or five-pound striped bass. I gave it to the
cook at Morton Inn."

"Hurry back now," she told him after he dressed,
loped down the stairs, and selected the fishing gear.
"I'd like us to eat at seven or seven-thirty. You going?"
she asked Allison.

"He needs his space, and I want to call Sydney."

To her surprise, Jake bent down and kissed her mouth in her aunt's presence. "Be back in an hour. Give Sydney my best," Jake said and left.

With her hands squarely on her hips, Frances looked at Allison, her expression that of disbelief. "I can't believe you didn't figure out the man you saw on the beach was the one you were traveling with almost every day."

"He didn't pass that close to me. Anyway, I barely glanced at his face; I was too busy ogling the rest of him." Laughter bubbled up in her throat and poured out as a giggle. "He wears clothes on the tour, so I had nothing for comparison."

"Do tell!" Frances rolled her eyes toward the ceiling. "You don't have to tell me how you found out he was the same man."

"Uh—"

"Keep it to yourself, child. I'm eighty, and I wouldn't be able to resist him, either. Lord knows, I wouldn't even want to, much less try."

Allison wanted to get off that subject. "Hmm. He'll be back here in a few minutes. I'd better put some clothes on. Any entertainment tonight?"

Frances stopped breading the catfish and stared at her niece. "Seems to me like you brought your entertainment with you. The band arrived this evening, but they're just practicing tonight over at the art center. They get paid for Saturday and Sunday, and you believe me they won't be blowing a single note till 12:01 tomorrow."

When Jake returned—his pride evident in the two bass and one pike dangling from the fishing rod—Allison apologized for the lack of entertainment, explaining that the band wouldn't play until Sunday afternoon. It struck her as odd that he seemed relieved, though that didn't make sense. But on more than one occasion, she had thought his behavior that of a man leading a double life. Her lower lip dropped.

Quickly, she closed her mouth, for he was attuned to her every gesture. "I am not going to start thinking like that," she said to herself. "I promised to report on what I see and hear during his working day, and not on what I surmise."

Chapter 9

"This is the best catfish I ever ate," Jake said at dinner, savoring his third helping. "This is the standard by which catfish should be judged."

"Talk that way, and she'll have you eating it till you pass out," Allison told him, pleased that he enjoyed her aunt's cooking.

"As long as there's a bed nearby, I wouldn't mind." He stopped eating long enough to ask Frances, "How did you, a Southern woman, happen to settle here?"

A smile of sweet memory lit Frances's face. "I sang with the big bands," she said, her eyes sparkling with remembrances of her younger days. "There wasn't a girl singer anywhere who could top Frances Wakefield."

Allison's head jerked up, and he realized she heard the gasp he hadn't been able to stifle. The woman was legendary, but he couldn't acknowledge knowing that without inviting questions from Allison, and maybe tipping her off about Mac Connelly.

"I'll be doggoned," he said. "You mean to tell me a celebrity can cook like this?"

"Honey, I haven't been a celebrity since the end of the fifties, almost half a century ago. Back there in the thirties, forties, and fifties, Idlewild was 'Black Eden.' All the greats came here. Count Basie, the Duke, Cab, Earl Hines, Mr. B., everybody. Right here in this resort, you could go to see Billie Holiday, Ella, and Lionel Hampton the same night.

"In the days of segregation, very few places that weren't black-owned booked black entertainers. They couldn't work in the clubs of Las Vegas and Hollywood, but they were welcome here, and they came. All of them. And black professionals and businessmen came here to enjoy them and luxuriate on some of the finest beaches in the country.

"Let me tell you, from the twenties through the fifties this resort rocked with talent. And a lot of those professionals who came here for vacation bought property here. It was nothing to see Dr. Du Bois and people like that walking around here. Integration changed it all. Our entertainers could work most anyplace, and blacks with money could stay where they liked.

"They all left Idlewild in droves and headed for Las Vegas, New York, and Hollywood. My husband and I had made our home here, so we stayed." With a faraway look in her eyes, she said, "We're bouncing back. Wait till tomorrow. You'll see."

Jake plowed his fingers through his hair. "I can't imagine anybody preferring Las Vegas to this place.

It's peaceful, and such natural beauty. First time I came here, I was awed."

"Well, a lot of 'em left, all right. You two want to play a couple of hands of pinochle? Haven't had a good game of cutthroat in ages."

After about an hour of losing to Frances, boredom crept in, a state with which he had no tolerance. "Now that you've beaten me to your satisfaction, Frances, I'd better start figuring out what I'll include in that one-hour lecture I'm giving Monday night in San Antonio."

He had to find out what time Saturday or Sunday the chief wanted to debrief him on his activities aboard the *Saint Marie,* and he needed time to prepare for that.

"You go right ahead, Jake. I'll have some hot chocolate on the stove for you, or you can open the fridge and get a beer or some white wine if you like. Make yourself at home."

"And don't forget to tell me good night," Allison called to him as he headed up the stairs.

He stopped, turned around, and asked her, "Are you suggesting I'm not rowing with both oars? How could I forget something so pleasant?" He placed his right hand over his heart. "Sweetheart, you wound me."

"He can talk when he wants to, all right," Frances said, enjoying the exchange. "He sure can. You go on do your work, honey. If you fall asleep, it won't kill her not to hear good night."

He thought she snickered, and a grin spread over his own face.

"I'll have breakfast and coffee ready by seven-thirty. And don't worry; the smell of those biscuits will get you out of that bed."

He teased for a few minutes, assured himself that

he hadn't displeased Allison, went into his room, and began working on his report to the chief.

Satisfied with what he'd accomplished, he knocked on Allison's door at a quarter of ten, knowing she wouldn't be asleep. "I'm here for my good-night kiss," he told her when she opened the door, and was rewarded with an open-arm invitation.

"Don't pour it on too thick, baby," he said. "We're circumspect here, remember?"

"You're never going to let me forget that, are you?"

"I wouldn't count on it, if I were you. I'll be down for breakfast at seven-thirty. Would you walk to the beach with me after we eat? I like it out there early mornings."

The back of her left hand grazed softly over his cheek. "If you promise to wear clothes, yes."

He stepped back, giving the impression of one deeply offended. "You don't like my G-string?"

"Trust me. I'm not going there."

He hated to leave her because he adored her most when she was in one of her playful, laughing moods, when her softness overrode everything else about her.

"Kiss me, love. See you in the morning?"

When he turned to leave, she pulled the hem of his T-shirt. "What kind of guy deserts a woman at her bed-room door?" She intrigued him when she mugged, as she did then.

"The kind who's been warned to be circumspect," he answered, kissed her, and went to his room. He had played with fire in his lifetime, and often, but only when he had the means of extinguishing it. If he had stayed with her five minutes longer, he'd have said, "Circum-spection be damned."

* * *

After a hearty Southern-style breakfast the next morning, Saturday, Allison and Jake strolled along the beach at Idlewild Lake, warm in their sweaters and their feelings for each other.

"I'm sorry you have to leave shortly," she told him, "but it means a lot to me that you came."

"Yeah," he said, shortening his steps to match her shorter ones as they strolled hand in hand. "We've done some serious bonding here. From now on, this will be *our place.* Let's plan to come back here, this winter, maybe when the small lake freezes. It *does* freeze, doesn't it?"

"I don't know for certain, but I think so."

"Do you ice-skate?" She nodded. "Good, then we'll do that."

Allison neither agreed nor disagreed, and she neither disputed him nor allowed his certainty to raise her hopes. Instead, she replied, "*Inshallah*—God willing, as the Muslims always say."

She pretended not to have read his quizzical expression, only placed an arm around his waist and turned toward Frances Upshaw's house.

"If you get into Washington by six-thirty," the chief told Jake when he called him two hours later at the airport in Reed City, "come straight here." Fearing that their conversations could be intercepted, Jake and the chief did not identify themselves or the chief's location when speaking by phone, a precaution that Jake occasionally found restraining, as he did then. It would have been easier for Jake if they could have met closer to the home of either one.

"I'd as soon not come to work tomorrow, and you're leaving Monday morning," the chief went on. "I'll wait here for you."

"That suits me, too, sir."

Twenty-five minutes after the plane landed in Washington, Jake knocked on the chief's office door.

"Sorry, we don't yet know precisely what Ring's role in this is, but I'd swear he's involved, and more than casually," the chief said. "His former lover works at the consulate there, and we suspect the two of them are doing a lucrative business."

"Did you pick him up?"

"Not yet. The agency is tracking both Ring and his contact at the consulate. We want to get the leader; a guy like Ring is a gofer. Someone's behind him. You did a fine job, Jacob."

"Thank you, sir." Having learned that his efforts were useless, Jake had stopped reminding the chief that he preferred to be called Jake.

"Going to Blues Alley tonight?"

"I had planned to. Why?"

"In that case, we'll have a couple of men there. Your Rockefeller Center nemesis—Mr. Harasser, we call him—went back twice, didn't see you, and hasn't been there lately. But his kind doesn't give up. Be careful."

"You mean they released him?" Jake didn't bother to disguise his feelings about the ridiculousness of letting the man go.

The chief rubbed his jaw, already a mass of stubble at seven in the evening. "No grounds for keeping him. So watch it."

At home, Jake checked his house, found nothing amiss, and prepared to go to Blues Alley. He donned a pair of brown pants, his well-worn tweed jacket with leather patches at the elbows, put on his old felt hat with the brim turned up in the back—a style he borrowed from the great jazz saxophonist Lester Young—got his guitar, and headed for the club. A block before reaching it, he put on his dark glasses.

"Man, did we miss *you!*" Buddy Dee said when Jake walked through the back door. "We had a guitarist here last night, but man, you wouldn't believe how poor the guy was. Take your seat. We've got just a couple of minutes before going on."

When the lights went up, Jake sent his gaze slowly over the patrons, looking for the one he considered his enemy. He didn't see the man, but this was one night in which he didn't plan to lose himself in his music.

Applause, stomping, whistles, and yells of "all right, Mac" greeted him before he or the band played a note. He expressed his thanks by bowing his head and touching the brim of his hat, got Buddy's downbeat, and sent his fingers flying over the strings in a hot rendition of "Honeysuckle Rose."

The more he played, the more the patrons demanded of him, but with his attention mainly on a man who might want to kill him, he couldn't lose himself in playing as he usually did, and therefore, because he couldn't let go and enjoy it, he soon tired. Finally, to let them know that they had exhausted him, he nodded to Buddy and played "Back Home in Indiana," his signature, and always his last song. He tipped his hat, looked over the audience once more, and waited for the lights to go down.

"This isn't working," Jake told the chief later that night, irritated at receiving a call after midnight. He wondered whether the man ever slept.

"Sorry. This just got to me, and I know it's a bad time, but we need you to testify at a closed Senate committee hearing. Just that one day is all I'm asking."

Jake raised himself up in bed and balanced his weight on his right elbow. "Yeah. You always make it sound as if the inconvenience you're proposing is the last unreasonable request I'll get. I'm scheduled to be in Texas."

"I know that. Cancel the last two days, will you? Authors do that all the time."

"Some of 'em. What about my reputation? The word will go out that I'm a no-show." And what about his relationship with Allison?

"We'll fix that."

"I don't doubt it," Jake said, though he didn't mean it charitably. "I'm sure you'll let me know the details."

He hung up and fought for hours to get back to sleep. He'd be willing to bet that Allison already had a dozen questions about his odd schedule changes and even more about his peculiar behavior on that cruise. And according to their agreement, she was entitled to put it in print. If only he could be sure he meant more to her than a sizzling story and a promotion.

Allison arrived at the Delta counter that morning dressed in a yellow handkerchief-weight linen pantsuit. Her Balmacaan raincoat lay folded atop her suitcase. As his loose, almost lazy gait brought him toward her, she fought back a premonition, unusual for her because she didn't worry about imagined unpleasantness.

"Hi," he said, not stopping until his lips touched her. "Got your ticket?"

Taken aback by his boldness, she could only nod. As had become his habit, he placed her bag atop his, grabbed the handle of his own suitcase, and started with her to the gate.

"What is it?" she asked, noticing his expression of concern.

"Just remembered something."

He stopped, took out his cell phone, and pushed a couple of buttons.

"Hi," he said to the person he called. "I'm at the airport. Yeah. Just getting to the gate. No, but if you need anything while I'm away, you know where to reach me." He appeared to listen carefully. "No, I didn't. I'd recognize him anywhere. You take care. Love you, Mom."

Relief flooded her, though she didn't think him so callous that he would telephone and speak with another woman while standing less than two feet from her. After they boarded the plane, she reflected on Jake's conversation with his mother and wondered at the lack of warmth in his voice.

"Would you believe my phone rang at midnight last night?" he asked her. "I almost never got back to sleep."

"Lay your head on my shoulder," she said after his third or fourth yawn, and patted the shoulder closest to him.

"Thanks." In a few minutes he was asleep, and didn't awaken until she checked to see whether his seat belt was fastened for landing.

"Feel better?"

His grin, sheepish and embarrassed, endeared him more to her. "Yes and no. I couldn't have kept my eyes open, but it would have been heaven if I could have stretched out. Where are we?"

"A few minutes from landing."

He checked the papers that he carried in the inside

pocket of his jacket. "A car should be waiting for us at the airport. The lecture is at six, so we ought to be able to get dinner around seven-thirty."

They checked in at the Hyatt Regency, and as the elevator took them up to their floors, he said, "Be sure and look out the window first thing. You'll get a nice surprise. I'm in room 940. Can we meet in the lobby for lunch in, say, forty-five minutes?"

She looked at her room key. "I'm in 740. Lunch sounds great." The elevator stopped and she was about to step out, when he put his foot at the door, leaned to her, and kissed her, flicking his tongue around the seams of her lips. "See you," he whispered before she could recover and welcome his tongue into her body.

"I owe you one," she said, "and it won't help you to mention the word *circumspect,* either."

A couple of doors down the spacious corridor she found her room, went inside, and walked straight to the window. *What a place for lovers!* She stepped out on her balcony and gazed down at the strollers along the Paseo del Rio, the famous cobblestones River Walk that snaked its way beside the winding San Antonio River, adorned on either side with trees, shrubs, ferns, flowers, hotels, restaurants, and assorted other buildings. She didn't think she had ever seen anything so idyllic as when a Yanaguana Cruiser—a flat boat—ambled past with a group of sightseers as its joyful burden.

She had phoned Sydney the night before, but got no answer, so she decided to use a part of her forty-five minutes talking with him.

"Wakefield," his deep and, to her amazement, officious voice said when he answered the phone—an attitude that she assumed was a part of his professional demeanor.

"Hi, Sydney. I'm down in San Antonio. How are you?"

"Me? I'm great. How's Jake?"

"Upstairs asleep, I guess. He slept all the way down from Washington."

"Hey! Go easy on the guy. If he needs to sleep, let him."

"I am. We just got here."

"Yeah? How's the romance shaping up? If he sat beside you and went to sleep, he must feel pretty comfortable with you."

"Maybe. Something's been bothering me. Jake breaks the tour with no excuse, except to tell me that something came up, and twice on the cruise he disappeared. In Martinique, he rushed us back to the boat an hour early, and we were the first passengers to return. All of a sudden after watching the passengers file in, he grabbed my hand and jumped the line. Then, he told me to go on to my stateroom and he'd see me later. The only explanation he gave was the hint of urgency in his voice."

"You're looking for something that isn't there. The man's a writer, and writers are always focused on that next book. How is he when the two of you are alone?"

"He's…uh, affectionate and loving. I couldn't believe he kissed me right in front of Aunt Frances."

His chuckles reached her through the wire. "What did she say about that?"

"Auntie? You know how laid-back she is. She didn't bat an eyelash. They liked each other. Spoken to Mom or Dad?"

"With Dad. But I haven't had the energy to talk with Mom. She wears me out just by the way she says hello."

Allison couldn't help laughing at Sydney's candidness, a trait he'd had since early childhood. "Tell me about it. I have to go; I haven't changed my clothes, and I'm meeting Jake for lunch in half an hour."

"Have a good time down there… And, Allison…"

"What is it?"

"Stop scrutinizing every blink of the guy's eyes. If you look for a problem, you'll find one. That man is honest and honorable, and you will not dispute me on that. When your relationship gets to the point where he starts talking about the future, he'll tell you everything. But if you pry into his life to get information for that article you're writing on him, kiss him goodbye. You listening to me?"

"Yes. I am."

"Take care of yourself, sis. Don't court trouble."

She hung up with his words still ringing in her ears.

After lunch in one of the hotel's restaurants, she strolled along the River Walk with Jacob Covington holding her hand, telling herself not to let the idyllic setting sweep her out of reality.

"Did you notice that every couple we meet, regardless of age, is holding hands?" she asked Jake.

"Impossible to miss it. Want a cruise along the river in a Yanaguana Cruiser? It's a great way to see the River Walk."

"I'd love it," she said. "How many times have you visited San Antonio?"

"Several."

When he didn't elaborate, she wondered if those visits were associated with a broken love affair. *It never pays to ask him direct questions,* she reminded herself, *unless he initiates the topic.*

Resting against his broad chest as the flat-bottomed boat glided slowly along the narrow stream, she wished she didn't love him, for she knew it had to end. Nothing beautiful in her life had ever lasted except Sydney. The more she thought of it, the more she hurt, and without considering her actions, she turned in his arms and buried her face in his chest.

At first, he seemed to relish her move, wrapping her closely to his body, but she remained there, never wanting to move, and he stepped back.

"Something isn't right with you. What is it?"

She laid her shoulders back, brushed the hair from her face, and smiled. "I just hate so terribly for…for this to end."

"This what? Being here, the tour, or…or…us?"

"Here, the tour. You know what I mean."

"I have a feeling it goes deeper, but you will eventually tell me."

When at last the cruiser returned them to the Hyatt Regency, she welcomed the opportunity for privacy in her room, if only for a few minutes. "What time do we meet?" she asked him.

"Five-fifteen in the lobby. If you'll excuse me, I'll look over my notes now."

"Of course." She said goodbye, noticed that he didn't kiss her, and wondered at the coolness he projected. Perhaps she imagined it.

His lecture and book signing that evening took place at a local high school. Although his audience consisted mostly of adults, more than a tenth were high school teenagers, juniors and seniors. On an earlier occasion when he spoke about his life, he had held her nearly spellbound, but she had attributed that to his subject matter. On this occasion, he mesmerized her with a talk she knew he had not planned, but had decided upon when he realized he had an opportunity to make a difference in the lives of thirty or forty African-American teenagers.

She took notes as fast as she could write, gave up, and turned on her recorder. Speaking directly to the youths, he told them not to use race as an excuse to fail in life, but to educate themselves, work hard, and meet every situation in life with honesty and integrity.

"Be kind to others, and lift up your less gifted brother or sister," he told them. "Don't aim to be good at what you do; aim to excel. Then, no one can stop you, and no one will *want* to stop you."

She stood aside while the audience surged toward him. He spoke to each youth, signed several hundred books, and shook hands with most everyone present. She thought it his most grueling engagement of the tour but it seemed to have invigorated him.

"I promised you we'd eat dinner around seven-thirty," he said as they were leaving the school, "and it's ten after nine. This looks like a nice restaurant; let's go in here."

After a relatively simple meal of blackened redfish, boiled parsley potatoes, and string beans, with peach ice cream for dessert, he reached across the table for her hand.

"This isn't going to sit well with you, and it certainly displeases me, but I have to leave tomorrow morning. It can't be helped, and I'm sorry. I'll change your ticket if you don't want to stay longer."

She supposed she looked a sight, as her mother often said, with her lower lip hanging down and her right eye narrowed to a slit. "Look, you've missed almost a third of your dates, and I'm facing three full pages of small newsprint in a standard-size newspaper. What the devil am I going to write? Most of what I know about you isn't printable."

"You must know that I wouldn't make these abrupt changes if I could avoid it."

She tried to squelch the anger that overtook her like a rising storm, but couldn't. "Maybe some day, you'll tell me—the woman, if not the writer—what you do in your other life."

He removed his hand, leaned back, and stared at her. And she saw nothing friendly in his gaze or in his demeanor. "It doesn't pay to get so fanciful. You've let your imagination run amok. Shall we go?"

Too late, she remembered Sydney's advice, but she was damned if she'd apologize. "Yes. Let's" was all she said until they reached the hotel's lobby.

"If you'll give me your ticket, I'll have it changed and leave it at the desk for you. When are you leaving?"

She thought for a minute. If she didn't give him the ticket, she would have to pay her fare back to Washington. "Tomorrow afternoon," she told him, got the ticket out of her handbag, and gave it to him.

"You can't imagine how sorry I am about this," he said, turned, and left.

"Jake!" she called after him, and her heart seemed to jump into her throat when he stopped, turned, and waited. He said nothing, and she knew it was her move.

She walked to him. "Jake, I'm sorry I caused this rift between us, but you must realize that I am frustrated. You said you can't help it. Well, I don't believe you would lie to me, but knowing you are honest about it doesn't ease my anxiety about getting the story I'm being paid for."

"I'm aware of that, and I'll do my best not to disappoint you again."

When he turned toward the elevator, without thinking, she said, "Whatever awaits you, go with God."

His eyes widened, and then a frown covered his face. "I… Thanks. Thanks a lot."

"My grandmother used to say that to me every time I left her house, and it always made me feel so safe," she said.

He reached for her hand and held it until they reached the door of her room. "I have to get a seven-ten flight, so I'm not going in. I'll leave your ticket at the desk."

Both of his arms encircled her, and for a brief second she felt the pressure of his mouth on hers. "We haven't cleared this up," he said, "but we will. I'll meet you at the airport Monday morning. Safe journey." He hugged her briefly, waited until she closed her room door, and left.

She told herself not to question his ability to get her ticket changed between ten in the evening and five in the morning when he had to leave the hotel. *Considering how much there is about him that I don't know, I may find out that he can walk on water.*

After breakfast the next morning, she stopped at the registration desk and asked whether she had mail. The clerk handed her a long white envelope addressed to her in what she assumed was Jake's bold handwriting. "I'd give anything to know how he did it," she said to herself, observing that he had booked a four o'clock direct flight. Puzzled, yet admiring him, she headed for the Alamo, the one site she wanted to visit.

Jake walked away from Allison, his heart heavy and his anger near the surface. Anger at the chief for disrupting his life, at himself for permitting it, and at Allison for not believing in him, although from his behavior on the tour, she had a right to question him. He hadn't wanted to leave her, and especially not with a chill hanging over them. He walked into his room, saw the message signal flashing on the phone, and, suspecting that the chief was his caller, called him back on his cell phone.

"Did you phone me?" Assured that he had, he asked, "What's up?"

"Just making sure you get to that hearing at eleven-thirty tomorrow morning."

"When I agree to do a thing, I do it," he replied, not bothering to show his annoyance. "She's not coming back with me. I want you to get her ticket changed for a three or four o'clock flight tomorrow." He read the ticket numbers to his boss. "I told her her ticket would be at the registration desk when I leave the hotel in the morning. I've never lied to her."

"Whew!" the chief said. "Man, you don't half do anything. I hope she knows how fortunate she is."

"Really? When I told her of your latest plan for me, she practically bit off my head. This is my last break in this tour. If the capitol is about to be burned, call someone else."

The long silence didn't impress him. "I see," the chief finally said. "I've only looked at this from the point of view of our needs here. No doubt this has been a burden for you."

"It's been a burden for the stores and event planners who purchased cartons of my books and had to dispose of them as best they could, and there's no telling what kind of story that paper will print if she loses confidence in me. And she has plenty of grounds."

When a fledgling agent, he would have considered himself reckless to speak to his boss in such a way, but after eleven years of faithful and selfless service with the same boss, he was entitled to speak his mind.

"Are you ever planning to tell her the whole story?"

"I'd need your permission. What do your other operatives tell their wives, for instance?"

"We'll discuss this when you come back. I had no idea I'd put you in such a predicament. The ticket will be there before you leave. See you tomorrow."

"A lot of good that does me right now," Jake said aloud and began to pack. The next morning, he stopped at the desk and assured himself that the exchanged ticket had arrived. The chief had ways of accomplishing the nearly impossible, and for this once, he was grateful.

He went from the airport in Washington directly to the Senate Office Building and walked into the chamber at eleven twenty-five for the closed hearing scheduled to begin at eleven-thirty.

Frustrated and increasingly agitated at her inability to get a grasp on Jake's public persona, which was so unlike the man she knew privately, Allison paced around her office at home, certain that she faced a hostile grilling from her boss and humiliation at being labeled incompetent. She understood why other reporters had managed to write nothing more than bland, uninteresting pieces on him. He shrouded himself in privacy, revealing only as much of himself as he deemed relevant.

She answered the telephone hoping to hear Jake's voice, but instead she heard the snarling words of her boss.

"I called you at the hotel and discovered you'd checked out. What have you got to say for yourself? I'm not spending my money to make it convenient for you and Covington. I—"

She interrupted him. "He had to cut the engagement short and left early this morning, but didn't tell me where he was going. He got my ticket changed, and I got back a couple of hours ago. For your information, I am sitting here working on this story when I should be asleep, tired as I am."

"Hmm. Well, as long as you're working at it. But I don't see you getting excited like you found out something good. I don't want a story telling me how great he is, the papers have been full of tripe like that on him. You find out what he's like when nobody's looking, and put it in that story. You hear me?"

She did, indeed. "I'm doing my best."

After musing over her dilemma as to what she could write that would be interesting to readers, she stopped short. *Oh yes, I will definitely do my best. It's my career I'm dealing with here. I know he went to college, but what year? Did he graduate with honors or not?*

The next morning, she got into her four-year-old Mercury Sable and headed for Maryland. *I'd better stop by Matty's Gourmet Shop and get some gingersnaps in case I get stranded,* she told herself, *and maybe I ought to fill up my tank.* She bought two boxes of her favorite snack food, a ham sandwich, and a bottle of water at Matty's, stopped by Shell, filled up her tank and bought the maps she would need, and set out for Reed Hollow, Maryland. If her luck held, Jake would have chosen some other time to visit his mother. Somehow, she didn't think his being there a possibility.

Around three that afternoon, she saw a wooden sign pointing to Reed Hollow and turned onto that road. Though it was paved and allowed for two-lane traffic, all else about it suggested that she would find a tiny hamlet, run-down housing, and few, if any, accommodations.

She stopped at a small general store that sat alone on the deserted road. "I'm looking for Mrs. Covington," she said to the old man behind the counter. He looked up at the ball of brown twine hanging from the ceiling, pulled a little harder, and cut the length he wanted. After tying a parcel that he had wrapped in brown paper, he pushed it aside, placed his hands flat on the counter, and looked at her.

"And why, might I ask, would you be looking for Annie Covington?"

Taken aback by the question, she told the truth. "I'm writing a story on her son, and I wanted to find out if she could add anything to what I've written."

He rubbed his whiskered chin and peered at her through his gold-framed glasses. "You mean young Jacob? We're right proud of him around here." He walked to the door. "Go down that way a piece till you see a big white silo, turn onto the road beside it, and drive till you see a white house. Can't miss it; only white house in these parts."

* * *

She brought the car to a stop in front of the white bungalow, said a prayer, and got out. If Annie Covington refused to talk with her, she would have lost more than information for a story; indeed, she already risked the complete rupture of relations with Jake. If his feelings for her weren't as strong as she believed, she would certainly lose him.

Annie Covington opened the door before Allison knocked. "Hello, there," she said. "I heard a strange car pull up and came to see who it was." She opened the screen door and stepped out on the porch.

"Mrs. Covington, I'm Allison Wakefield, and I've been accompanying Jake on his lecture and book-signing tour for a newspaper story I'm writing about him. I was won—"

When she smiled, Allison saw the strong resemblance between mother and son. As tall as Allison and with a well-proportioned, slim figure and streaks of gray hair at her temples, Annie Covington exuded charm, warmth, and friendliness.

"Come on in. Jake hasn't told me a thing about this. Hmm. Where'd you come from?" She led the way down an inlaid beige-and-brown-tiled floor to a living room that was tastefully furnished with brown-velvet-covered sofa and chairs, Persian carpets, and reproductions of Matisse and Price paintings. The huge stone fireplace struck her as most inviting.

"I'll bet this fireplace was Jake's idea," she said to his mother.

The woman turned and stared at her. "It definitely was, and if you know him that well, you're more to him than a reporter. Where do you live, and who told you I was in Reed Hollow?"

Impressed by the woman's astuteness and candor, she made up her mind to level with her, no matter what question she asked. "I live in Alexandria, Virginia, and I drove from there to here because I wanted to talk with you." She recounted how she found her. "Jake told me about his childhood, or some of it."

Annie Covington smiled. "I can imagine 'some of it' was all he gave you. He's very private, was so as a child. Getting personal information out of Jake is like pulling hens' teeth."

Good Lord, thought Allison, *so that's where he gets the twinkle!*

"If you've been driving all day, you must be hungry. The bathroom's at the end of the hall. I'll get you something to eat."

After washing her face and hands, Allison peeped into the kitchen. "Mind if I come in?"

"Goodness, no. I would have asked you to come back here while I fixed it, but I didn't know how you'd feel about sitting in the kitchen."

Allison sat at the kitchen table and turned the chair so that she could watch Jake's mother. "Mrs. Covington," she said, "my dear mother is such a snob that it's my great pleasure to be around someone who isn't. And if it's all right with you, I'll eat here at this table."

"You sure? I thought we'd eat in the dining room. My son's most proud of that room. Wait till you see it."

"Whatever you like. Can I help you with anything?"

"Thanks, but it'll be ready in a second. I just have to fry these crab cakes. That's one—"

"You're giving me crab cakes?"

"Why, yes, provided you like them."

"Like them? I'm crazy about them."

Annie beamed, her pleasure evident. "These are fresh; I pulled a couple of bushels out of the bay this morning. Just finished picking the meat out minutes before you drove up."

"I can hardly wait," Allison told her, her salivary glands already anticipating the taste. "No wonder Jake loves to fish. I'll bet the two of you fish together sometimes. How far is the bay from here?"

"Closest point's about a mile. Jake's got a nice boat that's docked about four miles from here. He likes to go out on the bay in his boat and catch the bigger fish. Of course, there aren't many of those left. The Chesapeake Bay has been fished to death, and parts of it need cleaning; a lot of weeds giving off carbon dioxide."

She put the food on a tray and took it into the dining room, went back into the kitchen and got plates, glasses, and utensils. "Come on," she said. "It's not much, but it'll keep you from starving." After setting the table, she beckoned Allison. They sat down, and Annie Covington reached out to hold the hand of her guest, bowed her head, and said grace.

"This is wonderful," Allison said of the crab cakes, potato salad, hot buttermilk biscuits, and sliced tomatoes. "Jake said he likes gourmet cooking, but that he loves soul food. I can see why. The biscuits are a miracle."

She marveled that they talked as if they knew each other well, attributing this mostly to Annie Covington's earthy charm and genuineness.

"I'll bring us some coffee in the living room and we can talk where it's comfortable," Annie said.

Allison glanced around from the walnut Thomasville dining set to the Royal Bakara carpet that nearly covered the large room, the sconces with electric candles on the off-white walls, and the big stone fireplace in a far corner that marked the room as a place of welcome.

"This is as comfortable as a room can be," she said, walking behind her host toward the living room.

Annie brought the coffee service and sat facing Allison. "Let's get this out of the way, dear," she said. "You're in love with Jake. Does he know it?"

Allison nearly spilled the coffee on her skirt. So they were going to be candid, and she was glad, because she felt more comfortable with her cards on the table.

"Yes, I am, and he knows it. What he doesn't know is that I'm here, and when he finds out he isn't going to flash that famous grin of his."

"I imagine not; he doesn't like to be crossed. Now, what can I tell you?"

She looked into the woman's eyes, kind and gentle, older versions of the eyes she loved so dearly. "I don't know how old he was the first day he went to school, what kind of grades he made, what he excelled at, whether he graduated with honors. None of that. Was he obedient as a child, or was he stubborn and hardheaded? What made him into the man he is today?"

Annie leaned back and crossed her right knee over her left one. "What kind of man do you think he is?"

Fair enough, Allison thought. *You can't answer a question unless you know what it means.* She opened her mouth and embarrassment flooded her. "He... he... I think he's a wonderful man, but I can't put that in my report."

The woman nodded. "Hmm. I see what you mean.

The woman who loves him is interfering with the gal who has to write a story on him. I don't envy you."

Annie folded her arms and began to talk—about their life before her husband died, Jake's life as a child, and the hardships they all endured. She closed her eyes as she spoke of Jake's honors, his graduation from high school as class valedictorian with a four-year fellowship to the university. Tears dripped from the corners of her eyes when she told of his graduation from college summa cum laude, of his subsequent graduate degree.

The moisture from her eyes pooled in her lap when she said, "Look at this house. It wasn't much more than a shack, but from the time Jake got his first paycheck, he set out to make my life as pleasant as he could. He rebuilt and furnished this place. I used to work until my fingers hurt, but not any longer. I don't need all the money he sends me. No woman could want a more faithful, more loyal son."

Allison stopped writing. "Nothing you've said surprises me. I know him to be an honorable man with laudable principles." She closed her notebook. "I'd better start back, though I am reluctant. I have loved this time with you. I hope Jake knows how fortunate he is to have you as his mother."

Annie stood, dabbing at her reddened eyes. "Stay the night. It's too late for you to start that long drive back. I have toothbrushes, I'll give you a gown, and you can wash your underwear and dry them in the dryer." She smiled. "I'd love for you to stay."

Supper consisted of stewed collards, fried chicken, candied sweet potatoes, and baked corn bread. "I've got apple turnovers for dessert," Annie said when Allison pulled her chair back.

She patted her belly. "Thanks, but I'm about to pop. I'll take a couple of those to eat on the way back, though."

"One thing I didn't tell you," Annie said as they cleared the table and straightened the kitchen. "I've got one complaint against my son." Guessing what that was, Allison didn't encourage her to continue. However, Annie evidently didn't need encouragement.

"I'm sixty," she said, "and if I'm ever going to have any grandchildren, I want them while I'm still young enough to enjoy them. But every time I mention it, my son changes the subject."

Allison couldn't suppress the laughter that finally spilled out of her. "Sorry," she said, "but if you heard him talk about that, you wouldn't worry. He says it's the one thing he can't contemplate living without, and that he will not compromise on it."

Annie dropped a plate in the sink and turned to face Allison. "Why on earth did he say that? Don't you want children?"

"Oh, yes, I do. He was letting me know his position on the matter. As I recall, he didn't ask how I felt about it."

"You've never married?" Allison shook her head. "Are these men crazy? I certainly hope Jake's got some sense."

They watched an old Humphrey Bogart movie, and at about nine-thirty Annie announced it was her bedtime. "By the way, Allison. Mind if I call you that?"

"Please do."

"What month were you born in?"

"February seventeenth is my birthday." Annie smiled. "You're smiling. Why?"

"Jake's part Leo and part Virgo. Great pairing with Aquarians."

Not wanting to show her hand, Allison joked, "My lips are sealed, Mrs. Covington."

"They may be sealed, but I hope that, given the chance, they'll unglue themselves long enough to say two words."

Allison wanted to hug the woman. Perplexed as to how she should respond, she took the toothbrush and nightgown Annie handed her and, on an impulse, kissed the woman's cheek.

"I'll find the laundry room. Good night and thanks for…for everything."

She showed Allison the guest room. "Good night, dear, and God bless you."

How will I tell him I did this? He will be mad enough to eat nails, and he might even attempt to break our relationship. But I'm not going to let him do that. I believe he loves me, and I can truthfully tell him, I didn't ask his mother anything he wouldn't want known.

She mused over those thoughts. Annie Covington hadn't said anything she wouldn't have said in Jake's presence. *She never mentioned where he works or what his occupation was before he wrote that book. Hmmm.*

The next morning, after the kind of breakfast she ate only at her aunt Frances's house, Allison prepared to leave. "Thanks for being so kind to me," she told Annie. "I mean, my own mother wouldn't have made me so comfortable or feel so welcomed."

A frown darkened Annie's countenance. "What a pity. Here's my phone number. I want you to call me when you get home, and please come back to see me."

The woman opened her arms and let Allison know the strength of a mother's affection.

Allison didn't say goodbye, because the words somehow seemed inappropriate. She took the bag Annie handed her, whispered her thanks, got into her car, and drove off without looking back. At the end of the road, she stopped, parked the car, and let the tears fall. What she wouldn't give to have a mother like Annie Covington!

Chapter 10

Jake walked out of the Senate hearing, stopped at the watercooler, and wet his throat. So intent had he been on answering the senators' questions as accurately as he could that he hadn't thought to drink the water provided for him. He knew he would be forgiven if he made an error, but he was also aware that, on some matters, his would be the only reliable information available to the committee, so he did his best.

"Fine job, Covington," a member of the committee said to him as he was leaving the area. "I don't know where you get the nerve to do some of the things you've done, but I am certainly grateful that you have it."

"Thank you, sir, but I'm not longer an undercover agent. Haven't been for the last four and a half years."

"I know," the man replied, "and it's a damned pity. I hope they do well by you over there."

"I've been promised a promotion when I return to duty full-time."

The senator took a business card from his pocket and handed it to Jake. "If it's not in your first paycheck, call me. I'll take care of it."

Jake thanked the man, and hoped he wouldn't have to resort to pressure to get what the chief volunteered. He'd never had to fight for a promotion; his work did that for him. He got his suitcase and topcoat from the cloakroom and headed for the exit. Outside in the clear, brisk, early September day, he walked half a dozen blocks for the exercise, hailed a taxi, and went home.

Three phone calls to Allison's home brought no answer, and although he wanted to call her at her office, he hesitated to cause her problems with her boss in the event that she was not at work. Sleepy, washed out, and with plenty of work to do but no interest in doing it, he dialed her number again and again. Finally, he left a message, "Almost every time I need you, I can't find you," fell across his bed, kicked off his shoes, and slept.

He awakened shortly after six in the evening, hungry and annoyed at himself for not having disrobed, gotten into bed, and favored himself with a proper rest. He dialed Allison's number again, but to no avail. Frustrated and fighting back fear for her well-being, he phoned the Hyatt Regency in San Antonio and learned that she had checked out that morning. A call to the airline yielded the information that she was aboard her flight to Washington and that the plane landed safely. Increasingly concerned, he considered telephoning her aunt Frances in Idlewild and thought better of it. He showered, made a peanut butter and jelly sandwich, got a glass of milk, and watched the evening news while he ate. But he absorbed nothing that he saw and heard, for he couldn't move his mind off Allison.

She said she wasn't interested in any other man, but that doesn't mean she isn't seeing one. Something's holding her back. I don't know her any better than she knows me.

"Oh, hell!" he said aloud. "Why am I being unfair to her? Maybe she went on a short assignment. Who knows? It will be time to worry if she doesn't meet me at the airport Monday morning."

Once more, concern for possible danger prevented him from immersing himself in his music as he did what he loved best, playing his guitar in Blues Alley with Buddy Dee's band. And Allison remained on his mind. At the end of the first set, glancing around the club, he saw the woman who usually visited the club with her, though her companion that night was a man, a familiar man. He shifted that around in his mind and decided it had no bearing on Allison's whereabouts.

The long and painful evening finally ended. He left the club—watchful and cautious as he did so—hailed a taxi, and headed home. After a fitful, restless night, he crawled out of bed, refreshed himself with a hot shower, made coffee, heated some frozen Belgian waffles in the toaster, poured maple syrup on them, and ate his breakfast. Ordinarily, he liked waffles, but not that morning; he forced them down.

I can't call her this early, he told himself. *It wouldn't be proper. She'll think I'm checking up on her.* Nonetheless, he was reaching for the telephone when it rang and his heartbeat picked up speed like a car with a jammed accelerator.

"Hello," he said, making an unsuccessful effort to keep his voice normal.

"Say, man. I thought I'd better get you early."

Jake let out a long sigh of disappointment. "What's up?" he asked Duncan Banks.

"Justine bought me this fantastic outdoor grill for my birthday. It's even got a spit that you can roast a twenty-pound turkey on. Man, this thing rocks. We're going to try it out this evening. Can you come over? It'll be just us. Our housekeeper's been marinating chops and chicken for a couple of days, and I don't know what else she'll have there for me to cook. Justine says if you don't come, you'll be on her blacklist."

"And we certainly don't want that. What time?"

"Come over about five. We'll catch up."

"All right. This wouldn't be your birthday, would it?"

"Well, yeah. According to my mother."

For the first time in two days, he found something to laugh about. "Occasionally, I forget that the Banks humor begins and ends with your sister, Leah."

"For heaven's sake, don't tell her that. She's smart-assed enough as it is."

"She'll be surprised to know that. See you around five."

He hung up and dialed Allison's number again, but got no response.

Out of sorts about Allison, and feeling the need to exercise, he decided to jog around the park, but remembered that he hadn't spoken with his mother since returning from San Antonio. He checked his watch, saw that it was just after nine—already late in the morning for his mother—and dialed her number.

"How are you, Mom?" he said when she answered.

"I'm just fine, son. I just came in from the bay with half a bushel of crabs, and I was about to put them to boil when the phone rang. Wind was a little brisk out there, but it felt good."

He thought he detected an airiness about her. "You sound great, Mom."

"And you don't. Maybe if you could get a few days on your boat before winter sets in, you'd perk up. Not sick, are you?"

"No. I'm fine."

"Well, if you are you don't sound like it. You ought to be rejoicing and thanking the Lord; your book's on two bestseller lists."

"I am, Mom." Perhaps he shouldn't have called her; she had the ability to detect his every mood. "I was about to go jogging and thought I'd call you."

"Now this doesn't sound a bit like you. What you need is a loving girl, but I'll bet you look right through the one who's perfect for ya."

"I don't know what you mean."

"Course you don't. Just like a man. Can't see the forest for the trees."

His antenna shot up. His mother excelled at hinting, dropping bits of information that she wanted you to have, when she had no intention of telling the whole story unless you asked her. In that way, she couldn't be accused of gossiping, and if she told you something you didn't want to hear, she could answer, "Well, you asked me."

"What are you getting at, Mom? Who and what are you talking about?"

"Oh, son, don't feign ignorance. I'm talking about Allison, that lovely girl you're touring with."

He jumped out of the chair, nearly jerking the phone cord from the wall socket. "What do you know about her?"

"She's a wonderful girl; that's what I know."

His fingers plowed through his hair, and he looked toward the ceiling, exasperated. "Mom, will you please stop this and answer me straight? What do you know about Allison?"

"If you're uptight right now, you deserve it. I'm always asking you to find a nice girl…"

He sat down and waited.

"…and bring her to see me. Well, I met her. We had a lovely visit. She spent the night with me and left here about an hour ago. I—"

"She *what?*"

"I said she left here about an hour ago."

Sweat poured from his forehead, and he took a handkerchief from his pocket and wiped the back of his neck. His mother was the one person he'd always counted on to be there for him, dependable and aboveboard. Now she… He corrected himself. Maybe he was losing his mind.

"Mom, would you please start at the beginning and tell me everything?"

"I will, but you relax. Allison said you'd get bent out of shape when you found out she came to see me. But I can't see why. She's a wonderful girl."

"Just start at the beginning, *please,* Mom."

He listened as his mother recalled Allison's visit with her, beginning with the minute she heard the Mercury Sable come to a halt in front of her house. She ended by saying, "I told her to come back to see me as soon as she can, and don't you scold her. You hear?"

Scold her. *Scold* her! He'd like to shake her. "You're telling me those are the only questions she asked you?"

"Right, and those are the only answers I gave her. Seems to me if she got close enough to you to love you, you could have told her when and where you were born."

"If she got... Wait a minute. I thought you said that was all you talked about."

"It was all. I guessed she was in love with you from the way she spoke about you, and she admitted it. All there was to it."

"I don't care. If she knew I wouldn't like what she did, she shouldn't have gone to see you without—"

Her snort, a wordless reprimand, didn't surprise him. "Don't say to me Allison should have asked your permission to do anything. She's thirty years old and doesn't need your permission or anybody else's."

"All right. Maybe I shouldn't have said that, but how could she go behind my back and—"

She interrupted him. "Jake, are you ashamed of me? If not, why are you upset?"

He related his agreement with Allison and added, "She violated the terms, and she's going to hear from me."

"Jake, are you in love with Allison?"

He remembered how tortured he'd been when he didn't know where she was and feared for her safety. "She...uh...she means a lot to me."

"Hogwash. I asked you if you love her."

"Yeah, but that doesn't mean I won't—"

"You won't do anything. Give her my love."

Jake hung up, walked over to the dining room window, and looked out on the yellowing trees. September and the beginning of his favorite season. A time when his mind always seemed to refresh itself, when he reaped a harvest of new ideas, like heading back to school after a summer of intellectual draught. He stared at the already changing foliage and saw nothing of the emerging season that interested him. Gone was his desire to jog or do anything other than confront Allison. He walked down the hall, opened the door, and sat on the balcony, enjoying the breeze that shot through him. What the devil possessed her do such a thing? Get into her car and drive from Washington to Reed Hollow and knock on his mother's front door?

Unable to put his mind on his work, he went into his storage closet, got a tub of varnish and a brush, and began to weatherproof the balcony's wooden floor, something he had been postponing for the past three years. He worked feverishly in an attempt to rid himself of his anger and get his mind off Allison. He accomplished neither. At four o'clock, he took a shower, dressed, called a taxi, and headed for Duncan's home.

The smell of food on the grill when he got out of the taxi reminded him that he hadn't eaten lunch, and he felt a pinch in his belly. He had barely touched the doorbell when Justine opened the door.

"I saw your taxi drive up," she said, evidently in response to his raised eyebrow. "I'm so glad you could come. We don't get to see you nearly as often as we'd like."

He kissed her cheek. "You and Dunc are too good to me. Where's Tonya?"

"Downstairs at the piano. She's not quite four, but considering how she loves that instrument, we may have a prodigy on our hands."

"Heaven forbid."

"That's what I say."

He let his gaze sweep over her and smiled inwardly. "Where's the old man?"

"Wait'll I tell him what you called him. He's out back dropping hot dogs on the grass."

"As long as he has some more."

"How's it going, man? These ribs are already getting tender. I've got some Cornish hens on the spit, and later I'll put the hot dogs and hamburgers on. That's corn and red potatoes wrapped in foil in that basket over there. I'll start 'em to roasting in a minute, and I'll grill some peppers, eggplant, and red onions. It ought to be good."

"Yeah, I don't doubt it. You're cooking enough for twenty people. Who else is coming?"

Duncan turned to face him. "Just us. You think it's too much?"

One look at Justine had told him she'd be eating for two, but even with that addition, he didn't see how they could consume so much food, and told Duncan as much.

Duncan allowed himself a careless shrug. "Oh, well. You'll take some home with you." He paused and seemed to scrutinize Jake. "You're pretty low-key today. Anything I can do?"

Jake didn't like thinking he was transparent. "Naah, man. Just one of those things."

A grin lightened Duncan's facial expression from serious to mocking. "I see. Why didn't you bring her with you? I told you this was informal."

"What makes you think it's a woman?"

"Considering the last conversation we had about this I figured by now she'd gotten to you." He cleared his throat. "That is, if she hadn't already. Smart as you are, any woman you get involved with must be a good woman. Let it happen, man. I wouldn't exchange my life with Justine for the Fort Knox vaults."

Jake leaned against a pear tree and heard himself telling Duncan Banks what his mother told him that morning. "I can't believe she'd do that. I've got a notion to drop her from the tour and out of my life. I trusted her."

"Hold it," Duncan said, waving the grilling tongs as if he were a conducting an orchestra. "Some of that's your fault. If you love each other, you should already have told her that much about yourself. I imagine loving blind must be frustrating, and especially for an intelligent person."

"My mother said something to that effect. Oh, hell. My life is complicated, and I try to separate the business from the social."

"And you're a maser at it. I don't ask questions, because we wouldn't be friends long if I did."

Jake slouched against the tree with his hands buried in his trouser pockets. "No, but I'd bet my hat there isn't much about me you don't know. A journalist of your stature has informants everywhere and knows where and how to get information."

"True," Duncan said, about the time Justine opened the door and stepped out on the porch. "Next time you come, bring her with you. I want to meet the woman who slowed you down." He walked over to Justine and kissed her quickly on the mouth. "Where's Tonya?" he asked her, letting Jake know they would finish their conversation another time.

"At the piano. Where else? That's all she wants to do," she told Jake. "If she isn't trying to play, she wants me to play."

"Is she studying music?"

"Yes, and doing well. I didn't want to start her lessons so early, but she gave me no choice."

"Make yourself comfortable, Jake, while I get my daughter," Duncan said.

"I don't know what I'd have done if you hadn't come, Jake. My husband is cooking enough for two dozen people."

"That's what I told him. Today's his birthday?"

"Yes. Wayne and Banks should be here any minute. It's a surprise."

Wayne and Banks Roundtree arrived, bringing their young son, Luke. Jake didn't know when, if ever before, he'd felt so out of place. He couldn't enter the banter and camaraderie that centered on family, on the joy that parents found in their children, couldn't loosen up with two men whose company he always enjoyed. Not even Banks's irreverence lightened his mood.

"Want to hear me play, Uncle Jake?" Tonya asked him.

He was about to say yes, if only to be relieved of his halfhearted participation in the conversation, but Duncan closed that avenue.

"Uncle Jake can hear you play next time he comes," Duncan told the child. "He wants to talk with us."

"I'll play for you next time, Uncle Jake." She gazed up at him, apologetically, he thought. "I don't know. My mummy is making a baby, and I may be a big sister. Then I'll have to help my mummy."

He hunkered before her and hugged her warm little body to him, and it seemed as if she made up for all the loneliness he felt. Lonely as he watched Wayne and Duncan bask in the love of their adoring wives and children. He told himself to snap out of it, released Tonya, and looked at Duncan.

"Is that so?" It was obvious to him, but he didn't think it proper to announce that fact.

"Sure thing. We're expecting a son in about four months. Get busy, man."

"Don't let them push you around, Jake," Banks said. "The only reason Wayne is married is that I took one look at him and decided he was mine."

"Don't you believe it, Jake," Wayne said. "I'm married because this woman got into me and wouldn't budge. It's the life, though. I wouldn't have it any other way."

Yes. The life he wanted more than anything else. After dinner, Justine produced Duncan's birthday cake and a bottle of Veuve Clicquot champagne, and he raised his glass in a toast that he meant with all his heart. "Happy birthday, Dunc. God's grace upon you and your family, and may it always give you joy."

He knew they were expecting something witty, even wicked, but that wasn't what he felt, and he was in no mood to pretend. As soon as he could do it gracefully, he made his excuses.

"Thanks for sharing, old man," he said to Duncan. "I wouldn't have missed it." He winked at Banks. "I'll match wits with you next time."

"I hope so," she said. "A solemn, no-nonsense Jacob Covington means I have to straighten up and act the same, and you can imagine how that thought pleases me."

He told them goodbye, walked outside, and called a taxi with the use of his cell phone.

Inside his house, he decided to talk with Allison that

night even if he had to spend the better part of it tracing her. However, she answered her phone the first time he dialed her number.

"Hello."

"Hello, Allison."

"Hi."

Silence. So she was waiting to hear what he had to say about her excursion to Reed Hollow. *Let her wait.* "I must have phoned you twenty times since I got back here. Can you imagine the scenarios my mind conjured up about where you might be? All of them unsettling. Couldn't you have phoned me, knowing I'd tried to reach you?"

"Well, yes…I could have, but somehow I didn't think to do it. Lodged somewhere in the archives of my mind was the certainty that you wouldn't be home, since you had an emergency."

"Did I say I had an emergency? I did not. Besides, I gave you my cell phone number. You weren't home at midnight or at nine this morning. I'm asking you for the second time whether there's another man in your life. If there is, tell me now and I'm out of here."

"There isn't anyone else."

"Then—"

"How can you demand what you either can't or won't give? You want to know where I was, but you're not about to tell me why you broke four lecture and signing dates in San Antonio. Don't you think I'm as much entitled to my privacy as you are to yours?"

"Yes, you are. However, if you thought I was entitled to privacy, why would you go to such lengths to invade it?" Her gasp reached him through the wires. Did she think his mother wouldn't tell him?

"I didn't invade your privacy. If you weren't so secretive, I could have gotten exactly the same information from your publisher or from the Library of Congress. For most people, dates of birth, first-day school attendance and graduations, colleges or universities attended, along with honors, are public records. If I left that out of the story, I'd never get another job. If you're angry, I'm sorry but I'm not going to apologize, because I loved your mother."

He stopped a mild expletive just before it passed his lips. Hadn't his mother and Duncan said as much? His conscience began to taunt him. *Don't be stubborn, man. It isn't worth turning your back, walking away from the only woman you have ever loved. Besides, one day soon, you're going to have to ask her forgiveness for a lot of things.*

"Yeah. The two of you must have had a ball together. She burned my ears off about you."

"You're blessed to have her as your mother, Jake. When I left her, I couldn't help crying. I got more love from her in eighteen hours than I had from my own mother in thirty years. My mother took care of Sydney and me in every way and made certain that we had every advantage, every opportunity, but, Jake, she doesn't have a maternal bone in her body. She's not loving. Your mother is love personified. I'm glad I went to see her."

"You promised to report only on my nine-to-five activities," he said, clinging to his stubbornness.

"Well, in that case, I can insert some salacious tidbits, not to speak of mystery, such as your sudden disappearance onboard ship while I went to get us some frozen yogurt. If you want me to stick to our agreement, I can do that."

He wasn't accustomed to being bested, and he had to admire her for it. "All right. Come off your high horse. What did the two of you do?"

"Nothing much," she told him after recounting the time spent with Annie Covington. "It was… Well, you know how she is. She just opened her heart to me the minute she opened the door. I was at home with her, and you should have tasted those crab cakes."

"I know all about those crab cakes, Allison. I don't even want to think about them. What are you doing this evening… I mean, can we see each other?"

"I'd love to see you. We can't stay out late, though. Where did you say we're going in the morning? I don't have my schedule handy."

"New Haven, so think in terms of autumn-weight clothing."

"Thanks. What time and where do we meet later on?"

"If it's all right with you, I'll be at your place at six. I'm…looking forward to seeing you."

After hanging up he mused over his last, banal words to her. *Looking forward to seeing you.* "Hell," he said, making his way to his office to settle at last into work, "I'm on my way out of my mind waiting to see her." Six o'clock found him ringing her doorbell.

Allison didn't know what to expect from Jake when he learned she had visited his mother, but she knew he would at the least take her to task for it. *No point in worrying about a new litter of kittens after the cat's been let out,* she said to herself, quoting her paternal grandmother.

She parked in her garage and took the package Annie Covington had given her into the house. She had never been able to control her curiosity, mainly because she loved surprises. In her little modern kitchen, the jewel of her home with its chrome appliances, beige marble countertops and yellow-brick walls, she placed the package on the counter and sniffed.

"I know what I'm having for my dinner," she said aloud, overjoyed to have the crab cakes.

After unpacking, she prepared to treat herself to a luxurious bubble bath and had started toward the bathroom when the telephone rang.

"Hello." Hearing Jake's beloved voice excited her, but she wouldn't say it pleased her, for she would have to tell him she had visited his mother, and there would be hell to pay. To her amazement, he had his say and then backed down. It seemed out of character, but for whatever reason he softened; she couldn't have been more grateful.

She didn't know where they were going, so she dressed casually, and when she opened the door to him it pleased her that he had done the same.

"Hi."

"Hi," she said and found she couldn't look into his eyes, not from guilt, but because the sight of him heated her blood. Her body telegraphed to her an unfamiliar message, reminding her that she had once known the power and pleasure of his hard, masculine thrusts—loving that made her a new and different woman—and that she needed to lie in his arms again. Raw and shocked at her feelings, she diverted her gaze, reached past him, and closed the door.

"Hi. Come in."

But as if her body had sent the same message to him, he grasped her arm, and she moved into him, relishing his strength as he locked her to him.

"I missed you," he said. "Last evening, I attended a party with close friends, and I was out of sorts. I didn't know where the hell you were, if you were in trouble, or what."

With her left hand she stroked the side of his face as his gaze bored into her. Then, she felt the hard pressure of his mouth and parted her lips to welcome him into her body. All she could think of while he loved her was the need to have him fill her with his heat and the driving power of his loins.

He stepped back from her. "We're of one accord here, sweetheart, but I need you to tell me what you meant when we separated in the lobby of the Hyatt Regency in San Antonio. I haven't lost sleep over it, but I don't believe in sweeping things under the rug."

She didn't hesitate, but took his hand and led him into her living room. "I was angry, Jake, and I struck out. I know it's a bad habit, and it's one I have trouble controlling."

"But you must already have been thinking that way."

"True, but I always gave you the benefit of the doubt."

"I see. All right." He looked at his watch. "It's getting too late for dinner and a movie."

A thought occurred to her. "If you don't mind being here alone for fifteen minutes, we can eat right here." She handed him a copy of *Once in a Lifetime.* "Read this. You'll love it." She kissed his forehead, grabbed her handbag, and was out of the door and headed for Matty's Gourmet Shop before he could react. She collected potato salad; corn on the cob; roasted red, orange, and green peppers; marinated shrimp; and buttermilk biscuits and was back in her house within twenty minutes.

"Luckily, Matty's was empty, and I've never seen that before."

"How can I help?"

She showed him the plates, glasses, and cutlery. "You can set the table." She put the biscuits and crab cakes in the oven to warm, heated the corn, and put the remainder of the food on serving plates.

"If I'd known you were coming, I'd have baked a cake," she said, parroting the famous saying.

"How much did you spend?"

She treated him to a withering look. "Nobody pays for the food served in my house but me. You buy when we eat at your place." She noticed that he was skilled in setting the table and complimented him on it.

"Why shouldn't I know how to set a table? I eat. I can cook, too. How about you?" It was a reasonable question, she conceded, but his tone in asking it suggested he expected a negative reply. She wasn't much good around a kitchen stove, and didn't think she should apologize for it.

"I have other attributes," she said.

His right eyebrow shot up, and then he laughed that broken-into-pieces laugh he had when he put his whole body into it, and although she loved to see him let himself go like that, at the moment she had an urge to swat him.

"I do have other talents," she said, "and it's not written anywhere that a woman has to know how to cook. Anyway, all the really great chefs are men."

"I didn't say a word."

"If you don't act nicer," she said, eyes narrowed and hands on hips, "I won't let you have any of my goodies."

When he sprawled out in the big, overstuffed chair and whooped, she had to work hard at controlling her exasperation. "What is wrong with you, Jake?"

He moved his head from side to side, hands up, palms out, and seemingly speechless. "Stop," he finally managed to say. "Please stop before you put *both* feet in it."

Perplexed at that, she knew she frowned, and she tried never to do that because her mother claimed that frowning aged a female, whether girl or woman, and had punished her for it several times.

"What did I say that amused you?"

His fingers plowed through his hair, and he shook his head slowly as if he were bemused. "I'm not going there, sweetheart. If I dared repeat what you said, I'd be laughing for another half hour. Do you think we can eat now?"

They put the food on the table, and when they sat down he picked up his fork. "Would you say the grace?" she asked him.

His eyes widened. "Oh. Oh. I see whose influence you're under."

"Well, you're always telling me how you were raised, so I figured…" She didn't bother to finish the thought.

Oh, how she loved to see him laugh, and he treated her to a good dose of it. He said the grace and then let his gaze travel over the food.

"This is a feast. I love shrimp. Say, what's that over

there?" He pointed to the crab cakes, served himself one, and put a forkful in his mouth.

"Hey. You didn't tell me you had these. These are my mother's crab cakes. Did she send them to me?"

It was her turn to laugh. "No, my dear, she did not. She didn't even tell me to give you any. But I graciously took pity on you, and I'm letting you eat up my favorite food in all the world."

He reached for another crab cake while still chewing on one. "What food is that?"

"Crab cakes, Maryland style. And I've never had any this good. Greater love hath no woman than to—"

He stopped chewing. "Don't joke about a thing like that."

"Who's joking? Sydney's the only other person I'd let taste these."

He did his best not to react to what she'd just said. "I miss these. I've loved them since before I could walk. This is really a treat." His smile blessed her as someone precious. "And such a surprise. Thanks."

After they cleaned the table and the kitchen, he asked her, "Do I get a doggie bag?"

"To eat on the plane tomorrow?"

"No. For my breakfast."

She put some crab cakes and biscuits in a small brown bag and handed them to him. "It's nine o'clock. Too late for a movie. We have to get up early."

He took the bag and stared down in her face. Her heart constricted when she saw the loneliness there. At least she thought it was loneliness. His desire was a thing she recognized, for she'd seen him exploding with it many times. But this...this almost pained look, this needful expression...

"Jake, if I put my arms around you, will it…will it help? Oh, Lord. Do you want to stay? Is that it?" She opened her arms, and he moved into them with such speed that she didn't know how it happened. He was a big man, tall and muscular, and she squeezed him to her until her arms hurt, until he pressed soft and tender kisses all over her face. She wanted to respond to him, to give him whatever he needed. If only she knew the wellspring of his angst! But he gave her no clue.

"You are so sweet. So sweet," he whispered. "I'll meet you at the check-in counter tomorrow morning at seven-thirty." Holding her hand tightly in his, he walked to the door.

"I'd better call a taxi for you."

"No. I want to walk for a few blocks. Then I'll call one." Abruptly, his arms went around her, and he hugged her close to him. "You…you're precious. I hate for the evening to end, because tomorrow your hair will be up in a knot at the back of your head and you'll have business written all over you. We only hurt each other when we're author and reporter. Maybe there's a message there somewhere. This is a short week, so we'll be back here Thursday noon. By the way, I'm getting an award Thursday evening at the Library of Congress. Will you go with me?"

"I'd be happy to. What's the award?"

"American Book Award."

"You're kidding. Congratulations, love. I'm so happy for you. This is… It's fantastic. I wouldn't miss it."

Jake walked ten blocks to Tucker Street where he saw a taxi, hailed it, and got in. "Fine night," the driver said. "Where to?"

Jake gave the driver his address. "Yep. Sure is." He couldn't have gotten his mind on a conversation if he had wanted to talk, and he didn't. He had stood there looking into the face of the woman who'd just told him that if she didn't love him she wouldn't have given him her crab cakes. *If she didn't love me.* Then she affirmed that she was not joking. As he looked at her, he came close to saying he wanted her to be his wife, to live and die with him. He didn't know why the words wouldn't come, and he couldn't help wondering if one day they would.

"You don't look the type to have woman trouble," the driver said. "Some guys get in this cab, and they got *no good* written all over them. Don't matter their color or the language they speak, I know they're no good. And they got no-good women. Then, there's guys like you. Gentlemen. Law-abiding. Upright citizens. My son's one of those, thank God, and I hope he's raising my grandson to be just like him. Get yourself a good woman, one who'll appreciate you. Well, here you are. Nice talking with you."

Jake thanked the old man and tipped him a five-dollar bill. He wasn't rich, but the man's jacket was ripped in the back, and that meant he could use an extra dollar. Since it was only nine-thirty, he phoned his mother.

"You didn't send me any crab cakes," he said after they greeted each other, "but I ate three of them anyway. Up to your usual high standards. How are you?"

"I'm just fine. I didn't tell her to give you any, but would have been disappointed if she hadn't. Does that mean you didn't pick a fight with her about coming to see me?"

He couldn't help laughing. "I did my best, but Allison fights back. You could say she put me in my place."

"Well, hallelujah! Next time you come down, bring her, will you? Jake, I'd feel the same way about her if you had never met her. Do you understand what I'm saying?"

"Yes. I'll ask her if she'll come with me."

"That's all you can do, except maybe make it permanent."

"I haven't gotten quite that far, Mom."

"That's all right, son. The Lord always answers my prayers, and I'll be praying."

He didn't want his mother to be disappointed, but it would never occur to him to marry a woman to please her.

Chapter 11

"I don't know how I did it," Allison said to herself when she returned home after three harrowing days with Jake in Connecticut. The strain of maintaining a professional demeanor during his nine public appearances, of working hard not to bare her soul to him whenever she looked him in the eye, and of finding excuses to avoid being alone with him had exhausted her. They had both realized the foolishness of making love at night and pretending a purely professional relationship during the day and, as if by mutual consent, had rejected that course. Knowing she was not alone in her frustration had done nothing to ease her stress.

Since it was only one o'clock in the afternoon, she still had time to visit Mother's Rest, improve the quality of life for at least one child, and get back home in time to relax and dress for her evening with Jake. She defrosted and heated the last three of the crab cakes Jake's mother had given her, baked a potato in the microwave, and ate it as quickly as she could. She put her kitchen in order, and even as she did so, her anticipation of the two hours that she would spend with a child at Mother's Rest seemed to peel away her tiredness and help her put her need for Jake into perspective.

"Am I glad to see you!" Nurse Zena Carter said to Allison when she opened the door. "I'm short of help today, and I've got one little eleven-month-old girl who's been fretting all day. I had the pediatrician look at her this morning, but the medicine he left hasn't calmed her."

"Does she have a fever?"

"She didn't have one an hour ago when I last looked at her, but I have fourteen children here, two nurses other than myself, and four sick ones. The doctor said they're suffering from different ailments, but no one is contagious."

Allison scrubbed and changed, put on the medical mask, and followed Zena. "This is Letice. I certainly hope you'll be able to comfort her."

Allison took the child, whose large brown eyes and dimpled brown cheeks won her heart immediately. She noticed that although the baby stared at her, she seemed not to relate to the new person holding her, so Allison walked the floor, patting the child, singing a lullaby to her. When the whimpering continued, she sat in the rocking chair and rocked as she sang to the little girl. She appreciated that each of the three visitation rooms, as they were called, provided the substitute mother privacy in bonding with the child in whatever way she could. Most sang or talked with the children, offering loving gestures of affection while holding them.

The hour passed quickly for Allison as always, for she was loath to part with the child. The heaviness in her heart intensified each time she looked into the little face, for though the little girl no longer whimpered, neither was she animated. Allison rang the bell for a nurse.

"She doesn't look right to me," Allison told the nurse. She put her hand on the child's forehead. "She's warmer, too. I think we should get her to a doctor."

"I don't see any point in calling the same doctor who came to see her this morning," the nurse said. "Put her in her bassinet and roll it to the side door. While I get my coat, call Nurse Carter on the intercom and tell her I'm taking Letice to the hospital."

"All right. May I go with you? Please, I—"

"All right. But hurry. Don't dress; just put on your coat."

Allison sat in the backseat with the bassinet in her lap and prayed that it wasn't too late for little Letice. For the next five hours, she waited and prayed with the nurse, whose name, she learned during the long evening, was Tiffany Jones.

"Tiffany, why don't they tell us something? I see them going in and out of the room. Why can't they give us just one word?"

"Yes," Tiffany said. "I'll be right back."

Allison sprang to her feet when she saw Tiffany coming toward her, tears staining her face and a doctor clutching her arm.

"This is one of those cases in which God was really merciful," the doctor told them. "If she had lived, she wouldn't have developed normally and would never have walked. Trust me. Her leaving here was a blessing. I'll send you the papers tomorrow."

Allison sat down, trying to digest what had happened. She had bonded with that little girl, had become more attached to her than to any of the other children she had nurtured. She grasped her stomach, symbolically sealing the hole inside her. With effort, she controlled the quiver of her lips and rubbed her arms for warmth.

"I'd better take you back to Mother's Rest, Allison," the nurse said. "I have to report to Ms. Carter, and you can get your clothes. I know you feel terrible, and I do, too. This is the first one we've lost."

Allison stood and forced a smile. "I suppose I should take comfort in what that doctor said, but—"

"You have to. It's no telling how long she'd been failing. We got her day before yesterday. Someone left her at the door, and she was warmly wrapped and clean. Whoever did that knew she couldn't make it."

After their report to Zena Carter, Allison dressed and prepared to leave. "Are you sure you're able to drive?" Zena asked her. "Maybe you should take a taxi. I can't leave the premises, because Tiffany is the only other nurse here."

"It isn't far, and I'll be all right. It hurts, but knowing she won't grow up deformed and an invalid is some solace. I'll be back as soon as I can."

Allison drove home slowly because she didn't trust her reflexes. She parked her car in her driveway and got out. Shock reverberated through her system, and her nerves rioted at the sight of a man standing at her door. Her first thought was of the man she saw when she and Jake were together at Rockefeller Center.

"Allison!" he called out to her, as if he knew he frightened her.

"Jake. What is it? Why are you…" She slapped her hand over her mouth. "Oh, my Lord, Jake. Honey, I forgot."

"Yes," he said, having closed the distance between them, "and you're going to tell me how you managed to do that. I mean, this night before I leave here."

"Come in." Inwardly, she was glad for his presence for she realized she hadn't flipped the switch that automatically lit the downstairs and the master bedroom when darkness fell.

She unlocked the door, and letting her know that he remembered her fear of darkness in a closed place, he stepped in front of her and turned on the light.

"What? Good grief, you've been crying. Allison, what's going on here?"

To his amazement, she locked her arms across her middle and bent over, as if in pain. Soul-rending pain. He picked her up, carried her into the living room, and sat with her in his lap, searching her face. What he saw were the tears cascading down her cheeks before she buried her face against his chest and sobbed. He rocked her and tried to soothe her while trying to adjust to his own perturbation at her loss of control.

"Talk to me, sweetheart. Let me help you." But her sobs seemed to grow more tortured. He didn't see how he could bear her suffering that way. Perhaps if he put her to bed or… He stood and went to her kitchen, still holding her as one would hold a baby, and set her on the counter.

"Did anything happen to Sydney?"

She shook her head, her puffed and reddened eyes

devoid of expression. "Oh, Jake. It… She was…such a beautiful little girl."

He put the kettle of water on the stove and turned on the gas jet as fear raced through him. What had she done? Thinking that she might have hit or, worse, killed a child with her car, he put an arm around her. "We can talk about it in a minute, soon as I make some coffee."

Fortunately, her kitchen was logically organized, and he quickly found what he needed to make the coffee. "Let's go back in the living room and talk," he said, carrying the coffeepot and two cups and deliberately allowing her to walk without his help.

"I hope you can drink it black." She nodded. He hated black coffee without sugar, but he'd drink it because his aim in making the coffee was to restore her calm. He put the coffeepot and the cups on the coffee table, poured a cupful for each of them, and took her hand.

"Did you have an accident?" She shook her head. "Can you tell me what happened?" he probed, nonplussed and increasingly apprehensive as to what she might tell him.

"I've never told anybody about this, not even my girlfriend Connie," she began, increasing his anxiety. "I'm a volunteer at a home for foundlings called Mother's Rest."

He listened to her incredible story of loving and of finding an outlet for her own maternal instincts by mothering and nurturing infants who, for a variety of reasons, didn't have mothers. His heart swelled with love for her as she recounted the joy she felt when the head nurse would place a child in her arms, hers for two hours.

"What happened today?"

"I got there around three o'clock planning to leave at five and be dressed and ready when you came for me at seven."

He thought his heart would break for her as she told him about the child she had lost that night, communicating to him without explicitly saying so that she felt as if she had lost her own child.

"I don't think I ever prayed so hard or so earnestly. I know I would be bitter if the doctor hadn't told us what her life would have been like if she had lived. Still…" Tears pooled in her eyes as she looked at him. "Jake, she was such a beautiful little baby, and she was the only one I ever had who just wouldn't respond to me."

"You'll have children of your own," he assured her, "and I see that you will be a wonderful mother."

"I've…stopped hoping," she said, her listlessness returning. "I'll be thirty-one in two months."

He tried to digest that information along with the other things he had learned about her that night. Things that he realized were an ingrained part of her, that would forever change his opinion of her as a woman dedicated to her career and to that alone. He wanted, needed a family, children of his own and a loving wife, more than he wanted anything, including the prize of scholar-in-residence at his alma mater. Deep down in his gut, he knew then that she wanted the same and would willingly give him the children he craved. And she loved him.

He wanted to get on his knees and ask her to marry him, but until he no longer had to keep secrets from her and until she stopped keeping secrets from him, common sense told him to wait. Yet, in every atom of his being, the need to bond with her asserted a powerful stimulus: he needed her.

"I'm so sorry, I missed being there when you received your award, Jake. And to think that I didn't even remember it. Did you make a speech? Tell me about it."

He gave silent thanks that she had been able to take her mind off the tragedy she had lived through earlier that evening. "I waited here for you until twenty minutes to eight, and when you didn't answer your telephone or your cell phone, I couldn't imagine what had happened or where you were. I was disappointed, worried, and hurt, if one can experience all those emotions at once.

"I don't remember much about the ceremony. I had a prepared speech, and believe me, I was glad I had memorized most of it. The trophy's in my briefcase, and along with it I got a check for ten thousand dollars that I'm going to endorse and send to my mother."

She was staring up at him now, her eyes wide with adoration, and something within him quickened. Without warning, she moved closer, rested her head on his shoulder, and placed her right arm across his waist.

"I wanted so badly to be with you tonight, and then…"

He stroked her back. He didn't dare hold her to him and love her as he longed to, for he didn't believe in exploiting a woman's vulnerability. "You couldn't be in two places at once, and I wouldn't have thought more of you if you had walked away from that child. We have to be who we are. This has given me a new insight into the person you are, and I'm grateful."

She sat up, leaving him bereft of her nearness. "We

haven't tasted this coffee. I'd better heat it and get you some milk and sugar," she said.

She returned with the coffee and a plate of gingersnaps. "I didn't have any dinner," she explained.

"Funny," he said. "I just remembered that I didn't, either. I had planned for us to have an elegant supper after the ceremony. That's water under the bridge. Hell, I love gingersnaps."

Allison held the cup suspended in her right hand. "You love gingersnaps? Jake, you almost never see me without some gingersnaps in my handbag or my briefcase. You can't imagine how I love these things. Crab cakes and gingersnaps. Wonder what else we both like to eat."

Savoring a cookie as if it were the delight of his life, he raised his left shoulder in a slight shrug. "I don't know, but I bet it's plenty. I'm getting the feeling that we're soul mates."

She leaned toward him and kissed his cheek, and when he didn't respond, she kissed the side of his mouth, happy to be with him.

He put his cup on the coffee table and locked his gaze on her. "Be careful, baby. I'm doing my damnedest to remember that you've had a rough night."

The memory suddenly of his arms strong around her, and of him deep within her, sent heat spiraling throughout her body, and she sucked in her breath. She tried to pull her gaze from his fierce and knowing look, the look that said, *I know you, I have possessed you, and I will have my way with you because you want me.* As if he willed it with the strength of his masculine aura, pulling her to him as a magnet asserts its mastery over a nail, she admitted surrender and let his fiery, passion-filled eyes seduce her.

Thoughts of the child lost to her that night fled like a swift-moving engine as he filled her five senses. The rumble of thunder overhead could have been the beat of his heart, the rising wind his breath. Memories of the sweet taste of his tongue in her mouth, and the scent of him, aroused and masculine, beset her, and she felt the muscles of her love channel contract and expand.

When she swallowed hard and crossed her knees, his hand gripped her thigh, and his eyes darkened from brown to obsidian. "If you want me, open your arms to me," he said, his voice dark and gravely. "I won't impose on you, but I've never wanted you as much as I want you this minute."

He tipped up her chin, and she willed herself to look into his eyes. "My God, sweetheart. I…"

She opened her arms, and he locked her to him. "Are you sure? I need to know that this is what you want."

"My whole being is tuned to you right now. I…I want you as much as you want me." She didn't know how she untied the bow tie and unbuttoned the tiny buttons on his shirt. The trembling of her fingers stunned her, but he stood patiently while she removed his shirt, folded it, and laid it across the back of the sofa and on top of his tuxedo jacket. When she grasped his hand and started upstairs to her bedroom, a nervous jitter overtook her and she stumbled on the stairs.

He lifted her and carried her up to the landing. "Where is your bedroom?" She pointed to his left, and within minutes, he removed her clothing and laid her on her bed. As he stood above her, his expression changed from adoration to hot fire in a second, like a shift of the wind.

If only he would… "Jake. Honey, what is it?"

"If I touched you now, I'd explode."

"I don't care. I don't want your self-control. I want to feel, to know you're mine. You don't have to be perfect, you just have to love me." She heard the words that came from her mouth and knew they were true. "Jake, come here to me. I'm on fire for you."

He kicked off his shoes, socks, and trousers, and she reached for the slip of fabric that protected him from her eyes. Emboldened by her passion, she jerked it down his thighs and let the massive organ spill into her hands. She felt herself rimming her lips with the tip of her tongue and knew what it did to him when he braced his left knee on the edge of the bed, and lowered his trembling frame into her arms.

When she tried to grasp him, he stilled her hand. "Slowly, sweetheart."

His lips brushed faint kisses over her forehead, eyes, ears, and then smothered her face with kisses. When she thought she could wait no longer, his mouth found hers, and at last she took him into her. He didn't linger there, but trailed his warm mouth over her neck and collarbone, promising and kindling in her a blazing fire. Her nipples hardened, and the muscles of her vagina clenched and expanded in a rhythm that made her want to beg him to ease the tension.

Her breath shortened almost to a pant, and she cupped her left breast, needing at least that much relief. "Please. I… Kiss me. Oh, Jake. Oh, my Lord," she screamed as his lips encircled the areola and slowly began to suckle. His fingers pinched her other nipple as he feasted, nourished himself. Nearly out of her mind, she began to rock her hips, and as if the motion excited him almost beyond control, he stilled her body with the weight of his big hand.

Her moans filled the room where he began kissing the insides of her thighs, nipping her belly, and promising her heaven and himself the feast of feasts.

"Honey, please get in me," she begged, but he ignored her, as she had known he would. She raised her body in an effort to force him, but he hooked her knees over his shoulders and bent to her. Her keening cry was her thanks when the warm marauding magic of his tongue threatened to send her over the edge. It didn't happen intentionally, but she knew for the first time what it meant to surrender completely to a man when the warm flushes attacked the bottoms of her feet and she lost the energy to urge him to her.

"You're mine," he told her, kissing his way up her body. He slipped on the condom and gazed down into her face. "Take me in, sweetheart." But she was already reaching for him and leading him to her lover's gate.

"Look at me. Don't close your eyes. Look at me." She opened her eyes and saw the fire and love in his. Then, he eased himself into her, filling her as she had longed to have him do. He paused for a minute to let her adjust. "Are you all right?" he asked in a voice that was nearly unrecognizable.

She nodded and her hips began to rock of their own volition. When he moved within her, her thighs began to tremble and almost at once the squeezing and pumping began.

"Let it happen, baby. Let me give you what you need."

She couldn't speak, so keyed up was she and so attuned to his every move. He eased a hand beneath her hips, brought her up to him, and gave her the driving force of his passion. Her whole body was one big flame. She thought it would consume her, but it didn't.

"Jake, I'm suspended here. If I don't burst, I'll... I'll die."

He increased the pressure and the speed. "You will. Be still and let me love you." She tried, but only for a minute. Then, suddenly it seemed as if her whole body were a massive balloon, swelling and swelling while she rode to his rhythm. And then she heard her own screams fill the room as she erupted in a violent spasm that sank her into a vortex of ecstasy.

"I love you. Oh, Jake, I love you so much."

His arms tightened around her." Allison. Baby, I love you. I love you." He gave her the essence of himself and came apart in her arms.

They lay locked together for a long time, not speaking. Softly and tenderly, she stroked the head that lay on her breast, while her heart galloped like a thoroughbred out of control, wondering if he knew what he said to her. Did he know that in the moment of his release, he'd told her he loved her, and would he ever say it again?

She wanted to kiss his eyes, his face, his lips, to tell him what she couldn't express in words, to show him how he had made her feel. His bulk wouldn't allow her to raise herself up, so she wrapped her arms more tightly around him, hugging him as best she could.

"How do you feel?" he asked at last. "Are you...all right?"

She nodded, forgetting that he couldn't see her, and he braced himself on his elbows and looked down at her.

"I want to know if you're…satisfied. How do you feel?"

"Strange," she said. "It was like being in a whirlwind, tossed in a thousand directions, sinking to the bottom, and coming to rest in heaven. It was wonderful, Jake, and I feel like a queen.

"What about you?" she asked him.

"Never worry about that, sweetheart. I told you when we were on the *Saint Marie* that you're perfect for me. That hasn't changed. If anything, I had it brought home to me even more forcibly a few minutes ago."

He separated them and swung his legs off the bed. "Be back in a second." He was back in a few minutes, and by the time he walked from the door to the bed in which she awaited him, looking at his nakedness had erased every thought but one from her mind.

"How late does that gourmet deli stay open?" he asked her, sliding between the sheets.

"Two o'clock in the morning," she answered, "but right now, nothing could be farther from my mind."

He sat up and leaned over her, his face ablaze in a grin. "You got something you want me to do?"

Play with her, would he? "Yeah. Provided you can manage it."

The laughter she loved to hear tumbled out of him until, wanting some of her own, she shifted beneath him, contracted her muscles, and had the pleasure of seeing his demeanor change in a second, as hot desire replaced mirth, and he bent to her lips.

"You're a wicked woman," he said, before sucking her nipple into his mouth, putting his hand between them, and finding the nub of her passion with his talented fingers.

When he had heated her to the boiling point, he asked her, "What do you want?"

She knew that if she didn't tell him, he would tease her mercilessly, but she held out as long as she could.

"Are you going to tell me?" he asked as her thighs began a quivering motion and heat seared the bottom of her feet.

Her moans grew louder, and she could stand it no longer. "You," she said. "I want you to make me feel like I did a few minutes ago."

Sensations plowed through her as his lips claimed her mouth and then, as if not satisfied that he'd drugged her nearly senseless, took her with him on a wild ride into the stratosphere.

"Wake up, sweetheart."

A feeling of lethargy stole over her and she stretched long and lazily like the sated female she was, warm and happy, his voice coming to her as if in a dream.

"I thought you'd want something to eat. Aren't you hungry?" he asked her. She turned over, grabbed the pillow, and hugged it to her. "Allison, are you awake?"

Was she awake? She bolted upright. "Jake. What are you doing? Oh, dear. I was sound asleep. You mean there's something for me to eat?"

"Sure thing. I was hungry when you got here hours ago, and you drained what little energy I had. I'm near starvation. I got us some sandwiches and apples at that gourmet shop. Everything else was sold out."

"I'm grateful for this. Can you spend the night?"

"I'd love to, and I want to, but in this closed community, that wouldn't do your reputation a bit of good.

Your neighbor watched me from her window while I waited for you. Are they all busybodies?"

"The older ones, yes."

She wanted to ask him what, if anything, he had planned for Saturday night, but decided against it. He hadn't given her the right to question his whereabouts. They finished the food, and he took the refuse to the kitchen.

"I'll call you tomorrow morning around ten. All right?"

She nodded, disappointed, but aware that if he made love with her all night, she wouldn't get enough of him. "Drive home carefully and safely."

"Thanks. I'll lock the door." He stood and gazed down at her with an expression that assured her he would rather not leave. Then he kissed her and left without another word.

"I never thought I'd back myself into a corner," Jake said to himself as he sat on his newly varnished balcony the next morning, sipping coffee that seemed cooler with each swallow. He needed some vigorous exercise; the heavy air was no help in clearing his thoughts.

Here I am, thirty-five years old, in love with a woman and sworn not to tell her or anybody else what I do for a living, and except for my superiors at the department, only my mother knows I was an undercover agent. Allison's a reporter, and she's writing a minibiography on me for her newspaper, so even if I trusted her not to write it in her story, I can't compromise her by asking her to keep a secret. So I can't share with her something so dear to me as my music, playing my guitar with Buddy and the band at Blues Alley. If she knew I compose classical music for the guitar, she might put two and two together and guess I'm Mac Connelly because he fascinates her. And State University would never honor a jazz musician.

He went inside, threw the cold coffee into the sink, put the cup in the dishwasher, and called his boss.

"Congratulations," the chief said. "I see in *The Post* that you got a big award. My hat's off to you."

Jake had to laugh. "Thank you, sir, but if I remember properly, you don't wear hats."

"The proverbial hat. You get the message. Think you can fax me your best recollection of what your nemesis looks like? I put two men on him and they've given me different descriptions. Only one matched the Rockefeller Center man. We have to know whether we're dealing with one man or two. Get it to me as soon as you can."

"Right on. Give me an hour." He wrote it out, adding that the man had tailed Allison on at least one occasion, and sent it off. Now, how was he going to avoid seeing Allison that night? It was Friday, and his fingers itched for a good workout with Buddy Dee and the band. He was willing to give up one night at the club, and from his understanding, it had better be Friday. On Saturday nights, women liked to be with their men. He hated lying and especially to Allison, so he decided on a partial truth.

"Hi, sweetheart," he said when she answered the telephone. "Did you dream about me?"

"Hi. I don't know. I slept so soundly that all I remember is putting my head on the pillow and waking up this morning."

He put on a face, though he knew it was wasted.

"Baby, you wound me; you were supposed to claw, scratch, and climb the walls in frustration because you didn't have me locked deep inside you."

"Whew. You're getting pretty bold. I scratched and clawed, waiting for you to do that. But after you lived up to your notices, I didn't have the energy to climb a wall, or even to scratch one."

He felt his body quicken and knew he'd better change the subject. "You know how to make a guy feel great. How about we skip tonight and see each other tomorrow evening? I need to work on my book proposal. After getting that award, my instincts tell me I should try something a little more ambitious than I started. Is that okay with you?"

It wasn't, he realized from her long pause. He waited. "All right," she said at last, "but what will we do tomorrow?"

"I have something in mind, but it may not work out. I should know by tomorrow noon."

A telephone call to Duncan settled it. "What happened to you after the awards, man?" Duncan asked him. "People were milling around anxious to congratulate you. What happened?"

He related to Duncan as much as he could of his need to find Allison, adding, "I know you'll treat that with discretion."

"Sure. Why don't you bring her over tonight? I want to meet her."

"How about tomorrow night?"

"Great. Tell her to come casual. We can have a barbecue on the grill. Five o'clock?"

"Right. If I don't call back, it's a deal."

He hung up and called Allison. "I hope you'll like

my friends," he said. "I don't call many people friend, very few, in fact, but he's one."

"I'm anxious to meet them." He imagined she wrinkled her nose when she said, "Imagine meeting your best friend in jeans and a T-shirt!"

"Look here, woman. He's not supposed to notice or care how you look. Get it?"

Her laughter rang through the wires. "I stand corrected, sir."

He hung up, welcoming the visit with Duncan and Justine because their loving relationship wouldn't give him the feeling of emptiness he had experienced the last time he visited them. This time, he would have his own loving woman.

By six o'clock that day, he had a reasonable proposal, or so he believed. Compared to the old one, it obligated him to write a more serious, more literary work than his first book, and he welcomed the challenge. He phoned a local restaurant for a roasted, herbed chicken, baked corn bread, and sautéed spinach, showered, dressed, and waited for the food. He'd get a full-time cook and housekeeper, if it didn't mean having the department's security force lurking around. In the meantime, he tuned his guitar and practiced scales to limber up his fingers.

After enjoying his dinner, he finished dressing, put on the old felt hat, got his guitar, and headed for Blues Alley. Buddy met him as he stepped in the back door.

"Man, you should see that crowd out there tonight. They're standing in the back. The manager's after me to get you here full-time as a regular member of the band, but I told him, 'Don't even dream it.'" His face bore an expression of hope. "I was right, wasn't I?"

"You know my situation, man. I'll be here when I can."

Buddy reached up to slap Jake on the back. "And any time you can get here rocks with me, you know that."

He got a glass of tea, which he used to suggest whiskey, took his seat onstage, put the tea on the floor beside him, and waited for the curtain to rise and the lights to dim.

"Want to go with Mark and me to Blues Alley tonight? According to *The Tribune,* Mac will be there," Connie said to Allison when they talked that afternoon.

"Great. What are you wearing? I know you'll dress up if you're with Mark."

"A simple street-length navy blue dress and a necklace. I have to, because Mark always wears a business suit and doesn't even own a pair of jeans."

"Okay. I'll wear my red wool dress with jewel neckline and long sleeves. Prim as Mary McLeod Bethune."

"Well, you don't have to go overboard. Meet you there at a quarter of eight. If you're late, come to our table. Mark's last name is Reddaway."

"Is this serious, Connie? You two seem inseparable."

Connie's voice softened, and she spoke in lowered tones. "We're serious, Allison. I didn't believe I could be so happy. What's going on with you and the author?"

"I'll know for sure when the tour is over, Connie. We still have a lot of stuff to clear away, but I'm praying we'll make it."

"I'll send up one for you, girl. See you later."

"How did you get a front-row table?" Allison asked Mark after greeting Connie and him. "This is wonderful."

"What would you like to drink?" Mark asked them.

"Gin and tonic for me," Connie said, causing Allison to raise an eyebrow. When the two of them went out together, Connie didn't drink anything stronger than Dr Pepper.

"White wine, please," Allison said, deciding that if she couldn't be with Jake, she might as well enjoy herself.

When the lights dimmed and the curtain went up, Allison expected Connie to comment on their closeness to Mac, but her friend sat there stonily as if they had never discussed the man. *Mark one down for you, Connie,* she said to herself.

"Mac's in the house tonight," Buddy Dee told the patrons. "Give it up for Mac." She noticed that Mac barely tipped his hat, glanced over the audience, and nodded to Buddy, who gave the downbeat. She sat back in her chair, ignoring Mark and Connie, and suddenly it occurred to her that, for the first time, she was not listening to the music, but focusing solely on Mac Connelly.

This is strange, she thought. *He manages not to look at this table, and we're directly in his line of vision, right in front of him.*

At the end of the piece, while the applause thundered, she saw him rub across his chin with his left hand. *Hmm.* She looked at his shoes—brown Gucci loafers—and swallowed hard.

It can't be, she told herself. *It's impossible.*

"You're awfully quiet tonight, Allison," Connie said. "I wonder why."

"He's in his orbit tonight. I don't think I ever heard him play like this, as if he broke out of jail and is enjoying his freedom. He's really *on* tonight," Mark said, relieving her of the need to answer Connie.

They sat through the first and second sets, but when the lights dimmed at the end, Allison didn't go up to speak with him. She knew he wouldn't be there, that he would elude her just as he did when she sent him a note asking for an interview.

She declined to go for a late supper with her friends, went home, got a handful of gingersnaps and a glass of milk, and turned on the television. But she couldn't focus on the television fare; her mind stayed with Mac Connelly. Same complexion, same long tapered fingers, and probably the same height and size. Same brown shoes. And he hadn't looked at her. Not once. Her right hand skimmed her jaw as she mused over the similarities.

"That's it," she said, jumping up from the chair. "That's it. A right-handed guitarist rubbing his chin with his left hand when he has both hands free." Jake always fingered his chin with his left hand, and she had so often wondered why he didn't rub it with his right hand. Jake Covington was Mac Connelly. She went to the phone and dialed his home phone number, and as she expected, got no answer.

What about that book proposal he's writing? Wait till I—

What about your own secret? the voice of her conscience demanded. *He's not keeping secrets from you any more than you are withholding a secret from him.*

What was she supposed to do with this knowledge? She'd sworn never again to withhold vital information about a person on whom she was assigned to report, not even if that person was a man she loved.

I'll keep it to myself, and maybe he'll tell me about this and the reasons for his sudden disappearances. She dropped back down into the chair. Washed out. Indignant. And not a little hurt. She didn't know how long she sat there reliving her every experience with him. Finally, she got up, checked the front door and the windows, and went upstairs. Nobody could convince her that Jacob Covington was anything but honest and honorable.

"I'll just have to see how it plays out."

"Damn the luck," Jake said, walking into his house and pitching the hat and brown tweed jacket to the back of the closet floor. "Sitting right in front of me and looking like a million bucks. I hope she didn't recognize me." However, it perplexed him that she didn't try to contact him as she'd done before. He brushed his left hand over his chin and lifted his shoulder in a slight shrug. Perhaps she left with her friends. In any case, he'd know sooner or later.

He rang her bell at four Sunday afternoon, and her dazzling smile bewitched him. Surely she wouldn't greet him so warmly if she had detected Mac Connelly's identity. His arms encircled her, and she offered him her lips.

"Go easy, honey," he said, unable to hold back a grin, "otherwise I'll be in trouble." He allowed himself the pleasure of flicking his tongue along the seam of her lips and letting her slowly draw him into her mouth. At once, his blood rushed toward his loins, and he broke the kiss. "Baby, you pack a wallop."

"You're the one who pours it on; I just react."

His lower lip dropped, and he imagined his face had

become one big question mark. "Next you'll tell me Adam seduced Eve."

With the look of an innocent, she said, "Of course he did. Walking around without even a fig leaf on, what would anybody expect poor Eve to do? Like that G-string you wear for bathing trunks. I didn't seduce you that morning in Idlewild, because I was so shocked at seeing you that I lost my wits."

"You won't convince me that you lost your wits. You might have been short on nerve, but wits, never. Ready to go?"

"You think I'm all right?"

He let his gaze drift over her black leather pants, skintight, her red silk-knit sweater, and her three-quarter-length leather coat. "All right? You could be on the cover of *Vogue*. From head to foot, perfect."

He could see that his words pleased her, and her softly uttered thanks let him know that she valued his approval.

Justine met them at the door. "I'm so glad to meet you, Allison. Jake promised he'd bring you, and we've been looking forward to this. Duncan's on the deck, grilling the dinner," she said to Jake. "Come on in."

They walked through the house and found Duncan on his knees looking for the grilling tongs. He found them, stood, and greeted Allison. "Thank you for coming, Allison. I've wanted to meet the woman who clipped this guy's wings."

She turned to him. "Is that what I did, Jake?"

"That's what he says, but he likes to exaggerate."

"Man, you hit the jackpot," Duncan said, "and that is definitely not an exaggeration."

Justine joined them, followed by Tonya, who ran to

Jake for a hug. "Uncle Jake, I have a new friend. He's studying the violin, and I'm studying the piano, and my daddy says it's all right if we get married but we have to wait until I finish college."

He ran his fingers through his hair, temporarily nonplussed. "Uh… How old are you, Tonya?"

"I'm four, and I'm going to be five."

"I see. And how old is this violinist?"

A smile brightened her face. "He's already five."

"I see. These things took a bit longer when I was growing up. Your daddy is a very wise man." He introduced her to Allison.

"Uncle Jake says I'm his best girl," Tonya informed her.

"I don't mind," Allison said. "You are a charming little girl."

"Thank you, Miss Allison. Next time you come, I'll ask my mummy and my daddy if I can play for you."

Allison hunkered before the little girl and put her arms around her, hugged her and said, "I'll be looking forward to hearing you play."

Seeing her holding that little girl brought to his mind pictures of her nurturing his own child, and it cost him a lot not to get on his knees and fold them both in his arms. *How different it is from the time I was last here,* he thought time and again. He had only to touch her to know that she held a piece of himself and always would. He ate the grilled food and drank the wine without giving them much thought. One more week, and the tour would be over. Ten days, and he would know the direction his life would take.

Chapter 12

At the airport that Monday morning, Allison called her boss. She adopted the habit of telling him at the airport where the tour would take her during the week so as to prevent his interference. He had asked to see the schedule, but she deliberately forgot to give it to him, fearing that he might add on an assignment for her that would cause her to miss one of Jake's lectures or a book signing.

"Montreal?" he asked, when she told him where she was headed. "I thought they spoke French up there. What are you laying on me? I'm not paying for hanky-panky; if you two want to get it on, let him pay for—"

"Bill, if you're concerned about my going to Montreal, why don't you check the tour schedule with Covington's publisher? I don't have to go all the way to Canada for what you're suggesting. The United States is a huge country."

"All right, all right. But this is costing me a fortune. Just bring me something good, I mean first-class. You get that? This is a last chance for you."

In more ways than one, she said to herself. To him, she said, "Bill, I can only do my best."

"That's all I'm asking. Just don't short me. If you find out he chases women, put it in there. And if he's lazy, doesn't show up for appointments, you'd better not leave it out. You understand?"

"I am not a child, Bill, and I know my job." Her shaking fingers could hardly set the receiver in its cradle. How she wished she had stayed home Friday night! This was one time in which ignorance was preferable.

Punctuality was one of Jake's traits that she admired and appreciated. He hadn't been late once since the tour began. She looked at her watch for the nth time. Boarding in half an hour. Where could he be? Her cell phone rang, and with her heart in her mouth she unzipped her handbag and pressed the code key.

"Allison Wakefield. Hello."

"My taxi is just pulling up to the airport, thanks to a four-car accident. You never saw such traffic. See you in a few minutes."

He reached the check-in counter fifteen minutes before boarding time, and she didn't think she had ever been so happy to see him.

"Hi. I was in such a hurry that the security personnel decided I was a risk, and they even examined my watch." He let out a long breath. "You can't imagine how happy I'll be midnight Friday when this is over."

"Hi. Yes, I can, because…" She whirled around at the sound of a scuffle behind her, and when Jake pushed her aside and jumped in front of her, she muffled a scream.

"What on earth?"

"Looks like our friend from Rockefeller Center just got picked off," he said, his voice as casual as if he were commenting on the weather.

"What was he doing here? I mean why is he after us?"

"Probably a celebrity hound. I have encountered some strange people since this book was published. I could write a book about it that would probably be more interesting than the one I wrote."

She wasn't placated. "Why was he trailing me that time?"

"Because he saw you with me and probably figured that if he could get close to you, he could get close to me. In this business, one has to be careful."

"Who apprehended him?"

He opened his wallet, took out his credit card, and placed it on the counter along with his photo ID. "My publisher takes good care of me."

"And thank God for that."

The telephone rang as she entered her hotel room. "Hello."

"Listen, babe," Bill Jenkins began, "get a pen and write this down. I want you to be at the opening of the World Wellington Hotel on Connecticut Avenue Saturday night coming. The tour's over, and I need you to cover that event. It's going to be the top hotel in Washington, and I want you to bring me a rave review."

Bristling at his order, she asked him, "What's your interest in that hotel?"

"I don't have one, but you give it five stars. I promised Roland I'd—"

"How dare you!" she said, interrupting him. "I told you I wouldn't lie for that man. Why should I? He means nothing to me now, and I regret that he ever did. I told you once that I wouldn't do it. Please don't mention it to me again."

She hung up and sat on the bench beside the table on which the phone rested, wondering how long that one mistake would plague her. Hadn't she paid enough? And now she had the unpleasant task of telling Jake what a fool she had been.

The phone rang and, thinking it might be Jake, she answered after the first ring. "How you doing, babe?" Her stomach churned at the sound of his voice. "If you think you can persuade me where Bill Jenkins failed, you're a sick man. And if the two of you don't stop pestering me, I'll send a freelance article to the local papers describing how you two tried to make me falsify a review of your hotel. I owe you one, fellow, and if you don't leave me alone, I will pay up, and I mean I'll do a grand job of it."

He hung up without answering her, and she didn't doubt that Bill would have to return the bribe he took in exchange for a rave review of that hotel.

She had no appetite for sightseeing, although she hadn't previously visited Montreal or, for that matter, any other place in Canada. They left his book signing with four hours of daylight left to spend as they chose.

"I think you've lost your enthusiasm for this, the tour, I mean," Jake said as they entered the hotel lobby.

"I'm trying to adjust to the fact that I won't see you

every day." It was more than that, and she didn't doubt that he knew it. He had given her no assurance that their relationship would not end with the tour.

"That, and we have a lot of cobwebs to clear away. Don't anticipate any unpleasantness, Allison. I suggest we enjoy every minute we have together. Life's too short to waste it on unpleasant thoughts. I want to see the famous Underground City and Old Montreal. Coming?"

She shook her head. "You go and enjoy it."

"This is so unlike you," he said. "You see depressed, even dejected. What's happened to you? You've been down ever since we got here. I sense something amiss, and it is not a small matter."

"Nothing I can't work out. Talking with my boss would depress anybody."

"Really!" He didn't believe her and made no attempt to camouflage that fact. "This noncommunication… this failure to open up happens too often for my taste," he told her.

Who was he to judge her? "Tell me about it. Me, too," she said, the bitterness there for him to hear and digest. "Have a good time on your tour of the Underground City. I'll be in my room."

Jake watched her walk toward the elevators, lacking her usual serenity and elegant carriage. Something wasn't right. And what did she mean, "Tell me about it. Me, too?" as if she had as much right as he to complain about the failure to open up? She did, but as careful as he was, how would she know that? He told himself to let it go for the time being and to think instead on the blessing he received that morning at the airport in Washington. And what a blessing!

"You didn't even see him," the chief had said when they spoke. "I know she's a beautiful woman, but she shouldn't have put such a film over your eyes that your forgot to watch your back."

And he had never done that before. "I suppose I relaxed after you put those two guards on me. Who is the guy, and what was his motive?"

"He'd been looking for you for four years. Remember that five-star job you did in Colombia? He's the guy you put out of business."

"Well, whatta you know? That didn't occur to me."

"He's out of the picture now; the feds caught him redhanded and with a loaded gun."

Perspiration dripped from his forehead. "Thanks. I'm taking the next two weeks off, and I hope you don't mind. No lectures, no handshaking, and no superficial smiles at strangers."

"Right on. Catch a few for me."

Over the years, he and the chief had learned to communicate by phone without identifying themselves or each other. It was a relationship that he enjoyed, but it was time to move on.

He had to find a way to bridge the chasm between Allison and himself, and he knew the department would not give him permission to tell her which agency he worked in or what he did. He rode an elevator to the basement level and headed for the shops and galleries beneath the city. Not one for window-shopping, nonetheless he browsed among the wares of the craftsmen, strolled through the department stores, bought a cone of peach ice cream, and wandered along until he saw bistro tables and chairs outside a restaurant where he sat to watch the passersby.

Hours passed, and without daylight as a guide, seven o'clock slipped up on him. Discovering that his cell phone was useless three levels belowground, he rushed up to street level and phoned Allison.

"Can we eat dinner together? Nothing special, but I'd like to eat with you."

"What time?"

He thought he detected relief in her voice and hoped he was right.

"Seven-thirty is good. Meet you in the lobby."

They ate in the little French restaurant situated off the hotel lobby, and all the while he watched her for an opportunity to begin a healing of their relationship. She wasn't depressed, he decided, but troubled. "Will you spend the coming weekend with me in Idlewild? I'll make all of the arrangements. As much as you mean to me, I can't let it all sour as it seems to be doing, and especially since I don't know why."

"I don't want to lose what we have, either, but I—"

"Not now. This will be out of the way in a couple of days, and the editor and author will no longer interfere with what we mean to each other. We'll have two whole days to talk and to understand each other. I think that's best."

"All right. We can fly from here to Reed City. Let's stay at the inn."

They spoke to each other as strangers, not as the passionate lovers they had been and, he prayed, would be again. He walked with her to her room, holding her hand, and when he reached her room door, he brushed his lips quickly over hers.

"See you at seven in the cafeteria."

She nodded, and went into her room.

* * *

Allison tried without success to recover their camaraderie and warmth, but in spite of her efforts, her mind remained on the decision she would have to make. Frustrated and saddened by what she had to do, she telephoned Sydney.

"It's about time you got in touch," he said. "You still on the tour?"

"It ends Friday."

"Yeah? How do you feel about that? I mean where do you two go from there?"

"I don't know, and I don't think he does, either. We don't want to break up but, Sydney, it's inevitable."

"Would you please tell me why? You're both single, and if you both want to remain together, what's stopping you?"

"I need your sworn confidence."

"On my life."

She told him about Mac Connelly, the abrupt changes in the tour schedule, the incidents on the cruise, and the fracas at the airport as they were leaving Washington. "I'm not going to cover it up; it's going in my story, and it will damage his chance at getting an honor from his university that he covets more than anything else. And, Sydney. He doesn't know anything about Roland and me and the trouble I got into. It's too much."

"Why do you have to include it?"

"How can you ask that when you know the shame I suffered because I didn't report Roland's criminal dealings? I rationalized that if I didn't have absolute proof, I couldn't report it. This time, I can't even rationalize my way out of it, and I don't want to."

"You love this guy?"

She knew he heard and understood the catch in her breath. "Yes, I love him, and he loves me."

"Well, hell! Why don't you give me a simple problem like how to fly to the moon under my own power?"

"I know. Sydney, I'm demoralized."

"Did you tell him you know he's that guitarist?"

"He wants us to spend the weekend in Idlewild trying to work things out. I'm hoping he'll tell me then."

"Look, sis, I wouldn't like to see you and Covington go your separate ways. There's a good explanation for his secretiveness. I'm sure of it, because I'd bet my life he's a man of integrity. But…well, you do what you have to do, and good luck."

"Thanks. Talk to you again soon."

She and Jake arrived in Idlewild around two o'clock that Friday afternoon, the tour behind them and, in her mind, only the Lord knew what was ahead of them.

After registering at Morton's Inn, she telephoned her aunt Frances and told her where she was and why. "We're not sharing a room, but we have to work out some personal problems, and I thought it best for us to stay here."

"All right with me, but I hope you get a minute to drop by before you leave. He's worth investing in. You hear?"

She did, indeed. "Yes, ma'am."

As soon as she unpacked, he called, wanting her to join him for a walk on the beach. "Wear a pair of sneakers, if you brought any," he said. She met him in the lobby, and they walked arm in arm along the beach.

"What happened since we were at Duncan and Justine's? I was practically eating out of your hand, swept up in you. Two days later, it had all evaporated, as if it had never happened. Gone like smoke in a puff of wind. Talk to me, Allison."

She faced him then and willed herself to look into the pain that his eyes had become. "I love you, Jake. What I feel for you is unqualified. But, Jake, I've looked at this from all sides, and I've come to the realization that there is no future for us, so I can't invest more of myself in our relationship."

He grabbed both of her shoulders. "If you love me and I know I love you, how can you say that? If I take you in my arms right now, I'll prove to you that we belong together."

She shook her head. "At Duncan and Justine's place, I was in a dreamworld. The… What's their last name? You didn't tell me."

"He's Duncan Banks," he said as if that weren't important.

"What Duncan Banks? Not the reporter."

"One and the same. Why?"

"N-nothing. I… We journalists bow when we hear his name, and I was talking to him as if he were an ordinary person."

She gulped and knew that her face lost color. Suppose he had recognized her name. She whirled around and looked toward the lake, lest Jake should read her emotions. Maybe the man recognized her name and was merely waiting for a chance to tell Jake about her. She rubbed and twisted her hands. Would she never be free of that scandal?

"He's as ordinary as they come," Jake said.

They sat on the bench beneath the old maple, and he nestled her close to him. "What did you want to be when you were little or a teenager?" he asked her.

"I wanted to be a professional singer, but my darling mother said ladies don't entertain people; other people entertain *them*. There went my dream. They wanted to send me to the University of Vermont to be a teacher, a proper position for a lady, but I rebelled and went to Howard University."

"And you asserted your independence by studying journalism."

"I guess so."

"I dreamed a lot of things for myself," he said, "but poverty is a master leveling agent. On the whole, I'm satisfied so far with the choices I made."

And so it went. The little that they divulged hardly passed for personal. Disappointed that he told her nothing that relieved her quandary, and unable to bring herself to open up to him and tell him about Roland, she suggested that they visit her aunt Frances. When he readily accepted, she knew he also regarded their sojourn in Idlewild as futile.

During the flight to Washington, she grappled with the demons that had tormented her since the tour began, intensified by his mysterious behavior and culminating in the revelation of Mac Connelly. She would surely lose him, but she believed in being straight. Her mind made up, she spent the remainder of the flight dealing with the pain.

At the airport in Washington Sunday afternoon, he hailed a taxi, put her luggage in the trunk, and turned to her. "I imagine you'll be busy writing your story—"

"Come home with me, Jake. Please. I have to talk."

His raised eyebrow suggested that she had wasted the opportunity to do that when they were in Idlewild.

She didn't waver from his gaze, fierce and inquiring, as it bored into her.

"All right," he said when the taxi driver honked the horn and yelled back, "You getting in or not?"

He brought her bags into the house, closed the door, but didn't sit down.

"Have a seat, Jake. This may take a while. You wanted to know what happened to cool our relationship. Any journalist worth hiring is a sharp and constant observer. I always questioned the frequent alterations of the tour, because they were so abrupt, and your disappearances during that cruise heightened my interest, if not my suspicions."

His expression didn't change, but she couldn't help noticing that he ground his teeth and a muscle in his jaw twitched, and she realized that he was either angry or anxious. But she had to tell him.

"Last Friday night, I realized that you and Mac Connelly are the same man, but you didn't trust me enough to tell me. And maybe that was a good thing, because I have to include that in my report."

He jerked forward. "You'd do that to me? The trustees at State University would never give their one seat of honor to a jazzman; they associate jazz and pop music with every sin known to man. You agreed to report on my nine-to-five activities plus all lectures, TV, and radio appearances. Now you tell me your word isn't worth a damn." He rose to leave.

"I haven't finished, Jake. That was your part; this is mine. I was twenty-four and on my first job with a major newspaper, assigned to write a minibiography on Roland Farr, an up-and-coming business executive and man-about-town. He was thirty-five years old, and I was no match for him. He seduced me in what I could later see as the most cunning of ways, claiming he didn't want us to get involved, but cleverly dragging me into his web. I noticed many suspicious things about him, but I was infatuated, so I told myself I couldn't prove it.

"I came across information that he was a part of a smuggling ring, the main source of his considerable income, but I discounted that, too, telling myself that there had to be a mistake. I excluded it from my report, which began on the front page of *The Post*. The next day, *The Star* printed a story on Farr that included everything I omitted, and documented it. My boss called me at two o'clock in the morning and told me I was fired. Farr was never indicted. This is my first job as a journalist since that humiliating experience. I promised myself I would never again cover for a man, no matter how much I loved him. A repeat of that fiasco would damage my career irreparably."

He got up and began walking the floor, his hands in his trousers pockets. "If you disclose my identity as Mac Connelly, I can forget about all I've worked so hard for. I'm sorry about what you've gone through with that poor excuse for a man, because I can imagine how you suffered.

"It's your choice. I wish you well." He walked out, taking with him her last chance at love, because she would never again allow herself to love.

A week later, she handed in her report to Bill Jenkins and left the office, not wanting anyone to see the tears that threatened to wash her face.

He telephoned her at home. "Great job, babe. There isn't a man anywhere who doesn't have a secret he wants hidden. Too bad you couldn't find out what he did all those times he sneaked away from you. You're in for a raise."

Two days later, Sunday, she opened a copy of *The Post*—which, to her surprise, carried a front-page story on Jacob Covington—and gasped. Unable to read beyond the sentence that began *Jacob Covington has proved to be a man with many secrets,* she folded the paper and put it on the top step to be discarded.

The next morning, as she sat in her office trying to think of a hook that would justify writing a story about skateboarding, her telephone rang.

"Allison Wakefield," she said in a disinterested manner, since she knew the caller would not be Jake.

"I'm Ron Parker, managing editor of *The Herald.* I'm impressed with that piece you did on Covington, sensitive and not out for the jugular. First-class reporting." She grasped her throat as if to prevent her heart's escape. "If you're not satisfied over there," he went on, "I'd like you to work for me."

"Well...are you sure you're Ronald Parker?"

"You bet. I'll be here all afternoon, if you're willing to discuss it."

Her common sense restored, she assured him that she'd be there at two, closed her computer, and sat there looking at it. She didn't want to climb up knowing she had pushed Jake's goal beyond his reach. But she also welcomed the opportunity to leave Bill Jenkins's smut mill. At five o'clock that afternoon, she walked into her house as features editor and occasional contributor to the features page of *The Herald,* one of the city's most influential newspapers. Bill Jenkins had objected to her leaving, but because he knew she had no options when he hired her, he hadn't given her a contract, only employment by assignment. Thus, he had no contractual hold on her.

She longed to share her good news with Jake, but

she didn't think he would welcome it. A phone call to Sydney went unanswered, and she didn't call Connie because her friend was on vacation with Mark Reddaway. She roamed around her house until she couldn't bear the sight of it, went out on her deck, and watched the autumn leaves drift to earth.

The occasion called for the best champagne to celebrate her return to the world of established journalists. Now, she could lunch at the Pen and Pencil, the Written Word, and other journalists' hangouts with head high, knowing she belonged. Once more, she would carry a press card. She bit her lips to stop their quivering. Damned if she would cry. She hadn't done that at the nadir of her career, and she wouldn't do it now.

She didn't examine the reason carefully; maybe she just wanted to know he was all right. She went to the telephone and dialed Annie Covington's number.

"How are you, dear?" Annie asked after their first obligatory words of greeting. "I mean, *how are you?*"

"Awful, Mrs. Covington. You couldn't imagine how awful."

"Yes, I can, but you brighten up. Jake will get whatever the Lord has in store for him. Why don't you come down here to see me this weekend?"

She didn't think it proper; maybe Jake would want to visit his mother and wouldn't want to see her. "Maybe Jake won't like it."

"He doesn't say who visits me. Besides, he's out on his boat. Been there for the last week. You come on."

Allison pondered the idea while they talked. She couldn't unburden her heart to her own mother, because Edna Wakefield knew almost nothing of compassion, but Annie Covington would welcome her with a mother's warmth and listen with compassion to the hurt that spilled out of her. Hurt because she had lost Jake, and hurt for the pain she caused him. She decided to go.

"I'm so glad you came," Annie said to Allison when she arrived the next day at noon, and locked her tight into her arms. "I've wanted to see you again. Now, you come on in here. I have something to tell you."

"What is it? Is Jake all right?"

"Yes, and…well, no."

Allison grabbed Annie's arm. "What's the matter with him? Tell me."

"Stop worrying, child. He's all right. Since yesterday, he's been fine…or almost. Come on into the kitchen. I made crab cakes for you."

Allison sat down before a plate of crab cakes and buttermilk biscuits and a glass of lemonade, but she barely touched her favorite food.

"Mrs. Covington, please tell me what's going on with Jake."

Annie pressed her palms to her thighs. "Well, seems a lot of newspapers picked up your story, they did some research, found out about his government work, and printed the entire story. So, thanks to the story you wrote, Jake's a national celebrity. A man called here all the way from Hollywood wanting to make a story of Jake's life. Looks like you did him a favor."

Allison shook her head. Unimpressed. "But the thing Jake wants most isn't a movie about his life, but an appointment as scholar-in-residence at his undergraduate university, and I ruined that for him. I wish I could… Did he mention me at all?"

Annie blew out a long breath and looked toward the ceiling. "You're just as foolish as Jake is. You're both miserable. He knows he's unhappy, but he's too stubborn to do anything about it, and you've heaped so much guilt on yourself—for no reason, I might add—that you can't make the first move."

"He won't want to hear from me."

"Really? Allison, I thought you were a smart woman. You only did your job, and he should be man enough to accept that fact. Eat your crab cake. His boat's docked about four miles from here. Drive on down the road for about a quarter of a mile, turn left into that lane, and drive till you see the boat."

"Can I take him some crab cakes?"

"Atta girl. Biscuits, too, and don't leave there till he's yours."

Allison didn't let herself think about whether or how Jake would receive her. No matter how it was resolved, she had to try, because she didn't want to live without him. She parked at the dock, and with no other car in sight, she figured he didn't have guests. If he did, she couldn't help it; she might not get the courage again to try making amends.

She didn't see a gangplank or even a board that she could use to get on the boat, so she picked up some pebbles and threw them at first one window, and then another. After about five minutes, when her arm had begun to tire, he stepped out on the deck and yelled, "Cut it out."

For a second she merely let her eyes feast on him as he stood there barefoot in a pair of tan shorts and a white T-shirt, scowling in displeasure. He turned to go back inside, and she called to him.

"Jake. May I come aboard? Please. I have to see you."

He whirled around and balanced himself against a post, as if groping for strength. "Allison. Where did you—"

"Jake, please hear what I have to say."

He gazed down at her from the distance as if making sure she was not an apparition. "Wait a minute."

He put in place a wooden plank, held out his hand, and waited for her to join him. "Don't be nervous," he said. "I'll catch you if you fall."

With those words ringing in her ears, the trip up to board the small yacht no longer unnerved her. She reached the boat, and he took her hand. She didn't know how long they stood in the spot staring at each other. She wanted to touch him, to hold him, but how could she?

Finally, in an effort to break the silence, she said, "I brought you some crab cakes and buttermilk biscuits."

At last, a smile covered his face and he took her hand, went with her inside, and closed the door.

"Did you come just to bring me these?"

She shook her head and didn't move her gaze from his. "I called your mother because I had to know where you were and how you were. She invited me to come see her, and I arrived this noon.

"If I asked forgiveness, Jake, it would be a lie. What I'm asking is whether there can be anything for us. I'm sorry that I hurt you. I've been in pain ever since you walked out of my house."

"Let's go in here and sit down," he said. "I didn't expect ever to be here with you like this, although I've wanted it badly. Needed you like… I went over what you told me about Farr and yourself maybe fifty times. I called Duncan and asked if he remembered it. He did; he said the press 'horsewhipped' you, and that he was pleased to know that you were working with me, because I wouldn't compromise you. He recognized you, but he wouldn't have mentioned it if I hadn't broached it to him.

"I couldn't ask you to withhold information, because I would have done what you did."

"But… Oh, Jake. It cost you so much."

His eyebrows shot up and his left hand fingered his chin. "Haven't you been reading the papers?"

"No. I haven't looked at a paper since I saw that exposé in *The Post*. I read the first sentence and threw the paper away."

"Then you don't know that I've resigned my job, and I've been appointed scholar-in-residence at State University?"

She nearly swallowed her tongue. *"What?"*

When he repeated it, she jumped out of her chair with her arms widespread, and he rose to meet her. "Thank God," she said over and over. "I'm so happy."

Until his arms tightened around her, being locked in them didn't register, so great was her relief and her joy that he wouldn't suffer because of her.

His hand moved up and down her back in gentle strokes, and she leaned back and looked into his face. "Jake. *Jake!*" she said, when her gaze caught his passion-filled eyes. With a violent shudder, his mouth was on her. Frissons of heat plowed through her, and the thumping of her heart turned into a mad gallop like the sound of wild horses' hooves.

"Open. Let me in," he said. "Oh, Allison, let me love you."

She stepped back. "Jake, I came here to deal with my future, not to patch up our relationship, but to ensure it. I don't want a little bit of you. I need all of you from now on."

He sat down and settled her in his lap. "For four years, I was an undercover agent for the government— I can't tell you which department—then I took on another, top-secret job. I was on leave for my book tour, but my boss at the department called on me whenever he needed me. I couldn't share it with you or anyone. At the end of our cruise, you saw me facilitate the capture of a woman and two men who had shared our table. If you value my life, you will never breathe a word of this.

"You know why I didn't tell you about Mac. He's a part of my life that is as essential to me as breathing. I'll still be on that stage every Friday and Saturday night that I can get there."

She tightened her arm on his shoulder. "But what about the university trustees?"

"They wanted me to give it up, but I held to my rights, and they accepted me without restrictions. If you hadn't published that story, all this may never have happened."

"I've got some good news, too." She told him about her new position.

"Now it's my turn to rejoice with you. I read your piece, and it impressed me that you are a fine writer. You don't know how glad I am that you're working once more for a first-class paper."

"I'm hungry," she said. "Can we warm the crab cakes and biscuits?

"Yes, indeed. I'm having a beer with mine." He looked at her. "What would you like?"

"Well...there's my favorite food, but seeing as how my favorite man—"

He held up both hands, palms out. "Hold it right there. One thing you never want to do is compete with crab cakes."

Nearly two hours later, he separated his body from hers and looked down into her face. "I had planned to say this while on one knee, but you've robbed me of every ounce of energy. I don't think I can move. Allison Wakefield, will you be my wife, and marry me soon?"

"I will. Oh, I will, but I need at least a month to—"

"Make it two weeks."

"But what about my friends and my family? Edna Wakefield will have a fit."

"I'll email your friends. If you tell your mother you're marrying a writer, she'll lose interest."

"Heavens," Allison said, laughing with happiness. "I didn't know you'd met her."

They laughed and hugged each other until moisture wet their cheeks.

"We came so close to losing this," he whispered.

"Yes. It frightens me to think of it."

Two weeks and three hours later, Edna Wakefield buttoned the last of the tiny pearl buttons in the back of Allison's ivory satin and lace wedding dress. No daughter of hers was going to be married in a court-house by a justice of the peace, she told Jake. The tiny church, which sat in the woods of a Vermont hamlet, was lighted with candles and decorated with white calla lilies. Lighted lanterns along both sides of the driveway approaching the church sparkled against the pristine white snow in which they sat.

At exactly 5:55 in the afternoon, the bells of the little church began to peal, Annie Covington took an aisle seat on the groom's side of the church, and Edna Wake-field immediately followed and sat on the bride's side of the church, a signal that the service would begin. Jake stepped to the altar with Duncan Banks, his best man, at his side. He turned to face the door, unwilling to wait any longer to see his bride. Connie walked in carry-ing yellow roses and wearing a pale yellow silk gown.

He stretched his neck looking for Allison, and at last she appeared walking between Sydney and her father, a vision in white and carrying his calla lilies.

"She's a real beauty," Duncan whispered.

Jake couldn't help grinning. He needed an outlet for his joy. "Yeah, she is that." He winked, deliberately that time. "So is Justine." Duncan's smile said he appreciated the comment.

"Who gives this woman to be wed?"

"We do," said Sydney and Arnold Wakefield, Allison's father.

And then she was beside him, holding his hand, promising to love him forever, locking her gaze on his eyes as he spoke his vow to her.

"I now pronounce you husband and wife."

Her smile, brilliant and sparkling, made his heart sing, and when his arms enfolded her, her lips, warm and sweet, returned his kiss.

"I love you, sweetheart."

"And I love you, now and always."

She took his arm, and they walked out of the church as their friends—Desiree and Rachel among them—tossed white rose in their path. Out of the church and into the rest of their lives together.

Finally, she was his wife. His for all time.

* * * * *

REQUEST YOUR FREE BOOKS!

2 FREE NOVELS PLUS 2 FREE GIFTS!

KIMANI™
ROMANCE

Love's ultimate destination!

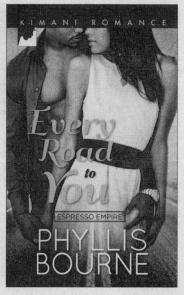